INSTRUMENTS OF DE…

"You?" snarled the monster into which Carnahan had turned. "You?"

He was beside Tyson; he seemed to have glided there without the agency of feet, so swift was his coming, and around Tyson's wrist settled a grip like steel bands shrinking into place. Over the shoulder of the maniac he saw the girl, sick and weak with horror. She could not even cry out. And Tyson looked calmly into the red eyes before him and wondered why he was not afraid to die. For he was very near death, he knew. Even in his full vigour it would have taxed him to meet this gaunt giant in his frenzy, but now that undernourishment and overwork had sapped his muscles—

He reached behind him, not daring to take his glance from the glowing eyes before him; he felt that if he flinched, if he winced, if he took his look away, the peril would be loosed and launched at his throat. That hand he sent groping blindly along the shelf behind him, seeking for anything which might serve as a weapon. The fingers closed on wood; he jerked out a violin, clutching the neck of the instrument with nervous strength. A foolish, flimsy weapon, but it might free him for a second from Carnahan....

Other *Leisure* Westerns by Max Brand:
THE OUTLAW TAMER
BULL HUNTER'S ROMANCE
BULL HUNTER
TIGER MAN
GUN GENTLEMEN
THE MUSTANG HERDER
WESTERN TOMMY
SPEEDY
THE WHITE WOLF
TROUBLE IN TIMBERLINE
TIMBAL GULCH TRAIL
THE BELLS OF SAN FILIPO
MARBLEFACE
THE RETURN OF THE RANCHER
RONICKY DOONE'S REWARD
RONICKY DOONE'S TREASURE
RONICKY DOONE
THE WHISPERING OUTLAW
THE SHADOW OF SILVER TIP
THE TRAP AT COMANCHE BEND
THE MOUNTAIN FUGITIVE

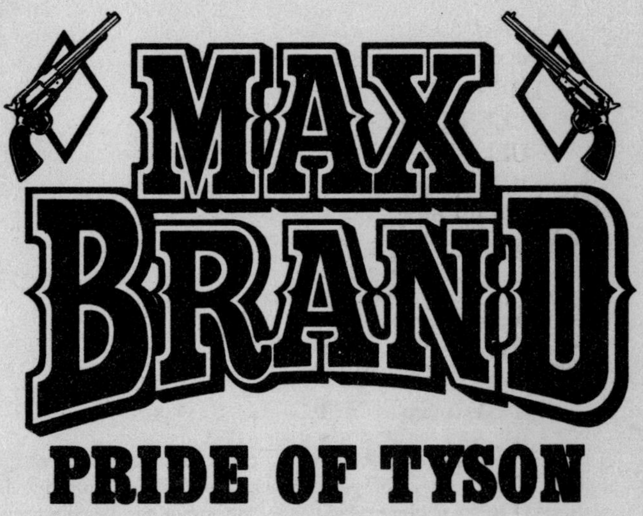

PRIDE OF TYSON

LEISURE BOOKS  NEW YORK CITY

A LEISURE BOOK®

November 1996

Published by special arrangement with Golden West Literary Agency.

Dorchester Publishing Co., Inc.
276 Fifth Avenue
New York, NY 10001

Printed in the United States of America.

PRIDE OF TYSON

One
Misgivings

Mrs. Garth frowned down at her sewing for a moment or two before she realised that the night was coming; then she laid her work over her lap, folded her bony hands, and looked out of the window.

First of all, with the readiness of long custom, she looked up to the dam, for she never ceased to wonder at it. She remembered when the space across the valley of the Chiluah, from La Cabeza to La Blanca, lay without a barrier; she remembered when the dam heaved up a low, massive, ragged ridge of masonry; and now it shot far up, binding the mountains together like a work of nature, and blotting out a great section of the sky with its stone curtain.

Very little remained to be done on it, she knew, yet it seemed incredible that the hands of men could ever complete the task and build to a smooth line the uneven top; but there were the giant agents at work, huge cranes, blackening now, and gaunt and ominous as gallows.

Mrs. Garth shook her head and her thin lips moved soundlessly; her left arm and hand moved to a singular position. For, very strangely, whenever she looked at the monstrous dam she thought of Edward in his soft baby clothes, and the foolish wisdom of the little pink face, and the small wrinkled hands groping at her. Now he was a giant, but even Atlas appeared a pygmy under the burden of the sky.

There always seemed only two periods in his life; and always she felt, vaguely, that she must share with him the burden of the building, and always she ached and failed at heart under the load. That was why she shook her head.

For the dam was only a symbol. She knew that out of that labour men expected the desert to bloom for many a mile south; she knew that the lips of a thousand men were already framing his praises, and whenever she thought of that she trembled for fear the whole work would fail—and then the shame.

Indeed, the schooling of her life unfitted her for accomplishment and care-free joy of creation; she was a graduate in pain.

Vaguely, though her head remained bowed, she knew that Diego the mozo was arranging things, carefully shifting dishes so that no noise might disturb her.

At last he turned, and the door closed upon his white figure. Mrs. Garth sighed and dropped her work.

She would have given a great deal to get rid of the guilty feeling which came over her when the servants were about. Of course they could afford help, and if she said the word Edward would flood the house with hired men; but it never seemed quite right to Mrs. Garth to have other human beings, free and independent souls, waiting upon her beck and call.

She looked at the tea-service now. That, also, distressed her. Such creamy-white, transparent stuff should rightfully be behind glass doors in a cabinet, and the tall, slender-throated silver pitchers had cost—heaven knew how much!

But Edward insisted on these things, for now and then he brought home men who could not stay for supper (dinner, they called it, oddly enough!) and he wished to serve them at tea in a style befitting the builder of the Chiluah dam.

Some of those backers of Edward's were such wonderful men! She shuddered at the thought of how their talk flowed from one end of the earth to the other, and how they had looked at her—thoughtfully—when she spoke. The eyes of Mrs. Garth grew wistful, and she sighed again until the stays of her fashionable corsets stopped her breath.

Time gradually blunted the sting of her self-consciousness, but today, for a very special reason, the old pain came back on her as keen thrusting as ever, and made her shrink from the wounding thoughts. The special reason lay on her lap beneath her sewing, and now she drew it out and looked again, stealthily, and after she put it back, she turned guilty eyes towards the door.

It was the photograph of a girl, and she had found it that day while she tidied up Edward's room. (All her domain of housework had shrunk to the care of that one chamber, except when Edward asked her to make Parker House rolls, bless the boy!)

The photograph of a girl, but what a photograph! It was one of those gum-prints with which fools ruin the work of the best camera, but which in skilful hands becomes a thing of art.

Just glinting in the soft, thick folds of the girl's hair—glinting *through* the hair, as sunshine does—the light slipped past her forehead and her eyes, caught at the firm, perfect line of the nose, played tenderly over the lips and chin, left the throat in obscurity, and fell, shining, on one shoulder and the swift curve of the breast.

One would think, almost, that the woman was undraped! decided Mrs. Garth; at least her drapery was much too scant for modesty.

Moonlight, Mrs. Garth faintly remembered, did such things to the face of a girl, and terrible things to the heart of a man. But what made her weak within was something which the camera caught in spirit, though no set lines could define it—an air of pride, of cool aloofness, of crystal purity as far removed from the pretty faces of other girls as the chilly summit of the mountain is removed from the desert it looks down upon, and mocks.

Her son Edward, for all his strength and bulk, had once lain against her breast, but what woman could have fondled such a girl as this?

The mist left the eyes of Mrs. Garth and a smile transformed the lean, withered face into something near akin to comeliness, for she heard, beyond the door, the thudding footfall of a heavy man—a quick step, which she knew was Edward's.

Two

The Turning of the Ways

A deep voice boomed—he was speaking to some servant—and then heavy laughter.

There he stood, filling the entrance, with heavy boots and shirtsleeves rolled to the elbows like a labouring man, except that an air of confident command fairly exuded from him.

"Evening, mother."

The sound filled the room; it should have had open space to echo through. He leaned above Mrs. Garth, brushed her forehead with his lips, and the next moment his big chair groaned faintly under his weight.

"Ain't there anyone with you, Ed?" she asked.

"Nobody tonight. And I'm too hungry to clean up before tea, if you don't mind."

Mrs. Garth reached out and patted his hand, furtively, as if there were a third person in the room who might see and correct her.

"I like to have you just this way," she assured him. She laughed a little, apologetically. "When you're all dressed up, you don't seem mine so much, Ed."

"You should have been at the dam a while back," he said. "I made a bet with big Joe, that Portuguese foreman, that I could sink a drill faster than he. That's why I'm late."

She looked at him with a touch of anxiety, keeping a lump of sugar suspended above the cup of tea.

"You won, Ed?"

"I'll tell a man I won. Hasn't been so long since I swung a sledge, at that, but, of course, Joe thought the boss was all theory and no practice. But I showed him." He chuckled reminiscently. "He took a single jack, but I used a double jack, and fairly walked away from him. He got so mad that in twenty minutes he threw down his drill and walked away."

"And forgot to pay his debt?"

"Of course I couldn't have taken the poor devil's money, mother."

Her lips tightened, her head bowed a little, and she started to speak, but apparently changing her mind, she passed over the cup in silence. Garth stirred it rapidly, and then dropped his spoon clattering on the saucer.

"Why don't we have a little more light, mother?"

"I'd forgotten about it." She pulled the cord of the floor lamp, and a soft glow swept across the room. "I was just sitting here thinking, Ed, and I forgot it was getting dark."

He nodded absently; he was looking about with satisfaction on the room.

"This rests a fellow's eyes," he declared. "I didn't

buy these things to keep 'em in the dark."

Indeed, the apartment was filled with costly furniture, filled almost to overflowing: the rich crimsons and blues and golds of the rug; the ivory woodwork; the bright cushions of the Louis Quatorze chairs; the glittering candelabra. Good taste reeled among these extremes, but Edward Garth enjoyed every feature of the room in detail.

His survey lasted for some moments. Then he swallowed his tea at a draught and rose from his chair, to stroll here and there.

"Isn't this a little bit of all right?" he boomed. "Honest, mother, I can hardly see myself here with all these things around me belonging to us. I keep imagining that we're back in the little old home."

"Weren't you tolerable comfortable there, Ed?"

"Comfortable?" He stopped short in his pacing and faced her. "Well, of course we had a place to eat and a place to sleep. But that was about all. Remember that terrible carpet in the parlour? The border of it was deep red, but the centre, where people had walked more and sat about, was faded almost brown. And you could see the underlining. And the boards in the kitchen floor were all hollowed out—with your scrubbing, dear old mother."

"Is that the way you feel, always, Ed?"

"Oh, no. It was all right in a way. Home, you know, and all that. But this is different."

He paused.

"That was all right for us then, but times have changed. We have to change with them."

"Clothes don't make the man, Ed."

He thrust his hands deep into his pockets and frowned down at her.

"Not in eighteen fifty," he said, "but this is the

twentieth century, and clothes go a long way—a mighty long way. Why, mother, think of the men I've known and met. All I know of them is their business side, dollars and cents, concrete and dynamite, but all the inside of them is shut away from me; I'm walled out. I don't see the insides of their homes and that's why I don't see the insides of their hearts. And why? Because I haven't any social graces. I can't tell stories. I keep harking back to shop. I use dollar signs for question marks."

Suddenly he strode across to her and caught her hands.

"Stop that sewing, please, I want you to listen and understand."

She lowered the cloth obediently and clasped her hands tightly together, for she was unnerved and feared that he might note their trembling.

"You've got to understand, because you've got to help."

He sat far forward on the edge of his chair, forgetful of himself, talking as he would have talked to his board of directors; his eyes gleamed, his face became ferocious, indomitable. It was like a cruel mask carven in rugged brown stone, so hard that it defied careful finishing. And he talked as if she were a hundred feet away.

"I've come to the turning of the ways, mother. The old method isn't good enough any more. When no one knew me it was different. I lack ease, poise, address; and I'm going to get 'em. D'you hear? I'm going to get 'em, and you're going to help me. Mother, we're going to start studying together!"

"Oh, Ed!" she cried, breathless as a girl, and her eyes shone.

"We're going to climb together."

She caught her hands up before her eyes while every muscle of her frail body relaxed, and her head rested against the back of the chair.

"What's happened?" he asked anxiously. "What's wrong?"

He drew down her hands, but he found in her eyes sadness too great for tears.

Three
Tyson

"It just means that you're right, Ed," she said steadily. "This is the turning point for you, and after this there ain't any way I can help you. I couldn't ever change my way of talking. And what would a girl like this think if she seen my hands?"

And she held out to Garth the picture which had lain under her sewing. While he took it, she watched him as keenly as the old Indian watched the distant smoke to make sure whether it were friend or foe, but her instant of hope vanished at once.

"Where did you get this?" he asked huskily.

"I found it in the pocket of your Sunday clothes—I mean in one of your best suits—when I got it ready for pressing."

She waited, and then sighed very guardedly, for he was too intent upon the picture to speak at once.

When he did lift his head, it was to say simply: "This is the girl I am going to marry."

It made her blink as though he had flashed an intolerable light in her face.

"You got engaged to her when you were back in New York this last time?"

He leaned back in his chair and smiled at her.

"Engaged? No, I've only met her once."

"Only once? Oh, Ed, and you talked about——"

He flushed, as though the very suggestion embarrassed him.

"Good Lord, mother, does she look like that sort of a girl? No, she probably hasn't thought of me once since I met her that time. But I'm going to have her."

He straightened in his chair.

"She's mine." His big arm shot out. "Look at that dam. If I can wall up the Chiluah I can capture one girl. I have to." He repeated it still more softly, but with an emphasis greater than shouting.

"I have to! The thought of her follows me. When I look at this picture the mere dream of ever having her makes me feel like a man on the edge of a great cliff; d'you understand?"

She sighed: "Oh, Ed, my dear! If she's what she looks to be, how can you have any claim on her?"

"Look at me!" he commanded, and stretched out his hands, palms up, as if he were about to sweep the empty air into his embrace. "I've got nothing. I have a little money, and a good future as an engineer, but that's worse than nothing in her eyes. All the hold I have on her is the will to own her. And, by God Almighty, I'm going to win her. There she is, three thousand miles away, and here I am, with empty hands; but I'm going to have her. I'm going to draw her out here. She's as good as mine already. I know it as surely as if I had second sight. Well, let her drop, mother. We will talk about something else."

"We'll talk about her," said his mother calmly. "Go ahead, Ed."

"I get too excited when I even think of her; makes me want to board an East-bound train."

"You can talk to me. That won't be hard. Why, Ed, I've seen this coming ever since you got back from New York. You tried to talk about how successful you were raising the money you needed, but all the time I knew you were thinking of something else. That's why you started buying more fine things for the house."

He looked about him with a kindling eye.

"Yes," he said, more to himself than to her, "when she comes out here—and I know she'll come—and sees this room in particular, she'll know that we're something more than she might think. Why, mother, I'll bet you that I spent more fixing up just this one room than they've spent on their whole house. Well, I'll tell you the story.

"I went with Winton to his club on Fifth Avenue one evening, and we dropped into the gymnasium for some exercise.. He suggested boxing, so we went out on the mat, but Winton was too slow and fat to do a thing, and after a while I hurt him a little—not meaning to. It seemed to anger him, though. After his nose stopped bleeding he looked over to a young chap who was throwing a medicine ball about, and asked him to put on the gloves with me.

"I thought it was a joke at first. The fellow didn't weigh within fifty pounds of me, I think, but he took the suggestion very seriously and came up and shook hands with me. His name was Tyson,

Henry Tyson, and he said he'd be glad to give me a chance to exercise; so he took Winton's gloves. Mind you, he was a lot shorter and more slender than I am, but when he faced me I began to worry a little.

"He stepped about like a thoroughbred saddle horse—you know how they walk as if there were coiled watch springs in their feet—and though his muscles weren't very large, they slid into each other like water running over stones. Besides, he had an eye which said he wouldn't fear his weight in wildcats. And when he went at me, mother, I thought that was what he was—just so much wildcat.

"At first he boxed easily, dancing about, slipping in and out, tapping me very gently here and there, and all the time I couldn't touch him with a glove. It irritated me, but I kept from hitting hard partly because he was so much smaller, and partly because I didn't want to muss up his golden hair or spoil his face—it would have been like smashing the face of a Grecian statue, you know.

"Then I saw Winton standing a little bit away, laughing, and I forgot myself for a second. My punch didn't go home, or Tyson would still be asleep, I suppose. Even as it was, my fist ploughed into his gloves and carried them back against his chest and sent him reeling away.

"I started to apologise, but Tyson came back at me as if I'd thrown a rubber ball against the wall. He came like a handsome devil, with a point of hellfire in each eye, and before I got my wits together, he'd hit me a dozen times from my forehead to my stomach. Not love taps, either. Every one of them stung me, and the last clipped me on the jaw and sent me staggering.

"Of course, after that it was a fight. I don't know a great deal about boxing, but you remember that I was always fighting when I was a youngster. So I knew the feel of a hard fist, and I knew how to hit quick and with my weight behind my arm. Understand?"

"Partly." Her old eyes were afire.

"But it was uphill work. He hit me ten times while I hit him once. I planted my feet, lowered my shoulders, and smashed away with all my might, but he ducked under some of the blows and sidestepped others, and blocked the rest, and all the time his fists kept up a tattoo on me. I still think that if we had not been fighting with big, soft gloves, he would have cut me to ribbons in the first five minutes.

"As it was, I weathered the storm. My wind was good; my muscles loosened up. I began to hit harder and faster just when Tyson began to pant. I could tell that he was going. His face grew red and then white about the mouth; his left arm—his guard arm, you see—went lower; and his breath came in quick, chugging gasps. He was terribly out of training. I suppose he was used to three- or four-minute bouts.

"After a while I began to get home punches—not clean hits, but partly blocked or partly sidestepped blows that whirled him here and there, and sometimes turned him half round. Then I noticed that he didn't step about with the same ease. His knees began to sag; his blows had so little force I didn't have to bother guarding them. At last a swing landed on his forehead, snapped back his head, and whacked him back against the wall—there should have been ropes about the mat.

"I stepped back, then, for I remembered how

much smaller he was. I stepped back and asked him to stop, but he merely laughed and came in again. Odd thing to watch him laughing with the blood from his mouth flicking across his face. He wasn't cut up badly, but there was enough red to streak his whole body, and as he came in at me, laughing that way, I felt something pretty close to fear. Yes, I knew that I had him—and yet I didn't know. I never saw such a look on the face of a man. I never saw such hunger in eyes.

"He came straight in, hitting straight and fast. You see this swollen lip? That's where one punch landed, and then I let him have it. He was wide open, and I put every ounce of my power behind the blow. It landed on the point of his jaw, and he whipped to one side and plunged to the mat, face down."

"Served him just right," snapped Mrs. Garth. "The way he'd been striking you, Eddie!"

Garth raised his hand.

"Don't say that. I felt like a cur when I saw what I'd done. Remember, he was not two-thirds my size, hardly; and I had begun the hard hitting. Besides, don't forget that if we had been using small, hard gloves, he would have chopped my face to ribbons, closed both my eyes and knocked out most of my teeth, I suppose, in the first five minutes.

"Well, all I could do was to pick him up and carry him to the showers, and the lightness of his body made me ashamed. I still wonder how he could have stood up to me for so long, in spite of his skill."

Garth paused.

"So that was how I met Henry Tyson."

"And then he took you to see his sister?"

"How did you guess that she was his sister?"

"Only from what you said about the face of the boy, and his yellow hair. I suppose her hair is like that?"

Four

Like to Like

"Like fine-spun metal," mused Garth, sighing. "Yes, he took me to see her. When he recovered consciousness he didn't bear me the slightest grudge—was all eagerness and curiosity about me, and that very night I had supper at his house.

"It was in Gramercy Park; a very select part of the city, where there are lots of homes of old families, and clubs, and things like that. It had a gravestone front, and the door was opened by a servant with a face like a saint and a cloud of white hair about it like a halo.

"Then I met Margaret. I won't talk about that; you've seen her picture; but all during the evening she kept eating into me the way acid eats into iron; I could feel myself dissolving. I tried to talk, but I was tongue-tied. I tried to be pleasant, but all I could think of was the weather. After a while I sat silent, hating myself, and during supper I knew that she thought no more about me than she did about a design on wallpaper.

"But out of that evening I learned one thing; she worshipped her brother. Love and admiration rolled together, and I was not very long in seeing that if I ever hoped to have any hold on her it would have to be through Henry Tyson. That was my cue.

"Mind you, the moment I looked at her, I knew I saw my wife. Odd feeling; sort of a nightmare thing in which you see safety but can't reach it. All the evening it seemed to me that I was reaching towards her—and my hands slipped off. She was so indifferent that she didn't even judge me—merely took me for granted as a new friend of her brother's.

"I tried to talk to her now and then; but after a while I merely sat and watched. She was not only different from any person I had ever met, but she lived in another sphere. That was one of the stinging things that got under my skin that night. Everything about the house was new to me.

"After supper we went into a front room and Margaret sat at the piano and played while she and Henry sang. Now her hair gleamed, and her hands and face flashed white; and now she was dim as the old pictures on the wall. She seemed to me to be moving back and forth from the past to the present.

"But most of all I noticed the eyes of young Tyson. They kept a sort of coldly polite observance upon me, but I saw that I mattered to him no more than the chair I sat in.

"They pretended to be playing for me, but I knew that they were playing for each other. For instance, they sang folk songs from the Hungarian and

French, and Italian boating songs—all dead stuff to me, but they knew the words as well as I know English.

"Afterward I spoke about one of the pictures. Portrait of an old fellow with an ugly face, but they would talk of nothing except how the thing was painted—well, I think that's what they mean by perspective."

His mother sighed and nodded.

"Well, son," she murmured, "the girl is three thousand miles away, most; and it'll be a long time before you can go to New York again. I'd say, put her out your mind; that kind of girl gets married young."

But Garth smiled on her, and then pointed out the window to the colossus of the dam, now dying out into the night.

"Do you think I can put that out of my mind?"

"The dam? There ain't any call to forget that, Eddie."

"She's so much more real and important than the dam—why, the dam is nothing. It's a thing of air, compared with Margaret Tyson."

His mother shook her head and compressed the thin, stubborn lips so that he frowned, watching her.

"There'll be no good come out of it, Eddie," she said gravely. "I can sit here and see that. You're wastin' your strength on dreams, boy.

"Listen to me, Eddie," she warned him, and she raised a lean, crooked, calloused forefinger. "Like takes to like. There was never anything said truer than that; and she ain't your like."

She smiled, and it maddened Garth.

"I'll tell you what I've done already. When I first saw the Tysons they intended to sail for Europe within ten days. The ten days have passed, and they haven't sailed. The ten days have passed; Henry Tyson is here, and Margaret Tyson is sure to come!"

Mrs. Garth stared with a grey face; suddenly she was very old, feeble.

"Eddie," she whispered, "she ain't comin' here—that girl?"

"Listen," he said triumphantly, "and I'll tell you how I worked it. I saw that in her own world I could never touch the girl's heart. But I thought that if I had her out here in *my* world it might be different, because I'm no good sitting down with my hands folded; but when I have a chance to work she might begin to see a little something in me."

"Unless she's blind!" snapped Mrs. Garth.

"I had to work fast. In ten days they were to sail. So I started to work my leverage, which was my hold on Hal Tyson, and that hold was his respect for the strength of my muscles. So that very first night I planted the seed. I told him the trouble with him was that his body had been built up in a gymnasium instead of by a little real labour. I talked to him about the dam and the country of the Chiluah.

"I got him enthusiastic. I told him about the dry, keen air, and what it does to the lungs of a man. It didn't take long. You'd understand if you could see the fellow, for he's like tinder, and ideas set him on fire. Before we went to bed—and I stayed with him that night—he shook hands with me, and said he was coming out, and within six months he'd promise to be able to thrash me."

Garth leaned back and chuckled softly. He added: "And he came West with me!"

"He's here now—working on the dam—a man like that?"

"Doing manual labour, yes—a man like that."

"How does he stand it?"

"Not very well. You see, the fellow's pride is a terrible thing. In the first place, his pride was terribly hurt because another man—even one as much larger as myself—had been able to strike him senseless; and the idea tortured him and made him writhe even when he was trying to smile. After that, when he said he would come, I wanted to make sure that he would stay, because he was the bait through which I hoped to bring Margaret out here. She and he had been as thick as blood all their lives, and I knew she could not stand it if he were away too long.

"But first I had to make sure that Hal Tyson would not leave too soon, so I induced him to sign a paper which I composed, in which he promised to live like a working man, accept no aid or money or gifts, other than his salary as a labourer, and to stay with his job for six months at least.

"It wasn't hard to make him do it. I drew up the paper half in jest, but he sticks to every letter of the law. He plays the game hard.

"The result is that I'm afraid he may wear himself out. He lives in a boardinghouse, and exists on his wages, though how he can after the life he has been accustomed to is a mystery—I can't explain.

"He takes this so seriously that I worry. He feels that it is a game between him and me, and if he should ever guess that I have done all this simply to get his sister out here he would call it underhanded—or something worse."

"And ain't it just a little underhanded, Eddie?"

"The means are justified by the end," scowled Garth. "When I have her, I don't care what Tyson thinks or feels. The bargain is fair. And now—I've got to dress for supper—dinner, I mean. Tell me first; you approve, or not?"

He took her old face between his hands and made her look up to him.

"Oh, Eddie," she murmured, "I misdoubt there'll be no good come out of it. She ain't your kind, nor is her brother."

Five
The Pilot

A thousand engineers had seen the Chiluah Valley, or at least heard of it. But none had ever dreamed that the grey desert might be reclaimed by the hoarding and careful expenditure of those muddy waters which swept down from the mountains.

After Garth formed his plan and began its execution, the thousand shrugged their shoulders and said: "Well, there's nothing wonderful about it. There flows the water, with steep natural walls on each side. Even a fool could plan a dam in such a site."

But to Garth the place seemed specially designed by Providence. From the breast of the higher mountains two ranges like two arms thrust out into the heart of the desert, terminating, as with fists, in two mountains, La Blanca and La Cabeza. Beyond these low peaks the desert stretched away, not gradually, in rolling foothills, but in a faintly undulating plain, slowly dropping away towards the south, the east, and the west.

Between those mountain arms ran the Chiluah, escaping past the peaks into the white desert, a muddy trickle during most of the year, but in the spring a roaring, pounding torrent of brown water crested with foam—water which yet held the chill of the mother snows.

It needed only a strong, tall dam stretching from Blanca to Cabeza to imprison the spring floods in the upper valley of the Chiluah and hold them ready for the remainder of the year; it needed only this to convert the bitter desert below into a green garden.

This was the vision which for many years had filled the eye of Garth, and now the dream was hurrying towards fulfilment. Across the gorge stretched the mighty wall of masonry, still growing. At that foot of La Blanca, which faced out on the desert, huddled the town of Blanca, where they lived who laboured on the great dam.

The dam itself, viewed from the desert side, was about finished. It lacked comparatively little of its destined height, and it was finished perfectly.

One gathered the feeling that this work had not to do with desert land reclaimed or any matter of dollars and cents; it was an affair of life and death.

And from a bird's-eye view it seemed a scene of mindless confusion, blind confusion, indeed, yet it could not be blindness which caused the tall structure to rise, massive, yet strangely graceful.

Far up the side of La Blanca, on a little shoulder that overlooked the whole, perched a shanty of rough boards, and in the top of the shanty there was a room with windows on three sides like the cabin of the helmsman, and in this room sat Edward Garth.

He sat at his table dressed like a mechanic. Many a one of his lowest subordinates, men who worked with the gangs of labourers, themselves newly risen from the ranks, had found comfort unspeakable in the work-worn hands of the big boss; so that they were enabled to stand upon both feet and hold their heads up and talk, man to man.

Accordingly, they loved him, and had faith in him and in his work. They understood him—because of those soiled hands, and other things; and they knew that he understood them.

The office was quiet, now, for the day shift was going off and the night shift had just come on; but the big boss was as tensed as ever during the day. He kept his mind ready like a pugilist in a battle, which went on day and night and night and day. Even now he was noting a detail on the left wing of the work, and someone would sweat for what he had seen in that instant. A door opened and closed. It was his secretary from the inner office.

"That fellow Tyson," complained the secretary, "is up here again—"

"Let him come in," said Garth, without turning his head from the window.

The secretary opened his lips to protest, but thought better of it almost at once and disappeared into his room. A moment later Tyson stepped in, cap in hand.

Six
Pride Finds a Model

"Here he is," announced the secretary, and closing the door slowly, he swept an interested, puzzled eye upon the common labourer who was able to see the big boss almost at will.

"Good evening, sir," said Tyson respectfully, stiffly, but the moment the door was fully closed, he advanced towards Garth with outstretched hand.

They made a study as Garth rose and shook hands, for if the world of white men had been combed with a conscious purpose, it would have been difficult to find two more exact opposites.

At first glance Garth was the more interesting of the pair through the emphasis of bulk, overshadowing the more meagre outline of Tyson, and the rugged intensity of his face. He might have stood for a sculptor's study of one of those Titans who had the heart of rival Olympic Zeus armed with nothing more than the strength of their hands; but Tyson was one of those whose faces excite, at once, and defy the painter.

If the first glance was for Garth, the second lingered on Tyson, the chin of Grecian roundness, the scrupulously chiselled nose, the large, dark, restless eyes, and the gold of the hair.

An influence radiated continually from him mingled of air and fire.

"Look, Garth!" he said, "I've something finer than a steam yacht or a blooded racehorse—twelve dollars—twelve round iron-boys of my own earning!"

He laughed joyously as he drew out the money and shook it rustling under the nose of Garth.

"Twelve dollars!" he continued. "I spent the last cent of my own money this morning. Thank the Lord this is Saturday and payday; otherwise I'd have had to go hungry I don't know how long."

"You don't mean to say you'd actually go without food, Tyson?" queried Garth.

It was easy to see that the younger man puzzled him.

"There's no other way out of it," answered Tyson contentedly. "I tell you what, I've gone through our bond a hundred times in the last ten days, trying to find some way out; but there isn't a single opening. I have to live by my own earnings for six months—or starve on 'em."

"But," protested Garth, "I didn't mean anything as severe as all that. When I drew up that little agreement——"

He stopped, for Tyson looked at him in open wonder.

"It isn't a matter of what *you* meant, Garth," he said. "The stuff is down in black and white, and it's plainly a matter of honour for me to stick by the letter of the law."

A faint tinge of red gathered in Garth's cheek. Every time he talked with Tyson he ran up against some obstacle like this within the first five minutes of chat. He could not wave his own thick hands without touching the fellow's hair-trigger pride.

"Confound it," said Garth, "honour is all very well, but I can't let you starve yourself on account of a silly prank—a bit of ink on a piece of paper. I simply wrote that to give you an idea of what you would have to do if you were *really* broke. What would happen, now, if someone were to pick your pocket when you go down to La Blanca tonight?"

The other winced at the bare suggestion.

"That would be the devil," he frowned. "However, I'd pull through."

"H-m!" muttered Garth.

"The point is," went on Tyson, "you're such a square shooter yourself, Garth, that you toe the mark, but your big heart can't bear the thought of another person suffering. The moment you squared off at me with the gloves, Garth, I looked through you. Your soul is made of glass, and the whole world can look through the window. You don't care, because every inch of your past is clean."

The man inside struck the consciousness of the big boss like the impact of a fist. It jarred him into wakefulnes. There sat Tyson, a common labourer on the dam, and yet he was a thousand miles aloof. No self-consciousness weighted him. It was harder to meet those clear, unstained eyes than it would have been to meet the stare of a tiger.

"Tiger!" Yes, that was the word. The same fearlessness. The same belief in one's own strength.

Some jungle creature which turns out of the path for nothing in creation. That was Tyson.

"Tyson!" said Garth suddenly. "I'll tell you what's in your mind."

"Well?"

"You're thinking of the end of the six months, when you're going to stand up to me with your bare fists—and thrash me if you can!"

Tyson locked his hands around one knee and threw back his head, laughing.

"Right!" he said. "Six months of hardening, and then we'll have another session."

Bewilderment made the brain of Garth spin. He could never follow the thought processes of this fellow. There was no malice about Tyson, now. He talked of fighting desperately with Garth as he would have talked of a friendly walk through the hills.

"Why the devil are you so set on it?" he asked with unrestrainable curiosity.

The smile died in the eyes of Tyson. He looked blankly at the other man as a man might look at a child who asks why the stars give light.

"I don't know, Garth. I really can't put it in words."

It left Garth floundering, in the nether-darkness. He felt his face grow warm as Tyson continued, studying Garth with that same aloofness, "You had me down—helpless—you—you beat me!"

He flushed suddenly, and his teeth set in a flash of white.

"I don't suppose that has ever happened before in the history of our family."

"No?" said Garth. He glanced complacently down to his burly hand. "Isn't that stretching it a bit, Tyson? Were *all* your family good fighters?"

"Fighters?" cried Tyson. "Fighters?"

What a ring came into his voice!

"Why, man, they followed the Black Prince—and they've been fighting ever since. Fighters? Old Sir Gregory——"

He stopped as short as though a knife had cut off the sentence. And Garth, in a flash of intuition, knew why. These things were not to be talked of to a rough engineer. Yes, Tyson might use the manhood of Garth as a model, but once one entered into the social world the old barrier stood as strong as adamant. The big man followed his line of thought to draw him out.

"Tyson, speaking of fighting, why don't you begin a war on your own account? If you're interested in engineering, for instance, why don't you study the work; begin on your own hook, so to speak? There's enough fighting represented in that dam, for instance, to occupy three generations of you—fighters!"

He said it with a fierce conviction, and then his heart sank as Tyson walked carelessly over towards the window and glanced out at the dam. Dismissed with a single look! He turned back to the big boss, and as he turned the light caught at his face and hardened it with shadows, and he seemed to Garth to be suddenly in a picture (the window was the frame) and looking down into the twentieth century out of a time of rapiers and ruffles and deadly courtesies.

"Oh," murmured Tyson good-naturedly, "this working about at the dam is interesting—very. But I wouldn't care to go in for this sort of thing in person. I'd rather look at the picture someone else has painted."

"Nonsense!" argued Garth, rather heated. He felt

like a small boy put into his place by a rebuff. "Come to supper tonight and talk it over. You're interested in this work too much to take such a casual attitude."

Tyson seemed suddenly embarrassed. His eyes grew thoughtful.

"Very kind of you to ask me," he murmured. "But I don't think I can dine with you this evening."

It was all in that word "dine," thought Garth. "Supper" in his home, and "dinner" in Tyson's. A very fragile difference, but the spider thread was strong enough to hold them apart as effectually as chains of iron. They stood in the same room, but each was in a different world, and Garth felt that no Columbus could ever cross that soundless sea of pride.

Seven
The Necktie

A little later Tyson went down the slope from the dam towards the town of La Blanca at its foot. The last of the workers on the day shift were sauntering with the slowness of the weary in the same direction, and up from La Blanca came the tag end of the workers of the night shift.

For night and day the labour at the dam went on. Every hour, now, counted heavily in the final reckoning, for if the dam failed of completion when the big spring floods commenced, a countless wealth of water might be lost to rush away through the unready sluice gates and wander off to utter waste on the unfinished canals that traced a tangled pattern across the desert.

Tyson walked with his hat in his hand, for the slant evening sun struck past La Blanca with only a pleasant warmth. On every side of him bobbed enormous sombreros, for nine-tenths of the labour on the dam was performed by imported peons.

Under the hats were round, brown faces, and the controlling colour note of the mob was drab. To be sure there was plenty of colour, crimsons and blues and purples, but dirt, and common time, had blended them all together. So a muddy river takes the turbulent colouring of a sunset and softens all the tones into its own mud-brown.

Now and then through the brown background loomed a lighter note—the tall form of a white foreman or mechanic. But these occasional figures did not interest Tyson. His eyes were upon the Mexicans, and they in turn volleyed back glances upon him with their glittering black eyes.

There was a childish curiosity in their manner, but no childish impudence. They knew the different classes of the "gringo," and they knew that Tyson belonged to the upper caste. Yet he did common drudgery, and that was enough to set their imaginations on fire. He had not been a day at the dam on the Chiluah before a thin stream of rumour went abroad among the peons that there was in their midst a man of mystery.

They began to make up tales about him; and in a day they were believing their own inventions. And it was not unpleasant to Tyson to feel those eyes of curiosity upon him.

He entered the outskirts of the town of La Blanca, which had grown up at the foot of the mountain. A bit of old Mexico, it was. Certainly there was nothing about the dam which stood as a greater tribute to the thorough and patient care of Garth.

To fill his great need of a vast mass of unskilled labour at a cheap price there was only the peon. But the peon does not like to work, and he does not like to stay in one place. His Indian blood speaks in both of these qualities. Garth trusted to his own indomitable will, working through capable overseers, to make them industrious; to hold them steadily to the job he summoned up for them at the mouth of the Chiluah cañon a true Mexican town.

To shop in such a marketplace was an inspiration—a joy, for in the stores were not the grim, high-priced gringo salesman, but their own compatriots, amiable, wheedling, robbing when they could, and yielding the palm to the able bargainer. The women looked forward to their day's shopping; it was the great event in every twenty-four hours.

And as for the men, the police were *not* in this hand-made city. Morals were one thing with Ed Garth; dam building was quite another. So he had brought in no police. He could not escape the office of a deputy United States marshal in the midst of the place, but the marshal was a good-natured sort. He had done his fighting in his youth; now he was quite willing to retire on his reputation.

So there grew up in a certain central portion of the little town a group of gambling houses where a man could joyously throw away in a few seconds all that he had acquired through six days of sweaty labour. Also, there were tobacco shops which displayed cigars of terrible and unknown powers and weird odours.

In a word, all that the heart of female or masculine Mexico could desire was present in this demi-Eden. The fame of La Blanca went abroad.

Dirt and squalor everywhere, but everywhere, also, life and happiness abounding. So it was no wonder that Tyson strolled at his leisure and made his way from street to street and plaza to plaza contentedly. He observed and he was observed. The very children in the streets ceased their tumbling and gaped at him as he passed, and silence was about him, while murmurs went before and behind.

So he came at length to the plaza mayor, and to the entrance of a clothing store with bright scarfs displayed in the window.

He passed idly into the store, and from case to case. The world has not neckwear to compare with the brilliance of the Mexican; before a case of scarfs and neckties Tyson paused, for his eyes had caught on a strip of silk heavily figured with gold and black—bright gold that was almost yellow, splotching the black with diamond-shaped spots like the markings of a snake's back. "How much?" he asked.

"Cinco pesos, señor."

"I'll take it. And that green affair?"

He took the two, shoved the parcel into his pocket, and wandered across the town at a more rapid gait towards the colonia, where lived the white element of the workers on the dam; overseers, bosses, skilled mechanics, engineers, and many others.

Eight
Room without Board

This white section of the town lay higher up the slope of La Blanca and could be reached more quickly from the dam, unless one chose, as Tyson generally did, to stroll through the peon quarters.

Tyson paused on the veranda of the rooming-house kept by Mrs. Irene Casey.

"A week or—a month?" asked Mrs. Casey, as she poised her pen above the receipt.

"A week," said Tyson.

"Room *and* board?" queried Mrs. Casey with an enticing smile.

Seeing that Tyson hesitated, she added quickly: "It ain't no bit of wonder that you're lookin' peaked and thin, young man, if you go on eating that Mex stuff. Time'll turn anybody's hair grey"—here she patted her own silver locks with something of a sigh—"but that Spanish cookin' ages the insides."

She filled out her argument with a gesture and

a look of graveyard solemnity.

"As a matter of fact, Mrs. Casey," said Tyson, and he gave her smile for smile, "I've about made up my mind——"

He felt for the coins in his pocket, but his fingers closed on one only. It was small, hardly larger than a nickel, and there came a grim and sudden realisation to Tyson that his worldly wealth was shrunk to a single five-dollar gold-piece.

He continued, not over-smoothly: "I've about made up my mind to board here, but I think I'll put it off for another week or so."

He slid the gold-piece carelessly across the table. Mrs. Casey picked it up slowly, the while she considered Tyson with a gloomy interest.

"Young man," she said solemnly, "the day'll come! You'll remember what I've told you—when you pay the doctor!"

"Three dollars for the room," she continued, dropping the money into her drawer and pushing back the change. "We all got to learn by experience. Can't take nobody else's advice. Well, I hope you don't come to no harm!"

Tyson stood weighing the change in his hand and the glance of Mrs. Casey softened as it dwelt on that uncalloused, inexperienced palm. Her eyes flashed up, prepared for kindliness, motherliness, and they dwelt in turn on the brightness of his eyes, careless, defiant.

"Good night!" said Mrs. Casey sharply.

Tyson nodded absent-mindedly in reply and turned away. When he reached his room upstairs the two dollar-pieces were still tightly gripped in his hand. A silver dollar is a comfortably broad coin; the weight and the size of these two were surpassingly cheerful to Tyson. But it occurred to him with depressing force that a week consists of seven days, and that two divided by seven leaves something under a third. It left for each of the intervening days until the next pay exactly twenty-eight and four-sevenths cents. This might have covered the amount of a single tip for an ordinary meal of Tyson's, but as the total means of subsistence for twenty-four hours—his mind went blank.

It was possible, perhaps, to live on bread and milk or even bread and water. Even then, it would be necessary to partake of only two meals a day. He must start by fasting on this first evening.

The odour of frying bacon has called the despondent failure from the thoughts of suicide to hopes of life and happiness; and it needs no long consultation on the pages of history to prove that the stomach is our least heroic part.

Tyson tightened his belt, but it did not aid him. His mouth watered, and a mist rose, clouding his eyes. Into his ear burst suddenly the roaring voice of his written contract with Garth, like a far-off waterfall: "You shall live by the labour of your hands!"

And he had agreed.

Suddenly Tyson drew out the brilliant necktie from his pocket and crumpled it into a ball to throw through the window. But before the burst of childish rage made him complete the act, his eye caught on the sheen of yellow-gold against the black.

He sat down again, scowling, and dropped the necktie across his knees. After all, there was an element of beauty in the thing, glaring though it might be. It lay now, silken to the touch, dropping across his legs like the body of a gorgeous snake. And considering the seven lean days which lay ahead of him, there was a sinister connotation in that luckless piece of silk.

He ran his fingers along its shining length, and smiled. The image of the snake had returned to him again in the gaudy colouring of the bit of silk. And there was not much of the philosopher about Henry Tyson, but his imagination had wings.

Nine
Ham and Eggs

He was up the next morning with the sun. There were no moments of miserable half sleep and half waking such as used to plague him in New York, but as soon as his eyes were open, he was out of bed with a leap, like a horse under the spur. And indeed there was an inner spur for Tyson.

Behind him lay a night of terrific dreams. He had been banqueting in his sleep, eating tremendously and drinking vastly, but suddenly realised that the food did not dull the edge of his appetite. Vast pasties, mountains of brown, crisp crust surmounting inner treasures of meat; sweetmeats; viands of three zones; all these had been stacked upon the board of his imaginings, and yet all of them could not appease his hunger.

A terrible sensation! Famine herself had lived in his bowels. The anguish of Tantalus was trebly his. And now that he wakened, there was a poignant reminder that the dreams had not been altogether things of air, for a keen pain lay somewhere in his vitals.

Shaving and bathing were the briefest of ceremonies this morning—the Sabbath morning when the fortunate breakfasted late and heartily, but early though Tyson was, the cooks in the kitchen below were earlier still, and as he tied his necktie the aroma of frying ham drifted keenly to him. A sharp pain struck through the midriff of Tyson, and his brain spun dizzily.

Yet, as he started to rush from the room, his eye caught on the yellow-and-black necktie, still draped over the back of the chair, he caught it up, and ran on, chuckling. The necktie was an omen.

On the street below he checked his run to a walk, but such a walk as would have taxed the powers of a trained athlete to keep pace with. And everything about him, the sweet coolness of the morning air itself, whetted the razor-edge of his hunger.

He had to go several blocks before he reached a restaurant, and the one which he eventually found was merely a hole in the wall, a lunch counter; but through the window he beheld a man in white cap and apron frying ham and eggs and hot cakes on a broad slab of iron. It was the goodliest sight which had ever met the eye of Henry Tyson.

He snapped his fingers at the waiter as he swung on to a stool.

"Ham!" said Tyson, and then choked. "And eggs"—he continued hoarsely—"and hot cakes. Stacks of 'em. Piles of 'em. And quick!"

The waiter stared at him, but he had seen hungry men before, and even while he stared a plate of bread and a pat of butter and knife and fork and spoon clattered upon the imitation-marble top of the counter. Butter—but that was a needless luxury; the teeth of Tyson were instantly in the bread.

The minute hand of the clock stole on past one little black line after another; and not until it had made a complete revolution of the dial did Tyson push back on his stool with a sigh of success. Automatically he reached into a coat pocket, but his hand came out empty. His hungry eye darted at a glass case filled with cigars and cigarettes. And among the cigarettes the first box which met his glance was his favourite Egyptian brand. A moment later he was drawing down great breaths of smoke.

"How much?" he asked, and puffed a cloud toward the ceiling.

"Eighty and twenty," said the waiter. "One buck."

The hand of Tyson, already in his pocket, closed convulsively on his entire capital. One from two left one.

"What!" he cried.

"Twenty for the cigarettes," said the waiter, prepared to argue. "And ham and eggs——"

"Never mind," groaned Tyson, and shoved the large, round dollar across the counter.

On the street again, however, his spirits rose instantly. The spring air, dry and cool, at this hour, fanned his forehead; he had eaten to repletion; the familiar thick, sweet smoke went deep into his lungs.

If there are three qualifications for mortal happiness, meat and tobacco are two of them. Tyson was happy. And in his mood of aimless content he wandered up the slope, past the dam, where cranes and derricks stood idle—for even a Garth could not work peons on Sunday—and up the valley of the Chiluah.

It was the first time he had gone up the stream for any distance, but now his careless mood led him on and on. Just above the dam the valley was sparsely wooded, but the trees thickened as he proceeded, mostly short-trunked and of species of which he knew nothing. Of course he knew the cottonwoods and the willows, particularly thick along the edges of the Chiluah, but the rest were new to him.

The leaves were a lighter and yellower green than any foliage with which he had been familiar in the East. And throughout the forest, in every open space, there was the inevitable cactus of the Southwest, sometimes broad, heavy leaves, close to the ground, sometimes tall and slender stalks armed with terrific thorns that could defy beast and birds and keep the worthless dry pith safe in the stem. Sometimes he found tiny shrubs bearing pears covered with an armour thick with reddish spines.

Through such patches as these he had to pick his way with care, for he knew that the thorns were often of sufficient strength to pierce the stoutest shoe-leather, and they made deep, poisonous wounds, like the teeth of a beast of prey. He had seen the effect of them on the feet of the peons.

He went on very leisurely. His mind moved sluggishly, for all his spare energy was wrapped around the good things in his stomach, and he still thought of the tasty ham, and his nostrils pulled down the cigarette smoke deeper and deeper.

In the same manner his eyes nibbled at the good things about him, and even in the burned basin of the Chiluah noted each variety—the changes in the outgrowths of rock, for instance. Sometimes they showed the red stains of copper ore, and now and again he picked up a fragment of quartz glittering with sparks of yellow.

Perhaps those very rocks had been broken off by the hammer of some prospector who had wandered up the Chiluah equipped with a set of drills, a mucking-spoon, and a single jack, ready to read the secrets of the stones, and hunting always for gold. How many had gone up this same valley on the still hunt for treasure, but finding their happiness more in the pursuit than in the actual possession of the metal. He had heard tales of those hardy men following a brave tomorrow around the world.

Some time, he decided, he would take time off and learn the signs of the rocks. And he would know what the varying colours of the soil meant. At this point in his musings he stopped and listened to the lazy sound of the church bells welling up from La Blanca, far, far behind him, and spreading in small waves, and breaking upon his ears with soft and irregular plashings. That sound died out and again the silence crept about him. He began to feel a mysterious sense of content—intimacy with nature.

Ten
The Whistler

It was, indeed, the most silent forest he had ever seen. He knew the hush of woodlands, but usually there are little sounds and noises which creep into one's consciousness by dim degrees. Once noted they continue—buzzing of insects, and bird voices diminutive in the distance. None of this here. It was not until he had lighted his second cigarette and paused with the thought of turning back that the hush was broken.

It was a musical duet of two whistling birds, sometimes long, solitary, inviting whistles, sometimes quick, down-pattering bursts of twittering. Towards this sound, cautiously, for sometimes it seemed near and again far off, Tyson made his way. It was at one of the times when the whistling seemed farthest away—indeed, when he was about to give up the futile hunt—that he found a further reason for turning back. A little creek, half a dozen paces in width, came murmuring across his path, sent from some spring in the hills above.

As he turned to leave, however, the whistling broke out again, near, loud, and, glancing up sharply, he saw one of the two birds perched in the top of a slender sapling—a top so slender that even the meagre weight of the bird kept it swaying here and there, and it was necessary for the bird to steady itself with frequent spreadings and flurries of the wings.

Never had Tyson seen plumage more brilliant. He made out yellow legs and a blue body, with a breast of gold and crimson and green, and wings shouldered with scarlet and commingled yellows. These were the details of the colours, but as the songster balanced with flurrying wings on the sapling top, the sun shifted and blended and mixed the colours till sometimes it seemed a solid flash of gold, then a blur of blue, then a glow of scarlet and again a mixture of all those rich colours beyond words to describe.

The feathers of his tiny crest were now so ruffled that they stood up almost on end, and as Tyson watched, the bird started that sharp scolding, looking down at the ground.

Tyson followed that glance and his eyes fell on a girl seated on the farther side of the creek. It startled him almost to fear, at first, for it seemed so inscrutable to him, and it struck on his fancy as if the girl were in fact the other bird turned to human flesh.

But obviously enough she was plain woman, and busy now with the most womanly of occupations. She had been washing her hair in the soft waters of the creek, apparently, and now she dried it in the sun—a black and silken mass so long that the hand with which she combed it could hardly reach to the ends.

She was a brown beauty. It was impossible to imagine a hat on that wild head, and the strong sun had tanned her deeply. Not her face and throat and agile hands alone; her dress was chiefly rags and tatters, a single garment, and where a thorn had rent it at the shoulder the skin looked out as dark as the hands or face. He might have thought her an Indian girl, but there was too generous a width between the eyes, the forehead was too broad and low, and, above all, there was a singular and speaking delicacy of the features, particularly of curves about the mouth.

Yet, in spite of eyes and mouth and hair she was not beautiful. She had not sufficient repose for real beauty. There was about her an unrest, the alertness of the wild. It danced in her eyes as visibly as the sparkling of the sun on the waters; it showed in the lightning, graceful movement of wrist and hand; and as she sat there, at ease, one felt that in the instant she could be on her feet and lost in the forest. Lost at a whirlwind speed that it would be folly to pursue.

Yet, the most perfect and Grecian repose and regularity of feature could not have given her a greater charm than this piquancy, this uncertainty, this aloofness. She was like a perfume thrown on the wind and blown into one's very soul. The eye of Tyson—a sharp, hungry eye—went from the brilliant bird to the girl beside the water and back again.

Suddenly, as the scolding of the blue beauty from the sapling reached a moment's pause, she tilted back her head, pursed her mouth, and whistled. It was an imitation so exact, so perfectly modulated, that Tyson held his breath to listen. The long strain, so light and sharp, broke, wavered, began again, rose, fell—the wild bird which calls for its mate, the weirdness of the pipe, the sharpness of the flute, the complaint of the violin, all gathered into the thin, sweet note.

The scene was blotted out for Tyson. He stood instantly in an English garden at full night, with the violets and the early roses breathing about him in the dark, and the shimmer of the lilies very faint by the pond, and the hedge gleaming under the moon, when the nightingale began its song.

The whistling ended; he was flung across six thousand miles of sea and land to the sunny valley of the Chiluah. He looked up to the bird on the sapling. It sat quite still, with its head cocked a little to one side as if it still listened—laughably like a connoisseur of music. Then the gleaming feathers of his throat swelled and bristled. He tucked back his crested head and began his long reply.

Her imitation had seemed perfect until the thin, pure reply of the bird began, and Tyson saw her frown with swift anger as the long, sweet note drew out. Before that first note died away, the slender hand of the girl darted out as swiftly as the head of a striking snake, and the next instant a stone struck the sapling under the very feet of the songster.

The bird was away, his scolding floating back behind him; and the girl stood up, shaking her fist after him, and stamping in a fury of angry disappointment. Her eyes were still blazing, her mouth still sulky, when she turned again and faced Tyson. She did not spring back from him, but she started, and remained there poised—the wind moved her hair aside, fluttered her dress—in a picture she would have seemed to be running already.

But the alarm passed as the reflection of a cloud whips across the surface of a narrow pool. She cast another angry glance in the direction of the bird.

"It was the wind that made me miss," she said. "It moved the tree."

"No," said Tyson, "your aim was too low."

Her anger rose like flame blown leaping by a touch of wind; instantly she was aglow.

She cried: "It was *not* too low! The wind——"

"I saw the stone strike," said Tyson. "It landed below the feet of the bird."

"No, no, no!" she stormed. "It did *not!*"

It thrilled him oddly to feel her opposition. Seeing her so angrily defiant, he was more sharply aware of her youth—the lines so slender at once, and so rounded. There is something in that age between girlhood and womanhood which carries home to the heart like music. He could not keep back the smile.

She leaned and stood erect again with a swiftness no eye could follow. In her hand she held another stone, and this one of formidable proportions.

"If you mock me——" she threatened.

"Well?" asked Tyson.

"I never miss *twice,*" said the girl.

He regarded the stone about which her fingers were tightening. The edges of it were uncomfortably jagged. But for some reason Tyson knew at once that he would have to come closer to the girl. He swept the stream with a glance.

A little above him the course of the water—which was everywhere comparatively shallow—was broken by stones which projected well above the surface. They were a risky distance apart, but a crossing might be managed.

"I'm coming over for a chat," said Tyson, and moved over opposite the stones.

"You'll stay where you are," responded the girl confidently.

"Are you sure?"

"Yes."

"What makes you so sure?"

"This."

She tossed up the stone and caught it again, deftly.

"You think I'm afraid of that?"

"All men are cowards," she announced with conviction.

She stood now with her arms akimbo and surveyed him with an insolently measuring glance.

"Who told you that?" he asked.

"Padre Miguel," she answered.

"He is a fool!" said Tyson.

"A fool!" she echoed, more in wonder than in anger. And then, shrugging her shoulders: "But you know he cannot hear you."

"I suppose it would be dangerous if he did?"

"Look at that branch."

She raised her arm, the ragged sleeve fell back to the shoulder.

"Well?"

"He would wither you like that—with a word!"

"Ah!" murmured Tyson, smiling once more.

"Are you mocking me again?"

"No, I'm mocking Padre Miguel."

"Do you know what comes to men who mock the padre?"

"Tell me."

"They are kept another hundred years in purgatory, and red fire is poured down their throats every day."

She made a grimace.

"Get your stone ready," said Tyson, "for I'm coming."

And instantly he was on the way.

Eleven

The Wisdom of the Padre

It was not altogether a simple task, for the stones were wet, and the least misjudgment of distance would send Tyson and his single suit of clothes headlong into the water and rolling along in the sharp current; but each spring he made was true to the fraction of an inch. Once, indeed, he slipped and staggered, but recovered himself with the address of a bird fluttered by an unexpected gust of wind. A second later he was safely upon the farther bank, and looked up to her.

She had retreated as swiftly as he came, and now she stood at the edge of the little clearing, her stone poised strongly above her shoulder, and her eyes afire with a stern light.

"If all *men* are the cowards," laughed Tyson, panting, "why are you *afraid?*"

"Afraid?" she echoed. "I'm never afraid."

"Then why do you run away?"

"Why do you dodge a snake?" she countered.

"Ah, then men are snakes! The good Padre Miguel has told you this, as well?"

"Yes."

"But how the deuce am I to talk with you if you stand over there with that infernal stone levelled at my head all the time?" he asked, with a touch of irritation.

"I have not asked you to talk to me," she said.

"And I suppose that's the very reason I want to."

Perhaps it was the heat of the sun, which was gradually increasing, or it may have been the continual threat of the poised stone. At any rate, Tyson dropped his hand into a pocket to bring out a handkerchief and wipe his forehead, but what the hand brought forth was the ominous yellow-and-black necktie. It dangled at full length from his fingers, flashing and twisting like a live thing in the sun.

"Oh!" cried the girl.

Her face was alight with a smile of eagerness. The stone dropped unheeded to the ground. She made a step towards him. Tyson grew strangely thoughtful. He considered the shining face of this stranger, the five dollars he had spent on this necktie, the single dollar remaining to his pocket, the six long days which would intervene before Saturday's pay.

"Do you like it?" And he flashed the silk in the sun.

"Oh!" she murmured again. Then, with the directness of a child: "Give it to me!"

He followed his first impulse and extended it towards her; he followed a second thought and closed his fingers over it. And at the same instant she snatched at it. They stood facing each other, each clutching an end of the tie. The girl was panting with excitement; it seemed to Tyson that her eyes alternately widened and expanded; she was like a hunted animal brought to bay. And he could not tell whether in the next minute she would turn and race off among the trees—or spring at his throat. It sent a tingling up his spine.

"I'll sell it to you," said Tyson.

She frowned.

"Not for a money price. But some things you can tell me."

"What things?"

"Why, your name, for instance."

"Rona Armitage Carnahan."

She jerked the necktie from his fingers and leaped away, but at the edge of the clearing, glancing back and seeing that he did not follow, she came to an abrupt halt and faced him again. The yellow-black of the silk was pressed to her breast.

Tyson sat down at the edge of the stream, cross-legged, his back to a broad stone. He began to whistle. It was all the inspiration of a moment, but it worked perfectly, for in a moment he knew from the corner of his eye that she was stealing back towards him with gliding, noiseless steps. His whistling was almost destroyed by the thought of this girl stalking *him*.

Her shadow fell over him. She was sitting upon the top of a nearby stone, frowning curiously down on him, the necktie still clasped in both hands.

"Why did you give me this?" she asked.

"I didn't give it. You took it, you know."

"Oh!" she cried softly. "Then I suppose I should give it back?"

Before he could speak she went on: "But I don't think I will."

"Padre Miguel will be very angry when you tell him," suggested Tyson gravely.

"Oh, he is always angry when I speak of a man, even of the Big Man."

"I knew," growled Tyson, "that there was a Big Man in it somewhere."

"But," she pursued thoughtfully. "I think you would have given it to me, anyway, in another minute. Wouldn't you?"

"I suppose I would," admitted Tyson.

"Why?"

"For the same reason I crossed the creek, I think."

She was silent a moment, her chin resting on her clenched fist, studying him.

"That's odd," she pronounced at last. "But you're different from the rest, aren't you?"

"Not quite so snaky?" he suggested.

"Not quite," she said grudgingly.

It came to him that she spoke amazingly pure English, this waif of the Chiluah. He turned a bit, so as to face her more squarely, and he took off his hat. At that she gave a delighted cry and clapped her hands together.

"What is it?" he asked.

"May I touch your head?"

"Why the deuce do you want to do that?"

"I'll do it ever so gently."

"Fire away, then!"

Her hand stole out, cautiously; her lips were parted in awe and delight. So she touched his hair and then snatched back her hand and studied the tips of her fingers.

"It isn't paint," she said, frankly amazed, and

then looked down to him with a new wonder: "What makes your hair so—yellow?"

"It just happens that way."

She frowned, like one who will not be put off with a light answer.

"Padre Miguel will tell me then." She edged closer to him on the rock, smiling. "You're funny, aren't you?" she suggested. "What's your name?"

"Henry Tyson."

She repeated: "Henry Tyson. That's different, too. What do you do?"

"I work on the dam."

She smiled incredulously.

"Don't you think I'm telling you the truth?"

"All men lie to women," said this child of the wilderness.

"The devil they do! Padre Miguel told you that also?"

"Of course."

"But why shouldn't I work on the dam?"

"You aren't the kind who work."

"Where do you see the signs?"

"Men who work have dull faces. They are like the faces of starved steers when there is no grass on the range in winter. But you, señor, have a little bright devil in each eye. But do not be afraid. I shall not tell the Padre Miguel! Oh, by no means!"

"Thank you," said Tyson. "It would anger him to know, of course."

"Oh, yes. He would drive the two little devils away."

"Naturally," assented Tyson dryly.

"But—shall I tell you a great secret?"

"Well?"

"I like those same points of fire—rather. They

are like eyes within eyes. Also, I will tell you another thing. Shall I?"

"By all means."

"When I raised the rock I was really hoping all the time that you would come across the stream, Señor Tyson."

"By jove!" murmured Tyson. "What a bully, frank sort you are! But, by the way, what are you going to do with that?"

"See!" she answered, and, gathering back her hair, she passed the bright band of the necktie round her head and tied it behind. It changed her amazingly; it made her instantly a wild Indian, untamed and untamable. She leaned above the water, and Tyson, glancing down, saw the image smiling up to her.

"I like it," she said, facing him again. "Don't you?"

"I'm glad I gave it to you," he said.

"Ah," she sighed, "that makes it perfect. If you are glad, then I shall not have to tell Padre Miguel."

"What would he do if he knew that you had—taken it?"

"He would only talk. But, ah, how the good padre talks! His words are little things, but they work into the flesh like thorns until they pierce the heart. Sometimes after he has talked to me I've lain awake all night and cried."

"I'd like to see this padre."

"The padre would not like you. He would send you away for ever, and I should be sorry. The hair of other men is not like gold, you see. And yet——"

She stopped, watching him with caution and curiosity.

"Why do you smile at me like that, Señor Tyson?"

"For the same reason that brought me across the creek?"

"Will you tell me?"

"Because you're so beautiful, Rona."

She sprang up, quick as fear, her finger at her lip, her eyes darting about like a hunted thing towards every covert of trees and rocks.

"If you had been heard!" she cried softly.

"What's wrong, in the name of heaven?"

"You must never again—never—call me beautiful! The padre knows everything—he is everywhere! If he heard you say that to me he—he would make you lose your way in the desert—he would make you wander for days and days without water!"

"Because I called you——"

But she sprang to him in terror and closed his mouth with her hand. He felt the quiver of her fingers; he saw her head turned, and the frightened glances once more seeking an eavesdropper.

"I saved you!" she panted, standing straight again.

"But tell me what's wrong in saying—that—to you?"

"How should I know what is wrong in it? But the padre has told me—oh, so many times and in so many terrible ways—that men who call me beautiful have devils in them. How can I know why?"

"I think I might like the padre, Rona."

"And yet," she said, and she leaned close, whispering: "I am *so* glad that I heard you say it."

She sat on her rock again and asked him seriously: "Am I very wicked?"

"You're delightful," said Tyson. "Is that permitted?"

"I suppose so," she said cautiously. "But I shan't ask the padre."

"No?"

"No, because something tells me he would say it is very wrong. I myself, señor, *feel* that it is wrong!"

"Explain yourself, Rona."

"Have you ever taken fire upon the end of two sticks, and played with it?"

"Never."

"It is great fun. You can dance with the fire, and in the night it is lovely to watch against the sky. But then the flame may drop down the sticks, very suddenly, and set your clothes all on fire. It is dangerous, you see. And talking with you, Señor Tyson, is like dancing with the fire."

She sat suddenly, stiffly erect.

"Hush!" she said, her lips framing the caution soundlessly. "Someone is watching us! I feel it!"

And Tyson, turning, saw a sight that made his blood run cold. For on the edge of the forest, leaning against a tree, was the strangest figure of a man he had ever seen. It was an old face, and yet it was framed in jet black hair—long, wild hair. His skin was sickly pale. His eyes were so bright a brown that they seemed red, and the man was laughing silently, like the grin of a wolfhound.

Tyson turned his head slowly back to the girl. She was already on her feet.

"He has come for me," she said. "Good-bye, Señor Tyson!"

And when Tyson rose he no longer saw the ghastly, laughing face beside the tree, but towards this place Rona walked and disappeared instantly among the foliage.

"Is that Padre Miguel?" muttered Tyson to himself, "or is it the Big Man?"

He kicked another stone out of his way, viciously, and then turned and looked back through the trees. Far away a bird began whistling.

"The devil take the girl," muttered Henry Tyson.

Twelve
Tequila?

Now that time meant so much to him, Garth lived under a tremendous strain, rising with the first light of day, and labouring incessantly until midnight and later. Sometimes for twenty-four hours at a stretch he did not close his eyes; many a day his only rest was an hour flat upon the floor with his arms thrown wide, crosswise. He had a vast reserve of muscular and nervous energy, and he drew upon it remorselessly to meet the crisis.

For without him work on the dam went helter-skelter. There was no assistant, no second to whom he could entrust the management for even a moment. Now a few days at top speed and a little luck in the delaying of the spring floods, and all would be well.

He multiplied himself, and the commonest labourer felt the eye and the inspiration of the big boss.

The casual observer could have noticed little difference in the roughly hewn face of Garth: he was a little thinner, that was all. But to the careful eyes, there was a long story in the bulge of the muscles at the base of the jaw, the hollowing of the cheek, the sinking and brightening of the eye: and the most careless of those who saw him daily noted a nervous habit growing upon him—a restless flexing and reflexing of his right hand that continued without ceasing, day and night, as if he were taking up the uncompleted labours of others who had failed.

Living in this atmosphere of endless strain, no success made him smile, no failure made him scowl. He kept an even front to all occasions.

So, on this Thursday afternoon, when Garth stopped with an exclamation and a scowl, the young engineer who was going the round of the works with the big boss looked upon him with astonishment and concern. The smashing of the fifty-ton crane the day before had not brought such an outburst from Ed Garth. He swept all things around him with a startled eye, but all seemed to be running without interruption or flaw; perhaps some singular intuition had brought news of disaster to the builder.

"What is it?" asked the engineer at last.

"Don't you hear, Harris?" cried the big man in one of his rare bursts of impatience.

The terrific clangour of steel on steel, stone on stone, the voices of engines and men—surely it was an uproar worthy of the heart of hell, but nothing which seemed out of place at the dam.

"Not a thing that's wrong."

"The singing, man!" cried Garth. "Damn it, don't you hear that singing?"

From the side of La Cabeza, at the base of the dam, it rose—a Mexican air which Harris did not know.

"Why," he said, "the Mex often sing while they're working, don't they? Thought it was a good sign?"

"They sing when they work—sometimes," growled Garth; "but they don't sing in the cement storehouse! And by God, that's where they're singing now!"

Beyond doubt that was the source of the music, now that Harris bent his ear to listen in that direction. He called up a picture of the storehouse—the sweltering heat which seemed magnified to oven intensity by the roof of corrugated iron—the wraiths of white cement dust that bite the skin and eat at the lungs.

It was surely impossible to conceive cheerful singing from such a place. To the cement house the unruly spirits were consigned—the most powerful and dangerous Yaquis, for instance—and ten days of that labour brought them forth limp of body and docile of spirit.

"It isn't possible!" cried Harris. "The devil himself couldn't sing in that place!"

"Tequila!" said Garth.

His nervous right hand balled itself into a mighty fist; the buffet of those broad, bony knuckles might have crushed plate-armour.

"There's been more smuggling of the stuff," he went on, "and if I catch the men that have done it I'll make them an example that'll cry to Heaven!" He concluded after an instant of gloomy silence: "Tequila!" and strode off towards the cement house with young Harris fairly running to keep up with the longer legs of his chief.

For if rum has been called "demon" among the

whites, tequila deserves the title of "Satan" among the Mexicans. It is the super-devil among drinks. It is distilled from that species of the maguey called zotol, which grows extensively in the state of Jalisco near the town of Tequila, hence its name.

It is like clear water in appearance; it has the power of liquid dynamite. With its peculiar and pungent odour and "green" taste, few white men like it. Even the native Mexican is apt to disguise its flavour.

First he sprinkles salt on his wrist, and prepares a slice of lemon. Then he tastes the salt, drinks the tequila, and sucks the lemon in rapid alternation without drawing breath between. Imbibed in this manner, the stuff is not unpleasant, and the peon loves it with a consuming passion.

A wineglass full will stagger the uninitiated, but the natives drink it copiously with little noticeable effect. Yet the effects of the intoxication last for many hours, and produce in the end a murderous and brooding depression. Mexicans drunk on tequila are like starved wolves; they turn their teeth on each other.

Several times cargoes of this liquid poison had been brought surreptitiously to the workers on the dam. One shipment resulted in a widespread strike. A second brought about a deadly knife fight that laid up twenty men in the hospital. So the word "tequila" had deep meaning for Garth. It had equal meaning for young Harris, and knowing the bare-handed methods of his chief, he blanched, and made sure that his revolver was loaded and ready for instant use.

In this manner they hurried to the cement house, and climbed up to the broad dirty platform. At the same time the plaintive strains of La Paloma rose from the depths of the building. It was a moment before they could take in the details of the situation.

On the platform on the farther side of the warehouse thousands of sacks of cement had recently been dumped, and these were being carted with hand trucks from the outside pile to the interior of the building. The white dust filled the place like a thick fog, and turned the labourers into ghostly figures, powdered from head to foot.

The endless chain of trucks turned steadily between the pile and the neat stacks of sacks inside; they could make out that in the weighted inward journey the men were silent—the breath jolted from their lungs, but as they turned back each man struck into the song of the moment. Garth regarded the scene with a sombre eye.

"What does it mean?" asked Harris, white of face.

"Mutiny inside of twenty-four hours," responded Garth curtly. "These brown devils are never happy except when they're planning mischief. Go find Rodriguez and ask him what he means by letting this run on unreported? No, I'll go with you!"

Rodriguez, a redoubtable half-breed famous for his grim temper and his skill with the knife, they found perched on a stack of empty sacks, his black hair powdered white with dust, his dark face similarly discoloured, and raised in a minstrel ecstasy while he boomed out the strains of La Paloma—"The Dove!" Across his knees he held a banjo with two strings missing, and kept some sort of accompaniment upon this instrument. The large hand of Garth fell upon the dusty shoulder of his overseer.

But to the astonishment of the big boss, Rodriguez turned his ugly face, still singing, and still singing he slowly swung himself down from the stack of sacks. It was not till that round of the song ended that he permitted himself to speak, or to be spoken to.

"What does it mean?" asked Garth, too astonished to show his anger at once. "Tequila? And you, too, Rodriguez?"

But the eye of Rodriguez was not dulled by the familiar, deadly film of tequila. He stared blankly on his chief.

"All this damned singing," went on Garth, with rising wrath, and his voice thundered over the wailing song. "What does it mean, Rodriguez? Are you all drunk? Is it tequila again?"

"Tequila?" laughed Rodriguez, shaking his head. "Ah, no, señor. It is El Oro!"

"The golden one?" growled Garth. "What the devil does he mean by that, Harris?" Then he turned again and bent a grim eye upon Rodriguez to make sure that there was no mockery in the man. The Mexican, be it known, loves a jest, but he is only too apt to point his jokes with a knife.

"Are you angry, Señor Garth?" said Rodriguez anxiously. "Is the singing bad? See!" And he gestured towards the line of truckmen. "Is it ever before known that they worked so fast?"

The labourers, indeed, were swinging along at a rapid pace.

"Too fast," rumbled Garth. "Too damned fast. Looks like tequila. And if it is—you'll sweat for it, Rodriguez."

"Tequila?" The eloquent shoulders of Rodriguez went up. "Liars have brought tales of me to the Señor Garth. No, it is not tequila. It is El Oro."

He pointed to a figure that passed singing, in a wraith of cement dust, trundling his hand truck along.

Thirteen
El Oro

"El Oro!" announced the foreman to Garth.

"El Oro—the Golden One," translated Garth for the benefit of Harris, and he stepped forward with the younger man at his side.

The name El Oro evidently came from the colour of the man's hair, for even through the cement dust it showed a bright yellow, shining where an occasional ray of sun slid between a crack in the roof of galvanised iron, and splashed upon the workers here and there. It was Henry Tyson, and Garth cursed once, briefly, and with profound emotion.

Tyson had an appearance of wild gaiety, viewed from a distance, with his head tilting back as he sang, but as he came opposite them on his loaded return journey towards the stacks of cement within, there was a pause in the music, and the face of Tyson set.

Garth saw that his face was pinched, the eyes

buried in shadow, the nostrils distended to catch deeper breaths of that acidly dusty air; and the lips drew in a thin, straight line. The moment before he seemed drunkenly happy. Now he was utterly sober, and seemed supported on his feet only by a great resolution. One moment he swaggered with the insolent gait of the self-contented; but as he retreated he seemed staggering, about to fall.

One thing Garth had noted above all. The clothes of Henry Tyson, once the pride of a Fifth Avenue tailor, were ruined beyond repair. If his pride lay at all in personal smartness, then surely that pride must have fallen utterly. His shirt, worn to tatters below the elbows by the friction of the rough sacks against the cloth, his trousers, his shoes, were layered thick with dust, and through the dust had worked his perspiration, gluing cement and cloth into a sort of brittle concrete. He was not even white. He was a grisly grey.

"Drunk as a lord," chuckled Harris.

"Drunk?" repeated Garth thoughtfully. "No, undernourished, I'd say." And he muttered to himself: "The pride of the devil, but why in the name of Heaven is he doing this?"

He broke off and turned back to Rodriguez.

From him he heard a strange tale. On Monday of this week, El Oro had come asking that he be given a place in the cement gang. It was surprising, for no white man had hitherto been consigned to that bitter labour. Rodriguez had asked questions, but El Oro had insisted that he wanted the job. He even seemed eager for it.

What was there to be done? The new man did his full share of the work, and if there were any particularly obnoxious jobs, El Oro gladly did them. Rodriguez had watched El Oro. He had seen the gringo laugh at his work. There were even tales going about. Some said that the hand of God was manifestly upon the man with the golden hair.

The rest of the gang had agreed from the first that it was a miracle that a white man should ask for such bitter labour, and they were almost afraid to work beside him. Nevertheless the days went on, Monday, Tuesday, Wednesday, Thursday, and nothing had happened.

It had seemed to Rodriguez, indeed, that El Oro was a very docile madman. But on the morning of this very day—the fourth—El Oro had suddenly staggered while he was wheeling his truck along, and fallen upon the floor. When they reached him, he lay like dead, but in a moment he was again upon his feet, brushed them aside, and went on again like mad with his truckload. Aye, he even burst into song.

The rest of the gang was then sorely stricken with fear. That one should sing in the cement house was like music in hell. But there was something infectious about the singing. Another caught up the tune. Then another. Before long the whole gang was in an uproar.

The work proceeded merrily. Men worked as if they loved their labour here in this white-misted, sweltering inferno. However, Rodriguez implored Garth to let El Oro stay. Let others say what they would, he, Rodriguez, and all his crew, were glad to have this merry wild man with them.

Garth remained for another moment, watching the far-off figure of Tyson, and bit his lip. He felt almost as if the credulous Mexicans were right. The hand of God was upon Tyson, and had maddened him. Why else should the foolish fellow choose this man-killing labour?

He waited until Tyson once more passed them, trundling along his hand truck, and singing again with such force that his gait became a swagger. Or was it weakness that made him unsteady.

Garth frowned more gloomily. If Margaret Tyson found her brother in this condition—always supposing that she really came out to the dam—would she not turn her blame upon Garth himself? He stepped out and laid a hand on the dusty shoulder of Henry Tyson.

It could not have been the weight of the hand alone. It must have been more the surprise at being stopped in this unceremonious fashion. But Tyson reeled back a step as he came to a halt. He stared at Garth with wide, unseeing eyes, as if he were frightened.

"What's this mean, Tyson?" asked the big man curtly.

"Don't you see?" and Tyson smiled wanly through the dust on his face, while the sweat from his forehead slowly furrowed the grey. "Work! Work, man! And I'm doing as much as the next man. Ask the boss, over there. Ask Rodriguez."

"As much as the next, and a little more, Tyson," growled Garth. "Let me be alone with him, will you, Harris?"

Harris obediently turned away. He was glad enough to get over to the side door and draw down deep breaths of the fresh air and brush away the fine grey silt from his clothes. He was not a particularly soft-handed man, but the depths of the foulest mine were nothing compared with this inferno of sharp-scented dust and heat pouring down from the iron roof. It was so hot, indeed, that it dried perspiration almost as soon as it started, and left the skin dry and salty.

"Too much work, Tyson," continued Garth, as soon as they were alone. "You look as if you need the doctor's attention now."

"Nonsense," said Tyson calmly, and looked the other in the eye. "I'm perfectly all right."

"Enjoying yourself, eh?" suggested Garth grimly.

"I'm carrying my end of the load—the hardest load I can find at the dam. Yes, I'm enjoying it!"

"Why the devil do you wabble on your feet, then? Come over here and sit down, man; you look positively ghastly."

"It's the dust on my face," said Tyson coolly. "Also, if I knock off work I'll have my wages docked and maybe get fired. If I'm fired that means I've broken my contract."

"Damn the contract," burst out Garth.

His glance sharpened.

"Tyson, when did you last eat?"

"Eh?" The other looked about him vaguely. "Why, at noon."

"What did you have?"

"Er—sandwiches. Cold ham sandwiches and hot coffee at the restaurant over there, with Mex soup to start on and half a pie to wind up."

He lied smoothly, smiling upon Garth.

"But why do you ask?"

"Because you look half starved."

"Merely getting down to weight. Always get lean."

"Tyson, you're lying like a villain. Confound it, man, you'll do yourself a permanent harm if you aren't careful!"

"Listen to me," said Tyson gravely. "If I can't prove that I can do a man's work with my hands, I'll never be able to look at myself in a mirror after this. If I have to admit that I'm a soft-muscled parlour athlete with a yellow heart, I'll hate myself the rest of my days. Why, Garth, if you were in my place you know you'd go through with the game in spite of hell!"

Big Ed Garth looked at Tyson thoughtfully. There was more mettle in the man than he had dreamed. This was sufficiently foolish, but there was something fine at the bottom of it.

"As a matter of fact," admitted Tyson, "what keeps me going is the thought that you'd never buckle on a job like this."

There it was again. The fellow had set up Garth as a sort of model—almost an ideal. For the second time a great desire welled up in Garth to make a clean breast of the whole affair—to tell Tyson, man to man, the underlying purpose for which he had been lured out to the Chiluah—to admit that he was serving no more important purpose than bait in a trap, as far as Garth was concerned.

And then Tyson was saying: "I've been writing to Margaret and telling her that I've taken everything that comes my way. Do you think I could face her if she came out here and found that I'd just quit? Eh?"

Garth moistened his dry lips.

"She's coming?" he asked sharply.

"I don't know. Her last letter sounded a good deal as if she'd take the next train. She's lonely."

For another moment Garth paused and fought temptation.

Then: "Take care of yourself," he said, and abruptly turned on his heel.

Fourteen
The Great Hunger

It was the crossing of the Rubicon for Garth. Grant that it was a small deception which he had practised upon Tyson in the beginning; the enthusiasm of the latter had made it a thing of moment. He had more than met Garth halfway. He was playing his game fair and square and hard. And Garth winced at the thought.

He tried to console himself. After all, what could he tell Tyson? That he was in love with his sister? He had only seen her once, and Tyson would think him mad. Better let the whole matter ride, and if Tyson ever found out—well, he would risk the consequences.

He paused at the door, and spoke to Rodriguez on the way out.

"That fellow back there—El Oro, you call him," he said. "Don't let him work himself to death. I'm interested in him."

And Rodriguez replied with a flash of teeth.

Now the whistle shrieked, soon after, the end of that day, and while the rest of the day shift hurried off from the cement house, Tyson sank on the heap of empty sacks beside the boss, Rodriguez.

He remained there beside the half-breed partly because he wished to talk to Rodriguez, more largely because his aching legs for the moment refused to carry him farther.

Monday, Tuesday, and Wednesday had seen Tyson eating a single meal of bread and milk, but vegetarians to the contrary, there is no doubt that working man is a carnivorous animal; and while Tyson was not actually famished, he was sadly weakened—visions of a barbecue he had once attended haunted him.

Even that meagre diet had consumed his money. There remained to him at the end of Wednesday a single twenty-five cent piece, and this he reserved until Friday. Thursday was his day of famine. Friday he ate bread and milk—a drop of water on the desert. Now this was the last day. Before noon of Saturday he would have his week's pay—incredible wealth! And the crisis would be passed.

To the test Tyson brought, to be sure, a strong and well-trained body, and nerves of steel; but there is a vital difference between the most strenuous athletic activity and the spiritless and monotonous drain of manual labour. He who has not had to swing a pick or wield a sledgehammer for eight or ten hours a day cannot understand the bitterness of the curse by which Adam was compelled to earn his bread by the sweat of his brow.

The air in the cement house was in itself a sufficient trial. The skin of his fingers, softened by sweat and filed away by the rough sacking, was soon worn to the flesh. It was painful to grip the sacks, and once gripped, being loosely filled, they evaded one's strength.

It was like attempting to lift the body of a man who lies limp. And on the journey across the rough boards of the flooring, the heavy hand truck jerked and twisted and tugged at his arms and jolted him light-headed and settled a peculiar nausea in the pit of his stomach.

Yet he managed to fight his way through the days, calling more and more heavily on his reserve strength of nerve and muscle. And so he came to the last grim day of famine.

Now, there is nothing appalling in the thought of a two days' fast; men have been known to live for forty days, partaking of nothing but water. But there is a vast difference between idle fasting and working fasting. Any automobile will coast down hill, but it takes a good engine to tug up a grade.

Tyson was pulling up a grade, and a stiff one. The loss of a single meal means a good deal to a labourer. It makes his knees buckle and puts a mist before his eyes. The loss of two meals in a single day is enough to lay out the most powerful.

It is no wonder that Tyson, after five days of agony, and one of them a day of no nourishment, felt his head sing, and began to see visions. Two things sustained him. One was pride; the other was the thought of Garth, upon which he fed as if on meat and wine.

But on this day even pride could not quite sustain him. He had fainted utterly away, as Rodriguez related to Garth.

After that a frenzy took him. He had lasted through all the torment. Was he to fail here at the very end? He fell back on the expedient of exhausted soldiers on a forced march; he began to sing, and the rhythm of the music enabled him to drag through the day.

A bitter day. At noon came the pay, but there was no time for Tyson to eat. Hardly had he received the money when the whistle blew one o'clock, and he had to go back to his last afternoon of effort.

He had expected that the afternoon would be harder than the morning, but it was not. The point was, that his health had not been seriously weakened by the trial. He was lean. His stomach lay flat against his back-bone. But it was the leanness of the hound. His heart and his lungs were sound. He did not dream it, but in case of need he could have done thrice as much. In fact, the fear of failure was more terrible to him than the actual hunger. The horrible fear of standing before Garth and admitting that he was beaten!

But the hours went more swiftly that afternoon. And at last the merciful whistle blew for the end of the day shift. It was like dew on the desert to Tyson!

Outside the warehouse he paused at the hydrant and stripped himself to the waist and bathed. Then he went down the slope towards La Blanca. On the way he kept his head high, and the money for the week's work clutched in his hand—he dared not appear weak before these peons who glanced aside at him, murmuring: "El Oro!"

And so he reached the restaurant. All he remembered of it afterwards was that there was a gust of warmth as he entered through the swinging doors. And in the breath of warmth there was a mingling of a thousand odours of food.

Food! He did not see the faces of the eaters around him. The table was a white smear before his eyes. All he knew was that food appeared on that smear, and he ate, ate, ate. His club brothers of Manhattan would have shuddered to watch his manners; but Tyson had lapsed a few thousand years and become merely a healthy, hungry animal, feeding heavily after the fasting.

After that he sat and smoked until his head cleared, his pulse grew more even. And not until that instant did the knowledge surge warm and sweet through his veins: he had won. He had played the part of the commonest labourer, and he was victorious!

When he left the restaurant and stepped into the street he was singing softly to himself, and walking in a happy haze, when he saw a thing that threw a sharp heat into him—like three fingers of whisky in an empty stomach.

For straight before him, a matter of a few paces away, came Rona Carnahan and a tall man whom he knew as Kennedy—Kennedy, who ran the largest gambling-house in La Blanca, and who was, furthermore, the star boarder at Mrs. Irene Casey's.

It flashed upon the mind of Tyson that this might be the "big man" of whom Rona had spoken, for at this very moment Kennedy was taking a package from the hands of Rona and tucking it under his arm with an air of unmistakable proprietorship.

Fifteen
Dangerous Laughter

Yet this was not what whipped the strength of anger through Tyson. It was the necktie of Kennedy—a very loud effect of yellow spots on a black background, like the back of a gaudy snake!

He stopped, glaring at them, but they walked heedlessly by. How should they take note of a common labourer covered with cement dust? Unreasoning, childish fury took Tyson by the throat. His necktie on the gambler!

A saving touch of the ridiculous suddenly cleared his mind with a gust of laughter. His eyes were still dancing as he hailed an urchin strolling past.

"Here, you!" he called. "You see that man and that girl down the street?"

"Sí, señor."

"Run after them. Take the man by the arm, yell at him that there's a riot in his house. Understand?

Here, take this quarter," and Tyson's money slipped into the grimy brown paw. "Hurry!"

"*Sí, sí,*" stammered the boy, his eyes large with the vision of the silver coin, and he repeated: "Señor Kennedy, a riot in your house! Much noise! Guns!"

"Fine!" grinned Tyson. "Now run for it!"

The urchin was off down the street as if winged by the wind, and Tyson saw his messenger catch Kennedy by the arm and shout something, gesturing wildly behind him. As for the gambler, he paused only long enough to thrust the package back into the hands of Rona Carnahan, and then turned and swung down the street with long strides. He passed Tyson with eyes grimly alight and lips compressed, and his right hand now and again touched at his hip pocket.

"A gambler," mused Tyson, "and a fighting man!"

He watched him out of sight around the corner, and then hurried after the girl. It was not easy to overtake her, for she walked with a light, swift stride, longer than a woman's, and quicker than a man's. As for Tyson, in the excitement of the moment he was keen as a hound on a trail; in another moment he was at the side of the girl.

She cast an inquisitive glance up at him, and he regretted with a tremendous falling of the heart that he had purchased this interview at the price of his last meal. For the beauty which had been hers in the wilderness was gone in the street of the town. A certain piquancy, and the largeness of the eyes, was that all?

Knowledge dawned in her face; she smiled up at him.

"Señor Tyson!"

Assuredly it was more than piquancy and the

sombre eyes; he forgot the lost quarter.

"The same Tyson," he nodded. "Here, I'll carry the parcel."

His touch recognised the familiar curve of the neck of a bottle. She read his surprise.

"Firewater," she admitted.

"Do you use the stuff?"

"Do you think there is a devil in me?" she asked angrily. "It is for my father."

"Father?" he said with a start. It was difficult to connect the girl with parents. Then he remembered, with a shudder, the man with the reddish eyes and the silent laugh like the grin of a wolfhound. "Then there is a devil in your father?"

"Oh, yes. A very thirsty one, Señor Tyson."

"Padre Miguel told you that?" he asked dryly.

"No, no, no, no! Once he saw me give the firewater to my father, and he made me say so many prayers—b-r-r—kneeling on a hard stone all the while—that my mind ached as hard as my knees before I was through. After that I was afraid to give any more firewater to father for a long time."

"But at last?"

"At last——"

She stopped short, for a youth, in passing, laughed at the odd attire of Rona, and threw a word of ridicule after her in Spanish. Her dress, to be sure, was enough to rouse laughter among a quieter people than Mexicans. She wore a bright blue calico dress scattered with big white polka dots, and gathered at the waist with a crimson sash. The dress was cut off just below the knees, and left the bare brown legs and sandalled feet free. Her headdress was a man's hat of soft, black felt, very wide-brimmed, and with a bright yellow feather thrusting up at one side. The spirit of the grotesque could not have been more fittingly arrayed.

In the meantime the boy had halted in the street behind them, and now stood, calling out his mockery and clapping a riding quirt against his bare legs.

"Listen!" gasped Rona, and set her teeth in unspeakable rage.

"Come along," advised Tyson. "Pay no attention to him."

But this was the unlucky instant chosen by the mocker to hurl his choicest and longest insult. Tyson could not follow the Spanish of it, but it set a sudden fire blazing in the eyes of Rona Carnahan.

She whirled and was after her tormentor. He had only time to shout once in alarm and cut at her with his whip—as well have struck at a cat! In an instant he was sprawling in the dust of the street, writhing, and the quirt in the strong hand of Rona lashed his half-naked body with strokes as loud as the cracking of a whip. Then he was up and raced down the street, shrieking in pain and terror, and every third or fourth step leaping into the air.

Rona hurled the quirt after him and stood clapping her hands, doubled up in an ecstasy of mirth. At length she came slowly back towards Tyson.

"It was an old whip and a very light one," she complained, "but three times, señor, I drew blood—once on the shoulders, and twice on the legs!"

And she let her eyes flicker half shut, and drew a long, slow breath of relish.

"If you had only had a blacksnake!" murmured Tyson.

"Ah, Señor Tyson, if I only had!" Then she

stopped and placed her arms akimbo, frowning at him aggressively. "Are *you* mocking me, señor?"

Her hat leaned in one direction, and the yellow feather in another, and a long lock of shining black hair gleamed over her shoulder.

"Never!" said Tyson fervently. "I have too much respect for my hide."

Yet for all his effort he could not repress a smile.

"You do mock me!" said the girl, softening suddenly. "But I don't mind it. I almost like it—in you, señor. Is not that strange?"

"But you were telling me how you did not give the firewater for a long time to your father, Rona."

"Yes. At first he was very sad. He would beg me for it. Once the tears went down his face, and my heart was sick and very small. But what could I do, Señor Tyson? I thought of the prayers of Padre Miguel, and the hard stones, señor!"

"Of course."

"Then he changed. He would be very angry. Once, twice, three times he caught me and he beat me. Usually he is like a child in my hands, but then he was a mountain lion. There is still a white mark on my shoulder—here!"

She pointed to the place.

"And still I remembered the many prayers, and the hard, hard stones. Well, he changed still again. He would sit in a corner and he could not look me in the eye, and he talked much of spiders with furry legs that were creeping up to spring on him. Sometimes he would yell very loud, and say that they were on him. But mostly he sat and watched them coming. And look, señor! I, also, could feel them coming by looking in his eyes! B-r-r!

"I brought the Padre Miguel, and he said that my father was sick and made him lie down in a blanket and said many prayers. After a while my father said nothing at all, but he would lie picking at the edge of the blanket and biting his fingers. And all the while his eyes went from side to side—so—so!"

"But still you thought of the prayers and the hard stones?"

"For a while, señor. Then I went to El Toro."

"Who is he?"

"An Indian I know. El Toro came to look, and he said that there was a devil in my father—a black devil that was very thirsty and needed the firewater to drink. So I went and got more firewater and brought it, and I did as El Toro told me—I gave him just a little bit in a cup. Ah, how he would cry and make a sad noise for more! But I never gave it.

"He beat me again, but I had hid the bottle and he could not find it, and I told him that if he beat me I would never, never give the devil another drop of firewater. So at that he was very much afraid. But after a while he saw no more spiders and he did not roll his eyes. And everyday I give him a little in the cup, twice. So when the devil found out that he could have no more, he took that little and left my father in peace."

"How does it come, Rona, that Padre Miguel, who knows so many things, did not know about this?"

"Foolish!" she said scornfully. "He is talking all day and all night with the angels and the blessed saints. But how should he know anything about the devils and their ways? Besides, this devil in my father is a very strong devil, for see what he brings for water?"

And she tapped the bottle in the arm of Tyson.

Sixteen
A Tale of a Face

They had left the outskirts of the town while she was talking, and now, rounding the dam, they circled down and then into the basin of the Chiluah. She was like a play to Henry Tyson. She walked at his side and yet she was upon a stage, and he sat among the audience in front and watched her from a distance.

It was a very odd feeling. Nothing like it had ever come into the life of Tyson before, for he had known many an attractive girl, but none like this child of the desert. Infinite, vague possibilities centred around her. That step, alert and buoyant as his own, promised to lead them into unknown adventures. Guided by her, he seemed about to enter a strange, enchanting realm.

The moment they reached the valley proper, she seemed to cast off all restraint, entering her own domain, and she accepted him as a part of it. She took off her hat, and walked along, swinging it in her hand. Her shining black hair had been gathered under the hat in an uninspired knot, from which sundry strands escaped, but now a single shake of her head sent a dark cataract over her shoulders.

"Where is the tie I gave you to bind around your hair, Rona?" asked Tyson, with some malice.

"That I have given away again," she returned carelessly.

"I am sorry for that," remarked Tyson, "because it's very bad luck to give away a gift."

"I could not help it," she answered. "You see, he liked it."

"Who?"

"The Big Man."

"Ah?"

"I am to marry him some day."

This was worse than the discovery of her parentage. If it was hard to imagine the girl living with a father, it was impossible to think of her obeying a husband.

"He will lead an active life," observed Tyson.

The girl halted. She faced him in her aggressive manner, arms akimbo, and then laid firm hold upon his shirt front.

"Hear me, señor," she said, in a voice as soft and velvety as the purr of a cat, "I have many times heard you laugh at me, and then Rona also has laughed. But still more times I have guessed at you laughing deeply and silently inside. I have seen a smile in your eyes. I do not like it, señor, and if I see that smile again——" She considered him searchingly from head to foot as one who sought a vulnerable point.

"Would you set the Big Man upon me?"

"I keep one friend with me always," she answered, and pushed down her broad belt enough to expose the hilt of a poniard.

"Then I shall keep at arm's length when I smile."

"A long arm," she said savagely, and then, infuriated by the continual glitter of his eyes, she snatched out the slender knife, caught it deftly by the point, and flung it from her, a whirling flash of light.

It was buried half a length of the blade in the trunk of a sapling, and Tyson heard its angry humming distinctly as it quivered in the wood. "Take warning, señor!" said Rona, and she drew the bright steel from the tree with a violent jerk.

"I would not laugh if I could help it," said Tyson, "but to confess the truth, Rona, there is a devil in me like the one in your father."

"A devil?" she cried, and recoiled a horrified pace.

"Your father's makes his throat dry, but mine is a mocking devil."

She crossed herself swiftly, and murmured something inaudible.

"I knew," she nodded at length, "that you were not like other men. Even Señor Kennedy is not like you."

"He lacks a devil, perhaps."

"It is true," she answered seriously.

"But he may have one before long."

"How do you mean that, señor?"

And her hand slipped under the broad sash.

"It was my devil that spoke in me," said Tyson, and he smiled openly upon her.

She stood on tiptoe, as if the force of her anger made her light as the wind; then she snapped her fingers above her head, and burst into laughter. It blended pleasantly with the woodland noises.

When she could speak: "Even Señor Kennedy would not have faced me then. You are brave!" More laughter, and then: "Why do I like you so much, señor?"

She swung closer to his side as they walked on.

"Is it I whom you like or the devil inside me, Rona?"

The wide black eyes glanced up and dwelt solemnly upon him.

"Indeed, Señor Tyson, I fear Padre Miguel will give me many prayers to tell, and my knees shall ache again from the hardness of the stone!"

She sighed.

"I do not wish to be wicked—no! no! But to be good always is like eating meat without salt. Is it not, señor?"

"Exactly."

At the mention of food his stomach clave to his ribs, and his head whirled.

"Well," he said, "as for the bit of silk, I hope it brings no bad luck to you. Perhaps there's a difference, since you gave it to the man you love."

"Love?" she echoed, and then her laughter went through a bright cadence again. "Ah, señor, I do not love him!" The agile fingers snapped. "Not so much as that!"

"The devil!" gasped Tyson.

"But he has seen the face."

"What's that?"

She frowned.

"You know very little, Señor Tyson."

"Almost nothing."

"You are smiling again! Well, I shall say one prayer for your devil tonight, señor—and two for myself! But I shall tell you about the face. Look back!"

She turned and pointed a rather melodramatic arm down the valley. La Blanca and La Cabeza rose doubly tall and very dark with the late sun behind them.

"You see the mountains?"

"Ah?"

"Would you ever guess that they are men?"

"Never!"

"Yet it is true. A very many days ago there lived two men, one in the west and one in the east. They were both so very tall and so very strong that no other warriors could stand against them. They were so big that they used whole pine trees to make a fishing rod, and they fished in a big water and pulled out fishes bigger than horses."

"Regular whales, eh?"

She flashed a sharp glance at him, and then went on, slowly, as though she dared him to smile again: "Six, ten, twenty of these fishes they would catch for a single meal, señor!"

She waited.

"Wonderful!"

She sighed with relief that he had not laughed.

"It is true. So El Toro has always told me, and never changed a single word in twenty tellings."

"Then it is gospel, of course. Go on, Rona."

"And when they left the great water they would kill in one day twenty bulls—and eat them, señor, for a meal! Think of *that!*"

"I *am* thinking of it!" groaned Tyson, and drew his belt still tighter, for there was a burning pain in his vitals. His newly appeased hunger had returned in no small measure.

"Does it seem possible?"

"Twenty bulls for a meal? Why, well roasted, with the trimmings—very possible indeed. To have lived in those days——"

It was impossible for him to continue; he was choked.

"Yet I suppose," she confided, "that they had only one meal in many days. Otherwise, they would have soon cleaned up the range, you see. I asked El Toro this, but he did not know.

"Now these great warriors went everywhere across the land, and as I have told you, señor, no one could stand against them. Their skin was so thick that the greatest chief could not drive an arrow through it, and they minded the prick of a spear no more than I mind dry stubble. So they went everywhere looking for someone to fight, and they had bad luck in finding him until at last the man in the west decided that he would fight the Great Spirit.

"So he began to pile mountains one on the other to climb up to the sky and pull down the great Manitou, and the Manitou watched him and grew afraid. Mind you, he was not afraid of fighting the man of the west, but if the mountains were once piled high enough, then every warrior on the earth could climb up to the happy hunting grounds, and there would be no one to pray any more to the Manitou. Which would have made him very lonely, Señor Tyson, would it not?"

"Naturally! A child could see that."

"Of course! So he thought a long time, and at last he came down in a dream to the warrior of the west and told him in the dream that there was a man in the east just as tall as he and just as great. So when the warrior of the west woke up the next day, he tore up the biggest oak he could find for a club, and started east to find the other giant.

"But the Manitou had come in the same sort of dream to the warrior of the east, and told him of the man of the west, and the man of the east woke up the next day and tore up the greatest rock he could find—the whole top of a mountain, señor! and he started west.

"So the two giants met—even here, señor! Ah, what a thing it must have been to see! Their heads were in the clouds. The birds of the air flew from all over the world to watch the giants fight. Oh, to have been here!"

And she clapped her hands in an ecstasy.

"The man of the west lifted his great oak tree, the father of all oak trees, and whirled it around his head, and the sound of it in the air was like the screaming of a whirlwind. And the warrior from the east heaved up his rock, and it blotted out the sun.

"But when the Manitou looked down on them he was sorry, for he saw they would kill each other at the first stroke; and he did not wish that the biggest men he had ever seen should die. So he thought what he should do.

"Then he went and lifted all the pile of mountains which the warrior of the west had made, and he brought it and dropped half of it on the man of the east, and buried him out of sight. Then he dropped the other half on the man from the west. And he was buried! The great spirit, you see, is very strong."

"He must be, Rona!"

"Now, the man of the east went to sleep, and he still sleeps. But the man of the west, he would not go to sleep, though there was such a great blanket of earth over him. No, señor, he began to fight and heave up his head, for he is a fierce giant, and so he has worked his head higher and higher until now it is almost out of the mountain.

"It is true! Now, many days ago the Comanches lived in all the valley of the Chiluah, and they learned that sometimes men can look at La Cabeza—that is the man of the west—and see at his top something that looks like a head. And they learned that the man who sees that face will in one year either marry the girl he loves or else die. You see, señor?"

Seventeen
The Bottle Breaks

"I begin to understand," murmured Tyson.

"Do you believe?"

He looked at her sharply, but her eyes were wide with apparent credulity.

"Why not?" he nodded. "Why not believe it? I've heard stranger things than that in my life."

But to his utter astonishment she burst into her soft, yet far-heard laughter.

"You believe? You are either a very great liar or a very great stupid, señor."

"Confound it, Rona, if you don't believe the thing yourself, why do you tell the story?"

She shrugged her shoulders, frowned, and then dismissed the troublesome question with a shake of her head.

"One never can tell," she answered. "There may be something true about it."

"And this fellow, this Kennedy, has seen the face? What is it?"

"It is seen at sunset when the shadows fall black across the valleys of La Cabeza. This, El Toro has told me."

"So it must be true. And had this Kennedy of yours heard the yarn before he saw the—face?"

"How should I know, señor? All I know is that he saw it, for he told me so. And should I let him die in a year! A man so young and so very big? Ah, no!"

"And Kennedy the—Kennedy is to marry you! When?"

"In a very few days. The year is almost at an end."

"You put it off to the last, eh?"

"Why not?"

"Well, I suppose you'll both be very happy. You like this Kennedy, eh?"

"He has much money. Yes, I like him."

"H-m-m!" mused Tyson.

"But you, you do *not* like him?"

"He may be very well—in his way."

"I have seen him shoot a little bird so high—as high above as that treetop—shoot it with a revolver, Señor Tyson."

"A bad man to meet on a dark night. I don't doubt it. Now what would you say, Rona, if I were to be wearing that same bit of yellow-and-black silk the next time I see you?"

"He would not give it to you," she said, shaking her head at the idea.

"And why not?"

"Because *I* gave it to him. That is clear."

"But if I took it?"

"Took it? From *him?*" She laughed softly as ever, but it was not a pleasant laugh to hear.

"I would like to see that time when you take it from the big man." Her cold and calculating eye swept him as though she were imagining the places where the bullets from the unerring gun of Kennedy would strike.

"Nevertheless," he said, "I shall be wearing that same tie the next time I see you."

Her eyes widened marvellously.

"Would you fight for it?" she whispered.

"Perhaps."

Then, as a little silence fell:

"Would you object to that?"

But for answer there was a little, contented sigh, and no words. It was so uncanny—it made the blood of Tyson run so cold—that he stared fixedly at the girl and paid no attention to his footing. The result was that his heel caught on a sharp, projecting rock, and he was flung to his knees; the bottle of whisky crashed into a thousand tinkling fragments. A wail from Rona brought him to his feet.

She was on her knees trying wildly to scoop up some of the precious stuff in the hollow of her hand. But the dry sand soaked up the fire-water in a single gulp.

It was then that she rose and fairly leaped at Tyson, the narrow blade of the stiletto glittering above her head.

Eighteen
Music—and Other Things

It would have been as easy to avoid her as to avoid the lunge of a snake; besides, he was too frozen with astonishment to move.

But her rush was checked even as she reached him. The chime of a bell floated down the Chiluah towards them, thin and small and far away, almost like a voice whistling on the wind.

The knife dropped from the nerveless hand of Rona, and clattered on the stones. She fell upon her knees, crumpling as though an invisible hand from above had smitten her to the earth. Sobs shook her terribly, and the sound of her weeping went through the heart of Tyson like the grief of a strong man whose strength is broken. There were words, too, in her weeping, and when he leaned, he heard, over and over: *"Madre dolorosa! Madre mia! Madre-cita!"*

Slowly the chiming of the well-matched bells

throbbed away to silence, and Henry Tyson heard the faint whisper of the girl at her prayers for the dead. It touched a chord of awe in him and set it trembling to listen to her, and all the loneliness of the desert fell about him, and he heard the faraway rustle of the Chiluah, until it seemed that the wild girl was kneeling at the very feet of her Maker.

She looked up, at length, her eyes starry with tears, and her lips trembled.

"Shall I ever be forgiven?" she whispered. "Tell me, señor, shall I ever be forgiven?"

To hear such words from her—it was like seeing a primitive Indian showing mercy to a wounded creature. Tyson caught his breath. He stooped and raised her to her feet.

"After all, there's no harm done. You were only trying to frighten me; you would never have used the knife, eh?"

"I don't know," she sighed. "That instant I hated you, Señor Tyson."

"Nonsense. You would have stopped at the last moment."

"Perhaps."

She looked wistfully at him.

"I wonder if God will think that, too?" she murmured.

Tyson had to struggle to keep from laughing aloud.

"Well," mourned the girl, "when the Padre Miguel hears of this I shall have six months of prayers and fastings. Because of you!"

She stared at him in gloomy anger.

"Why are you walking on with me? There is nothing for me to carry now. And if you go on, I may be wicked again. I feel something very bad in me."

He stopped.

"Do you want me to leave you, and go back?"

"No, no!" she cried suddenly. "I had forgot. *I* am not going to take the blame for breaking the bottle. Come; hurry! You shall face my father and tell him what has happened."

In the quickly coming dusk, they were almost upon the cabin before Henry Tyson noticed it. First they crossed a little rivulet lined with willows which looked like giants with enormous heads in the semi-dark, and when Tyson looked up, the cabin lay a few steps away.

The wall of the valley rose here in almost a cliff, and into an angle of this the cabin snuggled, protected from the wind on two sides by a natural wall.

Tyson made out the obscure, ragged outline of the house, and a crooked joint of stovepipe twisting above it. As they stepped into full view of the place he found one small window, faintly illumined, and the door sketched in roughly by a rectangular crack of light.

On this the girl knocked once, and then threw it open.

"Go in," she said to Tyson, and he stepped into the house.

It consisted of two rooms, or rather, one room and a wretched little cubby-hole of a lean-to curtained off from the main apartment by sacking, which was now drawn aside. It revealed what must have been the girl's sleeping place, for Tyson saw through the low aperture a flash of colour on the farther wall—perhaps a bright-coloured calendar—and the gleam of a mirror. Then, as if she resented the direction of his glance, the girl stepped across and jerked out the sacking, effectually blocking his vision.

The other and main room evidently served as living room, dining room, and kitchen. A wrecked table staggered against the wall on one side; opposite it, half a dozen ancient books lay on a small shelf; there in the corner was the roll of bedding, covered with a tarpaulin, where the father slept; and at the farther end stood the most important article of furniture—a rust-reddened stove.

These things Tyson observed in a single glance. He had no time for more, since the occupants of the place took his attention thereafter.

They were, in the first place, the man of the wolf-grin which had haunted his sleep since the first day he met Rona Carnahan, a big, gaunt man whose face was covered with an unrazored mass of shaggy hair; a man with uneasy, big brown eyes, which flashed a glance at Tyson and then flickered away and kept an outlook of suspicion upon him from the side. The other wore the vesture of a religious order, and Tyson put him down at once as the Padre Miguel himself.

He was a little, broad-shouldered man with a pale, ugly face. He looked more Irish than Spanish or Mexican. The keen sun of the southwest had not been able to tan his skin, the lichen whiteness of which suggested a lifetime spent in dungeon darkness. For the rest, a negligible nose turned up in a truly Celtic fashion, and there was an equally Irish mouth, with the long upper lip.

On the whole, Padre Miguel might have posed as a retired pugilist; his face had that battered look. Yet the eyes denied the rest of his features. For they were bright, steady, and wide open, with brimming kindliness. They fell first of all upon the hair which Tyson had uncovered as soon as he entered the place.

"This is Padre Miguel," began the girl, "and this, padre, is——"

"Señor Tyson," nodded the father.

He advanced with a kindly smile and took the hand of Tyson.

"We have heard of you every day since you met Rona in the woods," he said. "I am glad to know you, señor."

He spoke English with perfect understanding of the words, that was evident, but his pronunciation was a little strange, like that of one whose knowledge of a language has been chiefly drawn from books. Obviously he must have done most of his work in this land among the peons and the Indians.

"I'm equally glad to know you, Father Miguel," said Tyson. "To tell the truth, I've been almost worried about a man of such powers."

And he watched the padre keenly.

The latter flushed, and then made a little gesture of deprecation, saying: "Rona has been talking. She will do that, señor. She has told you about withered limbs, and——"

He paused and smiled, and Tyson gave an extra pressure of understanding to his hand.

"This is Señor Carnahan," continued the padre, turning away to the other.

Carnahan fumbled vaguely at his bearded chin, staring vaguely at the newcomer, as though he saw a form of misty thinness and could look through and through the younger man, while Tyson spoke his greeting.

"Father!" cut in Rona sharply, softly.

Carnahan started like one recalled from a

dream, and then advanced and took the hand of his guest.

"We have heard much of you, sir," he said, and Tyson's eyes opened as he heard the voice of the man—the unmistakable intonation of culture, "and of how you crossed a river—not quite so large as the Rubicon."

A lean, cold hand, barely touching that of Tyson, withdrew, and Carnahan pointed his little speech with a bow. At once the tattered clothes were forgotten; the unkempt beard appeared magically changed to a trim Van Dyck; the walls of the hovel fell away into an imaginary vista over soft, thick carpets, past massive, polished tables, and luxuriously upholstered chairs.

"Be seated, sir," continued the host. "Rona, a chair for Mr. Tyson."

He looked about him, smiling gently. Aside from a few boxes, the only thing in the shape of a seat was the one which had been recently occupied by the padre.

"This will do very well," said Tyson hastily, and took a box from a corner and drew it out.

He caught the anxious eye of the girl and the quizzical frown of the padre upon him, and nodded covertly, reassuringly.

"Are you comfortable there?" asked Carnahan cordially, as they settled down, Rona on the roll of bedding in the corner. "Rona, will you bring something for Mr. Tyson to smoke? What will you have, sir? Cigars? Cigarettes? Rona, my dear, you will find everything in my smoking-cabinet."

"Please don't trouble," interposed Tyson hurriedly.

"No trouble at all. Light or dark cigars, sir? What is your preference? If——"

"But I really don't wish to smoke just now."

"No? Well, well! For my part, I have grown attached to tobacco and brown papers. The knack of rolling them is difficult to learn, but now I amuse myself very often making them."

He illustrated this by instantly producing a little sack of tobacco and a package of the papers, and rolling his smoke deftly. A moment later it was between his lips.

While he lighted it, the padre looked again, quizzically, toward Tyson, and the latter nodded and smiled in understanding. Carnahan, apparently, thought himself seated in some finely appointed home. It was pitiful to watch him in his miserable rags, and a little ludicrous as well; and Tyson thought he understood the brooding look of sadness which he had sometimes noted in the eyes of Rona.

"I must go now," murmured the padre, rising. "Good evening, Señor Carnahan. Good night, Rona. Mr. Tyson, you must come to see the mission."

And so he was gone with bowed head through the door; and Tyson understood, with a flash of intuition, that the good man bore the burden of the sadness in that home upon his shoulders.

The moment the door closed, Carnahan leaned forward, the fragile cigarette crushing to shapelessness between his nervously contracted fingers.

"Did you get it?" he whispered to Rona. "Did you get it, girl?"

Tyson watched her eyes widen with horror, and fear, perhaps.

"I got it," she answered faintly.

Carnahan closed his eyes tightly and drew a vast breath of relief.

"I saw nothing when you came in," he said. "I didn't see that you carried anything. And I thought, for a moment—well, thank God! Quickly, Rona. Quickly! I have been dreaming of it!"

His long-fingered hand was fumbling at his throat through the beard.

"I got it," said the girl faintly, "but it was lost—the bottle was broken on the way."

The full import of what she said appeared to filter slowly into the mind of Carnahan. He sat with his lips still parted in that thirsty smile, but gradually they closed to a grim, set line, and into his brown eyes came that red light which Tyson had seen in them that other day—a nightmare thing to watch it grow. Carnahan rose from his box. He held out his hand towards his daughter with the fingers distended as stiffly as talons.

"You lost it? You broke the bottle! Then why did you come without it? By God, it's a plot against me! You're trying to drive me distracted. And I'm dying of it; dying of the fire within me. Why didn't you go back and get another bottle?"

"Because I hadn't enough money."

"You lie!" cried Carnahan in a terrible voice. "It's a plot. Oh, I see through you! It's a plot."

He made a long stride towards her, and she stood against the walls, cowering, literally paralysed with terror. The chills which ran through Tyson's own blood kept him motionless for an instant longer, then he called: "Mr. Carnahan, I'm guilty of this. I was carrying the bottle, and I dropped it."

Carnahan turned, and then Tyson understood the dumb fear of the girl; for he was facing a demoniac.

"You?" snarled the monster into which Carnahan had turned. "You?"

He was beside Tyson; he seemed to have glided there without the agency of feet, so swift was his coming, and around Tyson's wrist settled a grip like steel bands shrinking into place. Over the shoulder of the maniac he saw the girl, sick and weak with horror. She could not even cry out. And Tyson looked calmly into the red eyes before him and wondered why he was not afraid to die. For he was very near death, he knew. Even in his full vigour it would have taxed him to meet this gaunt giant in his frenzy, but now that undernourishment and overwork had sapped his muscles——

He reached behind him, not daring to take his glance from the glowing eyes before him; he felt that if he flinched, if he winced, if he took his look away, the peril would be loosed and launched at his throat. That hand he sent groping blindly along the shelf behind him, seeking for anything which might serve as a weapon. The fingers closed on wood; he jerked out a violin, clutching the neck of the instrument with nervous strength. A foolish, flimsy weapon, but it might free him for a second from Carnahan.

"Loosen your hand, Mr. Carnahan," he said quietly. "I warn you, loosen your hand!"

"A plot," said Carnahan thickly, "and you're in it. So's Rona. Everyone is in it. Everyone's against me!"

He leaned a little closer, his lips working.

"Stand away from me," cried Tyson. "I warn you for the last time, Mr. Carnahan."

And he swung the violin up to a striking position. At sight of it the face of Carnahan was transfigured to blank horror, terror.

"Give it to me!" he stammered in a panic. "Give

it to me. I shall not hurt you, man. Only give it to me."

He stepped back, and then held out his hands, imploring. There was an expression about his eyes, now, oddly like that of a mother who sees her infant in danger. Tyson hesitated an instant, and then placed the instrument in the hands of the madman. He was more curious than afraid, and he stared in bewilderment as he watched Carnahan take the violin into trembling hands, fumbling and stroking it.

"The fool! The fool!" whispered Carnahan. "He might have crushed you to bits, my beautiful!"

He settled it into place, cuddling it against his chin. His right hand fumbled on the shelf, blindly, and drew forth the bow, and forgetful of all else Carnahan drew the bow slowly across the strings.

The result was a low, prolonged note, delicate as a thread of light, and as piercing. Carnahan raised the bow and stood as one who listens intently; then his face flooded with unspeakable light. It fell like grace about him, and he smiled.

"She hears us," whispered the mad musician. "She hears us. We shall talk to her tonight!"

And cautiously, reverently, he approached the bow again to the strings, while all the while his eyes probed a gloomy corner as though a human figure stood there and Carnahan strove to charm it forth into the light of the single smoky lamp with the power of his music.

And slowly and reverently the singing of the violin rose, stole on the senses of Tyson, fascinating him, swelled, filled the room. He had never heard such purity of tone. There was no scraping or whining of the resin on the strings. It seemed as if Carnahan waved his hand through the empty air and brought forth the exquisite harmony, an improvisation of wonderful beauty. Sometimes in chorus two and three voices sang; then the G-string mourned in organ-like sorrow; and out of this sprang a thrilling, lyric note that sang at the very gate of heaven.

A hand fell on the arm of Tyson, and then the voice of Rona: "Go now before he notices you again."

"But you?" he whispered back.

"He is used to me. He'll play like this for hours now, if only I am here. Go now, quickly!"

"I don't dare to leave you."

"You must. I tell you, I am perfectly safe. Señor Tyson, you have been brave; you have helped me, and I shall never forget!"

She stood with one hand pressed against her breast, and he could look deeply into the misted eyes. For a single moment her beauty blended with the music, became one with it, and pierced Tyson to the heart.

Where was the wild, fierce girl who had walked with him up the valley that evening?

He turned from her, and went blindly out into the night.

Nineteen
The Insult

Out there he stood for an instant, with the music pouring out around him, transforming in his mind the squalor of the hut; until it seemed that a palace of light lay there behind him, a place of columns and marble vistas where the girl lived who had stood at his side a moment before.

He found himself standing with clenched hands and beating heart, and he had to shrug his shoulders and draw a deep breath to free himself from the fantasy. It was only a cabin on the desert valley of the Chiluah, and a madman playing to his wild daughter.

So he went on down the valley.

Behind him the singing of the violin grew smaller and smaller, and as it faded it seemed to Tyson to come from a point directly above him; to his excited fancy the music was dropping from the sky. And there was a great warmth and kindliness in his heart as he remembered the girl. He would never be able to dissociate that music from her face, he knew, and the sadness of it would haunt him.

His thoughts made the way to La Blanca short, and he swung thoughtfully up the stairs of Mrs. Irene Casey's boardinghouse to his room. He had hardly closed the door when a knock came on it, and he opened upon Kennedy, the gambler.

The big, lean fellow nodded casually in answer to Tyson's greeting, and then dropped into a chair, slowly. He surveyed his host with a calm eye while he produced and lighted a cigarette. It was not until he had flicked his own match away that he noticed Tyson.

"Smoke?"

"Thanks!"

He accepted the cigarette, lighted it, and drew a long breath deeply into his lungs. It threw him into the pleasant haze of nicotine. Into this daze broke the measured voice of the gambler.

"Got a little thing to talk over with you, partner. Won't take long. Just this; I fell for your play this evening with the girl. It was a pretty piece of work. It was like filling to a pair. But"—he leaned over, smiling, and resting a hand on his knee—"don't knife in there again. Get me?"

"I don't follow that," muttered Tyson. In fact, the words were meaningless sounds to him.

The gambler smiled again. He was perfectly tolerant and apparently good-natured about it.

"Listen!" he drawled. "Don't kid me like this. When I seen your hands I knew you was one of us. East or West, Bud, the profession ain't much different. Are you wise?"

Tyson looked vaguely down at his pale, agile hands.

"I'm West," went on the gambler, "but it don't foller that I'm green goods. Take the tip from me, partner. That girl is mine. I got her corralled, roped, tied, and branded—almost. Just ease away from her—that's all!"

The smoke from Tyson's cigarette curled idly up to the ceiling, his thoughts tangled mazily with the many-folded wraith.

"Well?" This came snapping sharply from Kennedy.

"What do you want me to say?"

"That you'll keep hands off!"

It came to Tyson that it might be exceedingly dangerous to irritate this man. Yet he enjoyed courting that danger.

"I gather," he murmured, "that you have a corner on Rona?"

"Right."

"Kennedy," said Tyson, "you're a bold man."

The gambler waited, like one who is slow to anger.

"You're a bold man," repeated the Easterner. "I'd as soon try to get a corner on the wind or the blue sky as to monopolise that girl."

"What you'd do," said Kennedy, slowly feeling his way into the argument, "ain't to the point. What I've already done is the thing that counts. M'frien', that girl is going to be my wife."

He did not say it exultantly, but merely as one who advances a decisive argument. Then he leaned back and smiled once more upon his host.

"You ain't the first," he went on, to let the other find a graceful way of retreat, "that's seen Rona and liked her and tried his hand. But they all found out damned quick that they was playin' a measly pair of deuces ag'in' a royal flush. D'you foller me, partner?"

Certainly nothing could be plainer, and Tyson realised with a pang that his interest in the girl was hopeless. That very fact made him for the first time ask himself how great that interest could be? For answer, he felt a sullen anger rise in him. It irritated him past words that this fellow should be so sure. Moreover, his eyes dwelt, fascinated, upon the bright yellow-and-black necktie of the gambler. He had promised Rona that he would be wearing that bit of silk the very next time he met her.

He managed to smile in return to his companion.

He said: "Has it ever occurred to you, my dear fellow, that a game isn't won until the last hand is played?"

The other frowned. But he refused to be angered. His self-content was as limitless as the ocean.

"Now just what d'you mean by that lead?"

"Why," said Tyson, "does Rona like El Toro?"

"He tells her queer yarns."

"Exactly. He amuses her. And why does she like Padre Miguel?"

"I dunno. Maybe because he amuses her, too."

"And why, Kennedy, does she like you?"

"Because I—look here, m' boy——"

"Because you amuse her, eh? Tut, tut, Kennedy, do you really dream that she takes you seriously?"

The cigarette, flicked from the fingers of Kennedy and thrown through the window, described, in the dark of the evening, a shining arc.

"You're quite right in calling it a game with her,"

went on Tyson. "It's all a game. You're one card—perhaps I'm another—she plays them as she sees fit. We amuse her—that's all."

Kennedy rose to his full height, his hands behind him.

"One week from to-day," he said, "we get married."

Tyson smiled.

"I said a week from today," in a rising voice.

The smile of Tyson persisted.

"By God!" muttered the gambler. "What d'you know?"

It was that continual smile which maddened him. He reached over, grasped the shoulder of Tyson with an iron hand, and dragged him to his feet facing the dying light from the window. Perhaps Tyson had never before been touched in that manner, and now his fingers twitched to be at the throat of the tall man.

"I know," he said—and he continued to smile straight in the face of the gambler—"that we're both in the pack. She may draw you—she may not."

"And you're in the game?"

"To stay, my friend!"

"You damned—rustler!" said Kennedy through his teeth, and struck Tyson across the face with his open hand.

The blow, in itself, was nothing, but it unbalanced and sent Tyson staggering back against the wall. There he stood for an instant, crouching a little, spreading his hands against the wall behind him to give impetus to his attack. As for Kennedy, he was bolt erect, a devil in his face, and his right hand clutching at a hip pocket.

Then—a knock at the door and a shrill voice: "Oh, Mr. Tyson, are ye there?"

Twenty
Roulette

"Come in," called Tyson.

Mrs. Irene Casey stood in the doorway. "Mr. Kennedy," she cried, "am I intrudin'?"

"I think our business can wait. It will even be better for waiting, eh, Kennedy?"

The hungry eye of the gambler was still measuring the other from head to foot, as if he had not yet settled on a vital place.

"Maybe it will," he growled.

"After all," said Tyson, "it will only take a moment to settle it."

"I'm glad you see that," nodded Kennedy, and he passed the tip of his tongue across his lips.

"Kennedy," said Mrs. Casey, "is it deviltry ye're up to?"

"Tut, tut! Not a bit," broke in Tyson. "It's only the matter of a small debt which I owe Kennedy, and he's pressing me to pay it. *Au revoir,* sir."

The door closed heavily behind the gambler, and Mrs. Casey turned a thoughtful glance from it to Tyson. With all his soul he was longing to be at Kennedy, but he wore the quietest of smiles.

"You men," moralised Mrs. Casey, "are like dogs that growl when you pass. My man Casey was like that—God rest him! Fightin' always, day and night. He'd rather have fought once than drunk red-eye twice, which was sayin' something with Casey. Well, I seen the look in Kennedy's eye when he come up here, and I come up after him."

She winked broadly.

"Son, keep clear av him! Don't be thankin' me. Good night!"

So she was gone, and Tyson was instantly down the stairs and out on the street. He wanted Kennedy. He wanted the man's blood. He wanted to damage him in any and every possible way; and, rather naturally, the first thing he thought of was the yellow-and-black necktie.

That belonged to Kennedy now, and he had promised Rona to take it from the big man. How he would get it, whether by force of gun or hand, he did not know. Above all, he continually remembered the heavy hand which had struck him across the face.

After that there was no doubt as to his destination: he headed straight for the gaming house of big Kennedy. Not that he knew exactly what he would do in the place. Certainly he could not gamble. Even if he had had money to stake, his oath to Garth kept him from using the proceeds. But in the house he would find Kennedy, and Kennedy meant trouble, and trouble tonight would be like meat and drink.

The gambling house was run with a shameless

openness, like the other palaces of chance in La Blanca; the only attempt to conceal its location was the establishment of a dozen easy entrances and exits. In this manner Kennedy avoided having a continual stream of patrons passing in and out at any one point. His house was like a sponge with many pores through which to draw the wealth of the town; once inside, a single pressure squeezed them dry of coin.

The place had been originally a stable of some pretensions, and the stalls were still clearly marked around the sides of the open court. On these four sides were the booths where the card games went on; but the freer space of the open court was turned over to the roulette wheel and dice, so that the crowds could circulate as freely as possible.

There is need of circulation around the roulette wheel. No one comes to the gaming house intending to play that mistress of misfortune; but everyone stands for a moment, in passing, and listens to the hum of the spinning wheel and marks the dizzy swirl of the colours.

He stands, he watches, he presses nearer to note how the unfortunates lose their money. And coming closer in this fashion, he cannot fail to note how the wheel comes to a drawling stop. It seems strange that the wheel should be so perfectly balanced and lubricated that it will pause at random. It seems certain that it must stop more often at a definite point on the circle. The newcomer watches and notes.

Behold! Once, twice, thrice in a half-dozen whirls the wheel stops on the black and on the eight. A system! A dollar to try it out—it is cheap. He lays the coin. He wins. He lays again on a single number, most daring of all chances, and behold!

the pointer rests on the eight. For every dollar he has wagered thirty-six pour into the hand of the gambler.

An hour later he leaves with downward head. He has emptied his pockets and pawned his watch for a tithe of its value. And still the wheel hums and spins behind him. Next payday he will return and exact vengeance. Luck cannot stay *always* against him!

Under the arch of the entrance Tyson stood and watched the scene. A motley crowd: white and brown, engineer and foreman and humble peon, they rubbed shoulders in this place. A swirling haze of cigarette smoke that mounted in lazy drifts disappeared, and above it was the blue-black of the sky with the golden stars burning their way down, lower and lower. A strange setting for the game, but in spite of the setting all was familiar to Tyson. No matter for the faces and the complexions; the eyes were the same the world over—narrowed, bright with hunger.

He knew that fat man in the white suit at the poker table yonder as well as if he had played against him. The large upper lip was pendulous, uncertain, and the china-blue eyes rolled wildly here and there now and again. He was winning heavily, Tyson knew. But he would lose it all before the evening was over.

Opposite sat a smiling youth who tossed his cards on the table with a flick of disdain. Tyson could almost tell to a dollar how much he had lost, and what sort of a letter he would write to his father explaining the loss. He was a young engineer, no doubt.

At the same table was a Mexican with a face pouched by unutterable weariness. The eyes of Tyson flashed as he recognised metal worthy of his sword. Automatically he reached into his pocket; but the wallet pinched flat under his fingers, and he groaned aloud.

He turned his glance to the central court. The crowd was small at this early hour; shortly there would hardly be breathing space, but now men drifted idly from place to place. Barefooted Mexican boys clad in thin white ran here and there carrying small trays covered with glasses. The size of the glasses proclaimed the dynamic quality of the liquor. That colourless stuff was *tequila,* or gin; the reddish-brown was whisky of uncertain quality and high proof.

Free drinks for the gamesters—the more they took the better. Yes, at this young hour free drinks for everyone; trade lagged. A tray was held up in front of Tyson, but he waved it aside. He needed a clear head this night.

For behind the roulette wheel he saw the tall form of Kennedy; and the light struck sharply on two things—the teeth of the gambler as he smiled, and the yellow and black of the necktie he wore. Rona Carnahan would look for that necktie around the throat of Tyson when they next met. Tyson moved forward involuntarily, and each step brought him, against his will, closer and closer to Kennedy. The proprietor stood behind the roulette wheel; the disc of light which the wheel made as it spun was all the advertisement that the game needed—that and the light clicking as it whirred more slowly towards the final pause.

Before the wheel the small and silent group was gathered—true roulette players, standing with their eyes fixed on the terrible little machine, wagering not more than once every dozen spins. But when they wagered, it was because they had figured out a little system which gave them at that instant a superior chance.

A typical roulette crowd, and, therefore, a crowd which was losing heavily: yet the fascination held them. Once in a while one of them ventured to play a single number, and always lost, but each time the other players held their breaths and gasped as the little pointer became stationary.

For they had witnessed the great opportunity—a chance so great that there was an element of the divine in it—thirty-six to one! Ten dollars wagered might bring to the lucky man three hundred and sixty! Aye, and if he left his money for a second trial he would be paid seventy-two for one, or twenty-five thousand nine hundred and twenty dollars—all in the space of a few seconds—fortune—by the bright spinning of a wheel.

Indeed, in this game against the wheel chance was dignified, and became worthy of the ponderings of a strongly contemplative mind. Perhaps this explained the philosophical calm of the men who stood about the wheel as Tyson approached. They were Mexicans, mostly, and all that good or bad fortune could elicit from them was a flash of teeth or a glint of eyes. Then they pushed their towering sombreros farther back and lapsed once more into the brown study.

It was one of these fellows that Tyson inadvertently shouldered as he made his way closer to the roulette wheel—a little man whose palm was as smooth with polished calluses as fine mahogany. He was so lean that his mouth puckered at the sides, and yet at the touch of Tyson's arm he glared up with a sudden ferocity which deeply appealed to the white man.

For he recognised, as it were, a kindred spirit—a hungry man playing the wheel. As for the Mexican, the angry light died instantly from his eyes—and his labour-withered arms waved through a graceful gesture of welcome.

"El Oro!" he murmured.

Tyson smiled down into the yellow face, and in a rush of warm brotherliness he wanted to take this poor fellow to one side and explain to him how little chance he had to beat the wheel—how sure he was of ruin if he kept at it. For though the wheel in theory gives no advantage to the house and affords an equal chance to the gambler, yet in fact it has a terrific advantage, for the wheel is a machine, and no man, however nerveless, can play for ever against it.

An illusion comes to him, a belief that one colour or one number, or one set of numbers, is more lucky than the rest. His reason may assure him perfectly that there is nothing but delusion in this belief, but nevertheless the idea haunts him. What gambler, for instance, will ever lay on thirteen or twenty-three? And yet the wheel stops as often upon these numbers as upon any others.

These are the things which give the machine the advantage. The gambler does not realise them; how could he dream that the very power which is emptying his pocket is the force of his own emotions, his temperament; and all that is of most use to him in other places serves to disarm him when he confronts the humming wheel.

But the least reflection, of course, assured Tyson that it would be worse than folly to lecture a Mexican; and now a withered brown hand was laid upon his arm, and those unhealthy eyes of black set in yellow were burning up to him.

"All is not well with me," said the peon, and his attempted smile was a convulsive twitching of the lips; "all is not well with me, Señor El Oro. I lose much money. The wheel sings the wrong tunes tonight. Ah, but the devil is always in Señor Kennedy. He is always sure to win. Yet if Señor El Oro were to lay my coins for me—"

He extended a ten-dollar gold piece with an inviting smile.

"If I should play the money for you—and lose it—will you stop play for tonight?"

The hand of the Mexican shook with eagerness; his eyes begged like the eyes of a dog. "Yes, yes! Do but play for me. Surely I am not a fool, nor the son of a fool, and I have no fear that you will lose—even to Señor Kennedy. And if you *do* lose"—he shuddered, and Tyson saw that he held the fellow's last coin—"it will be a plain judgment of God," finished the peon weakly, and he moistened his lips.

Twenty-One
The Necktie Returns

"We are playing the black, then," said Tyson coolly, and he placed the money; and while the wheel spun he looked from the ghastly face of the peon to the scornful complacency of Kennedy—the man who knew that no human being could win against his machine. The wheel slowed, the ball clicked into its place—the black had won. Tyson struck down the hungry hand of the peon as he reached for his winnings.

"Try again," he insisted, and looked fixedly at the chief gambler.

So intent was the gaze that Kennedy at last twitched his glance from a distant table where the stakes were running high, and pierced Tyson with his stare. Then Kennedy frowned and looked down; he was trying to recall the colourless face below him; he was trying to recall some great winning in the past which made the fellow stand there with that familiar hate in his eyes. And in his meditation he absent-mindedly stroked his necktie.

He was a very large man, this Kennedy. He had big bones that finished off his shoulders in sharp points, and his chest was thick. Great cords lined his throat, and when he turned his head these cords jumped out and quivered like banjo strings against his collar.

And he had large hands. There was no muscle in them. They were only bones and sinews; they could have been drawn with straight lines; there was black hair running down over the back of those hands almost to the big knuckles, and thickening into a veritable mane towards the wrist.

Tyson watched those hands for a while. He hardly heeded that the wheel had stopped on the black; he hardly noted the whimper of joy from the Mexican; he was only aware that Kennedy was now staring at him steadily. They were hating each other with a cordial vehemence.

After a time—ten seconds, ten ages, perhaps—the peon touched Tyson timidly on the arm. The white man looked down into a face that was strained with a joy more terrible than pain.

"Look!" said the peon, and pointed to a little heap of gold on the black. "Shall I not take it now? We have won—so many times—shall we tempt the dear God again?"

"Take your money and go home," said Tyson, not unkindly, for he was grateful for the interruption of the duel of glances between him and Kennedy. He considered the little man more in detail as the latter scooped up his gold and then extended the larger half towards his benefactor.

"No, no!" smiled Tyson.

"Ah, señor!" pleaded the peon; "only a single

coin—for a souvenir of one who shall pray for you daily—and his children shall pray for you!"

"Not a single cent," replied Tyson. "As for you"—and here he frowned—"you have now enough money to redeem the jewels of your wife which you pawned."

The peon was agape; he clutched his breast with both agonised hands.

"Our Lady of Gaudalupe has told you all!" he gasped. 'Ah, señor! Ah, Señor El Oro!"

"Not a soul shall know of it," said Tyson, keeping back his smile, "if you go instantly to the pawnshop and redeem the jewellery—and take your wife home some—er—what do you call them—reboso? Good! Off with you!"

"I travel on wings!" panted the little peon, and Tyson turned again to the roulette wheel. As he did so, something tugged lightly at the bottom of his coat. He glanced down; then he slipped his hand into the pocket and brought out a five-dollar goldpiece; the peon had left his souvenir.

Tyson turned; the little man was nowhere in sight. Then he moved to restore the gold to the roulette wheel that had originally lost it; for by the terms of his contract he must not accept either the winnings of chance or charity. Yet he paused with the gold piece gripped hard into the palm of his hand:

Five dollars would do a number of things. One might buy fifty loaves of bread; or great steaks, seared above and below to retain the rich juices; or—he stopped in his count of possibilities. A given word is a little thing, but now his promise encompassed Tyson like the surrounding barrels of cannon. Let chance, which had given him the money, receive it again.

He stepped forward to lay his coin, and he placed it where he was sure to lose—on a single number. As he stepped back again he was aware of a sudden focussing of eyes upon him, and a murmur about him; first he saw that his wager was the only one that was laid. Then he perceived that the gamesters before the roulette wheel had ceased all operations to watch him; he met a circle of curious, half-jealous, half-reverent glances, and he heard the strange nickname again: "El Oro!"

The wheel hummed to a pause; he heard the voice of Kennedy, sharpened now by the first touch of emotion, calling his number. Then he saw the proprietor waiting for him to collect his winnings.

His hands itched after that gold. He forgot the food and his own burning hunger, but the passion of the gambler caught him up; he had to fight it down. His given word tied his hands behind him.

So he said, smiling oddly up to the face of tall Kennedy: "Stake it all on the same number—against the necktie you're wearing, sir!"

It was rare to see Kennedy shaken, but now he first flushed and then frowned, and was shaking his head when he caught the murmur of the peons: "He will not dare; he will not risk even his necktie; it is El Oro he plays against!"

The wisest man in the world may be tempted by the idle taunt of a child.

"I take you," said Kennedy, and spun the wheel. For there was only one chance in seventy-two, after all, that Elo Oro could win. And the wheel hummed, and the spokes whirled into one unbroken flash, which in turn grew dim and dimmer, and then broke into sections, and finally was turning slowly, slowly, until it entered on what was plainly the last circle it could make.

And at a snail's pace the pointer crept on—and on—Tyson heard someone praying in swift Spanish, and he heard another voice beside him cursing in the same soft speech; and he was suddenly aware how fiercely he desired to win—that necktie. When the eyes of Rona fell upon the yellow-and-black pattern, what would she say?

He had won. A blur across his own vision did not enable him to make sure with his own eyes, but first he heard a harsh outbreak of joyous exclamations from the Mexicans, and then he saw the strong, pale hands of Kennedy go up to his throat and tear the necktie loose. The bright silk was dangled before his eyes, and as he took it he heard Kennedy say: "Another score, Señor Tyson. But the longest reckoning can be paid in one lump sum, eh?"

But Tyson could not answer. The retort came up in his throat and stuck there; he was too happy for talk.

Twenty-Two

Success

A certain measure of success makes men cruel. The best of us are flavoured with viciousness in varying proportions; if we are kindly one moment we strike an average with satire or irony the next. The politician snarls at his wife's supper, and thus erases from his mouth the lines of good nature which the practice of the day has engraved there; we are all more or less children, and smash our toys for the pleasure—if no other—of self-torture.

Now Edward Garth was winning. The dam was nearly done. He was already receiving congratulatory letters. Engineers were coming thousands of miles to see this masterpiece in the making. Scientific magazines sent out representatives to write articles about the Napoleon of the thirsty desert.

To be sure, Garth did not take time off to taste these pleasures. He was in sight of his goal, but his ship was still in deep water, and might conceivably sink before he touched the shore.

He had the confidence, then, of success, and he had the spur of danger goading him on remorselessly to full speed. He would have been more than human if moral considerations had not to some extent fallen by the wayside.

Ordinarily, he would never have stooped to double-dealing with Tyson or anyone else, for the name of "Honest" Ed Garth was not an empty one, but now the end began to justify the means, in his eyes. After all, his crime against Tyson was a more or less imaginary one. No harm was done to the man, and as for his sister, it was certainly not a dangerous plot against her—his attempt to bring her out to the Chiluah.

But when he made these deductions he overlooked one thing: one cannot do gratuitous wrong to another without poisoning one's own mind. He still felt the distance between himself and Tyson. It was as strong when he talked to the man in the cement house as it had been when he sat at Tyson's table in the New York house in Gramercy Park. That perfect breeding and graceful manner of Tyson's became something of a personal insult.

Eight hours of sound sleep would have cleared the brain of Garth and reduced him to the normal; as it was, he felt a danger in the flamelike pride of Tyson. The fellow actually looked up to him—but only as a model of muscular manhood. If Tyson dreamed for an instant that the roughhanded engineer aspired to his sister's hand—ah, there would be the rub!

Something of this was passing through the mind of Garth as he sat in his office this evening. He had dined with a great consulting engineer and two men of money—overlords of the street—and now he was back in harness. For the dinner he had had to don a Tuxedo, but when he sat again in the office he lapsed to the normal, rolled up his sleeves to the hairy elbows, tore off his high collar, and turned in the neck of his shirt. He could think better in such a costume. A stiff-bosomed shirt cramped his mind.

Something went wrong outside; it brought half a dozen of his lesser bosses into the office, and for ten minutes Garth was shouting at them from blueprints and pinching home his ideas with a brandished fist. He finished with a little profane exhortation that brought them out of their chairs like horses under the spur and curb, and then they were gone, pell-mell, through the door, and clattering down the high, wooden stairway.

He turned back, perspiring, when he heard the sound of a woman's voice from his secretary's room, the waiting chamber.

The sound of it stopped him—held him poised and waiting for he knew not what. It was like the pause on the football field just before the kickoff, with the two teams scattered on the green, each man crouched and waiting, and all the crowded bleachers breathless with expectation. The door opened; his secretary was announcing a lady to see Mr. Garth.

A lady? What did the secretary mean by the inflection, the singular drawl with which he lingered over the word? And there was a peculiar meaning suggestive of criticism in the eyes which he fixed upon his chief.

"Show her in," growled Garth.

The secretary turned away, and then came back. He seemed in a silent distress.

"Well?" asked Garth.

"Shall I bring you your collar and coat?" suggested the man.

Blood leaped in the veins of Garth. It was not the first time he had sensed an incipient contempt in this smooth-spoken, trimly dressed youngster. It was a continual reminder of Tyson, in some subtle manner.

"To hell with collar and coat," roared Garth. "Show her in. Is this a drawing room?"

The secretary vanished through the door as if impelled by a strong hand, and in the brief pause Garth remembered that his oath must have rung with perfect clearness into the outer room. He dropped into his chair. It fortified him with official importance to be thus ensconced behind a desk; and then he saw Margaret Tyson in the door.

Into the second before he went to greet her Garth crowded some intense thought. First he wanted to shout aloud with triumph. Then he remembered Henry Tyson with a touch of cold shame.

But, after all, what was that? Margaret Tyson stood in his office; Margaret Tyson was at the valley of the Chiluah; Margaret Tyson was in his country—the country of the strong hand and the fighting man. If he could have known that this thing would be before the night was over—if he could have gone to Tyson and made a clean breast of it—the entire harmless artifice which had now won its fruits—no, it was too late for that. He remembered the face of Tyson when the latter had refused to dine with the big boss. Pride!

Garth had moved from behind his desk; he was shaking hands with her. He was aware that Margaret looked first at his hand and then at his face as he greeted her. And it made him see that his hand was very soiled, and that her yellow gloves were very fresh.

It was still worse when she raised her eyes, for the bright glance went through and through him, and he was conscious that there were dark, soiled places in his soul of souls.

He asked her to sit down, and she thanked him graciously; but no sooner was she seated than something in her cool composure made him tremendously ill at ease. He stood grotesquely, in the middle of the floor, with his feet braced wide apart as though he stepped on the bridge of a sea-tossed ship; and his hands dangled, vast and useless. So he went behind the desk to cover his confusion.

He was no sooner seated than he regretted the move keenly. Would she think that he had taken up the position the better to impress her with his official significance? A faint shadow of a smile was touching at the corners of her mouth, and his heart sank. Moreover, the protecting desk did not cover his collarless neck, nor his unkempt hair. Margaret was glancing out of the window. There was nothing but blank dark outside; was she pretending that she did not notice?

It had seemed an age to the disturbed mind of Garth, but it was really only an instant after she sat down that she spoke: "You're busy, Mr. Garth. I only want to find out Hal's address. I've been writing to him, general delivery, you see, for he's been expecting to move. Can you give it to me?"

The very sound of her voice troubled him, as darkness had frightened him with the terror of the unknown in his childhood. She threw him back upon an aggressive defensive in which he felt a foolish desire to talk about things he had done, show himself in action, justify his existence. But here, under her eyes and in his own office, he was helpless.

"I have his street address," he said, and he scribbled the house number on a card and shoved it across the desk.

He saw her hesitate an instant, and then she rose and took the card. Sweat poured out under the armpits of Garth. He should have carried the card to her.

"Thank you," she was saying, as she glanced at the card. "I'll keep you no longer from your work."

She was going towards the door. For a frantic instant there welled in Garth a terror that he might find nothing in his empty brain—nothing to speak to her, and detain her. She was passing between his very fingers like the water of a mirage.

"Wait!" he cried, a little hoarsely, rising.

She turned to him, her eyebrows politely raised. "Yes?"

Why the devil was she so poised? Why did her colour come and go for no reason? Why were her eyes so mistily bright?

"You're staying at my mother's house while you're in La Blanca, of course, Miss Tyson?"

"That's very kind of you. But I suppose I'll be with Hal, you know."

"You couldn't possibly," he went on, breathing more easily now. "Tyson lives in a little boarding-house. He wants to. He's leading the hard life, you know."

Garth laughed uncertainly, but the girl nodded.

"I know about that. But if he can stay there, I can, as well."

"You really mustn't. I'll be hurt if you don't come to us. So will my mother. She knows of the pleasant time I spent with you in New York. Besides, we have loads of room."

He was so insistently earnest that the girl looked at him with a rather sharp touch of curiosity.

"But it would upset Mrs. Garth to have me come at such an hour. Tomorrow, if I may——"

He brushed away her objections with a wave of his big arm. He had come quite close to her now, a towering figure, forgetful of his disarray, and to the girl he seemed a figure strong enough to take the burden of Atlas.

"You'll upset nothing. There are half a dozen rooms that can be put at your disposal in five minutes. You'll come? Of course you will. I'll take you down right now."

He began to roll down his sleeves.

"You mustn't do that." And she raised a hand to stop him. He may have amused her a little, but he also pleased her. He could see it in her eyes; feel the new cordiality in her voice. "I want to see Hal by myself the first time—look in and surprise him."

"All right. Halloo, McIntosh!"

The secretary appeared at the door.

"Mac, will you take Miss Tyson in the machine wherever she wants to go? She has the address with her. And bring her around to my house when she's ready. Miss Tyson, may I present Mr. McIntosh?"

While McIntosh was bowing Garth suddenly wanted to wring the fellow's neck. He was not in the least embarrassed by the girl's beauty. He seemed to take her as a matter of course. Garth would have given nameless things for that same cocksureness.

"I'll see you later, then?" he went on to Margaret.

"Indeed, yes. You're sure I won't disturb your

mother if I come in a little late? I may be quite a while with Hal."

"Take your time. Take your time. Nothing will disturb mother. She used to run——" he was about to say "boardinghouse" when he checked himself. "She'll take care of you. You'll find your brother thin. Been working too hard, and I'm afraid he shows it."

"Good night, then. And thank you so much."

A little rising inflection in the middle of the speech sent a thrill through Garth. He could only nod in silence, and then they were gone.

He watched them covertly through the partly opened door. McIntosh was already chatting comfortably with her. Confound the fellow! He would bear watching. Never could tell about these smooth self-satisfied ones.

The rattle of the automobile starting; then the engine fell into a smooth humming, and slid away, and a fragment of pleasant laughter blew back to Garth.

Twenty-Three
Brother and Sister

McIntosh abused the advantageous position of his mission shamelessly. It was bad enough to discover that the headlights were not focussing, and get down and pretend to straighten them; it was worse to twice think that a tyre was soft; but it was perfectly inexcusable to develop engine trouble in the outskirts of La Blanca and call Margaret out of the car to ask her opinion on a matter of the magneto.

However, there were palliating circumstances. The girl wore a carefully tailored suit and a tailored hat with only one spot of colour in it; her new gloves, plumply filled, and with straight seams and unwrinkled wrists, gave her whole tone a touch of the Puritanical. The collar of her shirtwaist turned back in a white fluff from her throat, and it needed only one touch of softness to make her blossom. She had the colour and the unexpected beauty of the century plant—fabled to bloom only once in a hundred years.

But at last McIntosh could delay no longer, and Margaret stood in Mrs. Casey's hall alone. The hall light hung above and behind her, and Mrs. Casey squinted to make her out.

"I could call Tyson down into the parlour," she suggested, "but there's a couple of gents in there now havin' a quiet glass of beer. You see?"

"I will see him in his room," was the answer. "I am his sister."

"I ain't heard——" began Irene Casey, frowning, but here Margaret turned impatiently, and in so doing the light fell more fully on her face. "Oh," murmured Mrs. Casey, "I guess it's all right. I got to be careful, you know; my house has got a name!" she continued by way of apology. "Just step up this way."

And she led up the stairs. Under the ample pressure of Mrs. Casey's step the boards groaned, and she stirred up from the carpet a faintly pungent dust—the desert alkali that clings like a perfume. Moreover, there lingered about that stairway innumerable odours of strong laundry soap, and the fragrances of cooking, all embalmed and crowded together until the air was heavy with the ghosts of meals long past and forgotten.

Margaret followed her captain to the hall above, where a pendent electric light, nearly burned out, made a spot of yellow around which the dark hung heavily and seemed to stir like smoke.

"Here you are," said Mrs. Casey, and paused with her stout hand suspended in air before she knocked. "The young gent ain't in top spirits, ma'am. Ain't he sort of sickly by nature? Between you and me, I lay it to the cheap Mex chow he's been living on. As I was sayin' to him myself the other day: 'A white man,' says I, 'needs a white man's food.' Now, if I'm wrong, just call me a liar!"

She waited another instant, but receiving no challenge, she at length allowed her hand to fall heavily on the door; the vigour of the knock shook the wooden frame and resounded through the hall. There was no response.

"Maybe he's asleep," said Mrs. Casey.

"I really must see him," answered Margaret Tyson, and with this she pushed past Mrs. Casey and set the door ajar. Inside, all was dark as a blindfold. It was like the presence of deeper night pushing out at them.

"Hal," cried Margaret, not loudly, but with a tremulous vibrancy. "Hal!"

Margaret stepped fully into the room.

"Lady," cautioned Mrs. Casey, "be quiet. Men ain't nacherl when they wake up quick."

"Halloo!" called a hoarse voice from the middle of the dark. Then the bedsprings creaked, a foot thudded softly on the floor, a light snapped on.

He stood with his arm still raised towards the light above his head. He had lain down in his shirt and trousers, merely kicking off his shoes; the pattern of the rough spread was clearly designed in red along the side of his face; his hair stood on end; and the chalky apparition squinted at them, blinking at the flare of light.

"Now, ain't that a pretty picture," grumbled Mrs. Casey; but here Margaret calmly shut the door behind her.

Now, it was a very clean and well-kept room as rooms went in La Blanca. The strip of matting by the bed had once been a bright and cheerful spot, though now the shuffling of unnumbered feet had worn away the design, and the original reds and greens were oddly blended in that common over-tone of grey.

The bed itself had, on a time, been neatly en-amelled in white over the iron, and indeed there were still patches of white here and there upon the frame, though usually in a peeling state. The wash-stand was like the rest of the room: time, not Mrs. Casey, was at fault. The lip of the pitcher was roughly broken away, exposing the brown stuff of the earthenware, and a jagged crack darted down the fair, smooth belly of the pitcher.

The wallpaper was on three sides regularly and pleasantly green, with a design in gold, but on a fourth side some torrential rain, leaking, perhaps, from the floor of the room above, had washed out the green and the gold, and streaked that portion of the wall with grisly browns.

It was along this wall, therefore, that the prac-tical common sense of Mrs. Casey had concen-trated the pictures. Three nymphs danced in a discreetly misty woodland; neighbouring, a big Newfoundland held guard over a little kitten, his brows wrinkled with supernal and defiant wisdom; and there was a four-poster showing a girl with a shower of straw-coloured hair down her back and several choice stalks of wheat between the whitest of white teeth; while nearby was a print of George Washington—forehead singularly narrow and his jaw most amazingly large.

It chanced that now the smile of the selfless pa-triot looked over the head of Tyson and straight into the eyes of Margaret; and it freed her, strangely, from the hysteria that had leaped up in her throat when she first saw Hal. She recovered slowly from the first shock. That wavering, gaunt-faced man was not the one she knew. He was not clean.

Twenty-Four
The Builder

Indeed, he showed that he had been through the fire. For the long test through which he had just passed showed plainly. And how could she tell the leanness of hard training and gaunt muscles, and the staggering of sleep, from the meagreness of starvation and the weakness of under-nourishment?

"Hal!" Margaret cried, "what in the name of Heaven have you been doing?"

Then her arms were around his neck.

"Hal, dear," she said over and over, her voice beginning to tremble with grief and anger, "what have they been doing to you?"

He extricated himself slowly and stared at her. There was no mirror to make him understand her horror.

"What's all this pity about?" Tyson said, frowning a little. "But, oh, it's good to see you. Don't stand so horrified. I'm not a ghost. Gad, I'm hard as iron!"

He flexed his arms to try his muscles, and smiled down at her. Now that the sleep was leaving him, he could see her clearly for the first time, and as they sat down, he rested his head against the back of the chair and feasted his eyes upon her. She was all that he had been missing, to Tyson. She was a breath of fresh air, a vision which he had almost forgotten in the sweat and slime of the cement house.

"Hard day," he explained, "and I hit the bed without changing my clothes. Awfully fagged, you see."

Margaret drew her chair beside him and took his hand. "Now," she asked, with the quiet insistence which he remembered in her, usually—"now, Hal, will you tell me what this is about?"

"My trip West?" he asked vaguely.

"Why does this Mr. Garth keep you out here in the desert?" she asked, and all the time her eyes examining him, and behind her eyes there was a promise of danger for someone. The fighting blood of the Tysons was in her in full measure, as Hal knew well enough.

"He doesn't keep me here, Margaret. I stay of my own free will."

"He only told me that you were thin—not like this!" she said angrily. "Why hasn't he sent a doctor to you?"

"Ah?" muttered Tyson. "You've talked with him. Did he say that I was weakening on the job?"

He chuckled.

"He only said that you were working too hard."

"Ah?"

His eyes shone with gratification.

"But why has he let you get in this condition?"

Her voice rang dangerously. "The rough-handed vulgarian!"

Tyson queried: "Didn't I write to you that I was trying myself out at a man's work?"

"It was an amusing letter," said Margaret Tyson. She turned his palm up. "Oh, Hal!"

The rough sacking of the cement had torn away the skin inside his hand and left it almost raw, and there were blisters at the fingertips.

"Manual labour?" said Margaret.

He began to laugh again. It pleased him to see how completely she had misjudged him. She thought of him as of a sort of hothouse, decorated species of man, not fit for the labours of the world.

"And Mr. Garth knows you're in this condition?" asked the girl with ominous calm.

"I tell you, he has nothing to do with it, except that he first suggested that I come out here."

"What in the world, Hal, could make you torture yourself of your own free will?"

"I want to show you something," he murmured, rising. "Come over to the window."

He pushed back the curtain and remained clinging to it for support. With the other hand he gestured out over the desert.

"Look!" he commanded.

The view carried down over the roofs of La Blanca and then shelved rapidly away across the desert. In the infinite distance the grey-black of the sky met the blue-black of the land, and everywhere the desert was dotted with lights; some of them moved, but almost as slowly as stars, at that distance; and those lights which were farthest away seemed solitary, single rays. It looked like a harbour, with ships at anchor.

"It's the work of the night shift," he said. "I see

it every evening from this window. And when I'm tired out, as I am now, it puts new life into me. Do you wonder that I stay with this game?"

"I'm trying to understand," said Margaret, "but you never were interested in things like this before."

"You never can tell what sort of a soldier a man will make until he gets into a war," answered Tyson calmly. "But out here I feel as if I were one of the ranks—a unit in a marching column. Can you guess at what I mean?"

She lifted her face from the desert scene to Tyson, and winced as she saw his sunken eyes.

"There is something fine in it," she admitted. "It means so much to you, Hal?"

"I'm a small part—the very smallest part," he said, humbly, "but for the first time in my life I'm a constructive, not a destructive force. That means a good deal."

He encountered her critical eyes, shrewd with suspicion.

"Don't laugh at me," he challenged. "I feel rather deeply about all this."

She looked away, smiling.

"And Garth?" she queried.

Tyson drew a quick breath, and then looked straight in the eyes of Margaret.

"I suppose you think it's odd that such a fellow could influence me?"

"He seems rather—*queer,*" she suggested. "Not exactly your sort of man."

"You don't know him," replied Tyson quickly. "You see the rust; you don't see the finely tempered steel that lies underneath. Oh, there's mettle in that man!"

He nodded in silent conviction. "He has qualities

you would never dream from hearing him talk. You must see him in action. A pile driver is a blunt and ugly thing in action, but when it drops it shakes the earth. This isn't an age for heroics in the ordinary sense of the term, but perhaps you'll understand me when I say that Garth is truly one of the heroes of the industrial world.

"If you take a deep breath as you stand here at the window you'll taste the alkali in the air. Think, Margaret! In six months when someone stands at this same window and draws the same kind of breath he will taste the scent of green, growing things. Growing things on the desert! And that's what Garth will have done! Think of it! The power of a man who can affect the very quality of the air."

She nodded dubiously, but something of his excitement was beginning to affect her. She was very lovely, standing against the black of the night with her eyes commencing to gleam.

"I'll look at him in a different manner when I meet him again. But it's hard to get past his exterior. I'm afraid that I haven't much insight."

"Possibly not," he said dryly. "But don't bother your head about him. He's purely a man's man."

"Tell me more about him."

"You're open to conviction?"

"At least, I'm interested."

"Haven't I told you enough about him?"

"But I should think that you'd love to speak of him. If you are the soldier, he's the general."

"I could talk with you all night," he said, "and never leave the subject of Garth. In fact, he hasn't been out of my mind this fortnight. Never for half an hour at a time. I even dream of him."

"If I didn't know you, Hal, I'd call this hero worship."

"He'll have the same effect on you, once you get past his exterior. Consider the man who came out here and looked at this white stretch of burning, useless sand with a muddy trickle in the midst of it, and out of that caught the idea of the dam. Something in that?"

"There is something in him," she said thoughtfully, "but I was inclined to call it mere mass of physical strength."

"Listen to me. Once he started he met the most terrific difficulties. His labour merely to finance the dam was enough to fill the lives of two ordinary men. But then the mechanical troubles. He had to build this entire town and make it like a true bit of Mexico to hold his employees. Then the dam itself. It was a terrible task to haul fuel to the dam; no railroad came within twenty miles until he built his own branch, and even operation of the branch line was an expensive thing. They had worked for several months and it seemed hopeless."

Tyson was so wrapped up in his subject that he forgot to watch the effect on Margaret. She was looking far away, like one who struggles to understand difficult music.

"Garth went to the upper waters of the Chiluah, tunnelled a whole mountain, brought two streams together, carried them to a cliff's edge, and erected an electrical plant. Hence the electric light in this room!" And he pointed to the little globe.

She smiled at his enthusiasm, but the smile went out quickly. She felt as if Tyson was probing the soul of that big, clumsy man, and the result was a revelation.

"Hard work over?" and the eye of Tyson hardened and brightened. "No, the worst lies ahead of him. He has to have the dam completed before the spring floods strike down the valley. If he loses that first rush of water he might as well leave the gates of the dam open for another year. Yes, if he is a week late with his work this year is thrown away.

"So he is fighting every minute. He labours day and night. He drives his men with whips, you might say. Yet he has to keep his labour contented while he wrings the last possible drop of effort from them.

"And think what a terrible danger hangs over him all the time. If the rains come before he is done! Suppose some little thing should hold up the completion of the dam for a few days—ruin! It is like a magnificent and strong machine that can be ruined by the dropping of a single little bolt! What a tragedy that would be—the dropping of the little bolt."

He left the window. He began to walk spiritedly up and down the room.

The critical gleam had left the eyes of Margaret Tyson, for as her brother talked she saw a new vision of this Garth, this heavy-handed son of the soil. She and Henry Tyson had grown up in close intimacy, more as man to man in friendship than as brother and sister, and her whole urge was to follow him in his likes and dislikes. So that now she dropped that barrier she had raised against Garth—that barrier of good taste—and prepared to find the good in the man, beneath the rough exterior.

More than the words of her brother described Garth, she felt the man in the change which had come over Henry. Before, he had been a pleasant and amiable wastrel. Now he was a force, for good or for evil. It seemed to her that she had only known the surface of Henry before; now he was stirred up from the depths.

Her earlier alarm was dissipated now that excitement had sent the blood pumping into his cheeks and given surety to his poise and balance. He was rather worn than exhausted.

"I'll go now," she said, "and let you sleep. Mr. Garth has asked me to stay at his house. I'm going to watch him with a sharp eye, Hal. If he's a tithe as great as you say, he's worth knowing."

He would have followed her down to the front door, but she waved him back, and he heard her heels tapping lightly down the stairs.

Twenty Five
Golden Silence

Garth's hours at the dam this night were cut short, for after Margaret left, his brain refused to function. Finally he hurried into his clothes and went back to La Blanca; he must prepare his mother for the arrival of Margaret.

He found her in her own room in a dressing-gown, finishing the reading of her chapter in the Bible, which always closed the day's duties with her. Indeed, life was simply a compound of duties to Mrs. Garth. It was never what she wished, but what she *ought* to do that governed her actions. He went to her, raised her face between his big hands, and kissed her withered, patient forehead.

"Mother!" he cried, stepping back from her, "what do you think has happened?"

There was just a flicker of emotion in her face, like the play of light across the ceiling when the headlights of an automobile flash past the window.

"It ain't hard to guess, Eddie," she said. "The girl has come?"

"Now, how in the world did you guess that?"

"Well, you got a kind of foolish look, Ed," she answered, a little dryly.

He laughed boisterously.

"She's not only come, but she's going to stay with us. Think of that!" he added. "Aren't you happy about it?"

"Comin' here?" she repeated vaguely. "Why, Eddie, how in the world can I talk to a girl like that?"

He did not hear her.

"Get into your clothes, mother. Please. She'll be here any moment; with her brother now. What room'll we put her in? D'you think that room facing on the south—that corner room—will—"

Mrs. Garth rose. She had a way of taking command of things in a crisis.

"Eddie, you go downstairs and sit down. Don't be worryin' about anything. I'll take care of the room for her."

"But I want to see how—" he persisted.

"Eddie," she said sharply, "there ain't call for you to help me run this house. You go downstairs, and everything'll be all right."

Force of habit made him obey, but he paused at the door.

"Put on one of your best dresses, will you, mother?"

"I'll put on something good enough. Get along with you."

After he was gone her assumed coolness disappeared, and she fell into a tremor. She went to the wardrobe and turned on the light and looked over the array of gowns and dresses and coats which

Edward had insisted upon for her. She had put it off from day to day until he compelled her to go shopping. She *had* to be properly dressed when she entertained some of those formidable associates of her son.

The result was that she fell into the hands of an enterprising clerk who fitted Mrs. Garth out from head to heel. The prices were right enough, but the gowns ranged through filmy things which might have become a débutante to singularly coloured creations such as are usually worn by women of "a certain class."

Mrs. Garth had no great liking for such clothes. But she felt that since the outlay in money had been so great she must not neglect any of the gowns. So she wore them in rotation, one after the other, with a religious regularity.

As she looked them over now she squinted her eyes and strove to imagine what Miss Tyson would be wearing. All that she could think of was the picture, with the suggestion of a very low neck.

Mrs. Garth, by instinct, set about looking for a dress with a high collar attached, following an unvoiced thought which bade her put the newcomer in her place. She wanted something sufficiently severe and also sufficiently impressive.

What she chose was a black gown thickly spangled. Over the arms and shoulders and bosom it was heavy lace, and a tall lace collar propped up her head. It wasn't an easy dress to get into, but Mrs. Garth managed the labour and reviewed herself with some complacency in the glass. The waistline was quite high, and the dress fell off into a sweeping, abbreviated train effect.

Mrs. Garth, when she turned suddenly, found the cloth swishing silkenly around her legs, and the picture was very much like pictures she had seen in magazines—of actresses and others of renown.

She decided that dress would do—plain, but just rich enough, but *full* of style. She gave her hair another approving pat, tossed her shawl over the spangled shoulders, and went to look at the bedroom. It was not the corner room of which Edward had spoken. That was her room of state, and certainly should not be wasted upon any sprig of a girl. She chose, instead, one of the side rooms, an ample apartment.

Moreover, the furnishings struck the eye more impressively than did the corner room of state. The heavy blue carpet figured with red roses seemed to Mrs. Garth quite the most cheerful pattern she had ever seen upon a floor. The walls were yellow and brown—quite different from the carpet—but a success in a different way.

Moreover, Miss Tyson, even if she did come from New York, could search the world over before she'd find another chair more imposing and comfortable than the Morris in the corner with the cushions of bright green plush. Mrs. Garth was particularly partial to green. She had read somewhere that it was good for the eyes—rested the optic nerve.

Yes, the room was quite all right in every way except that Miss Tyson must not be left to think them an unliterary household. Mrs. Garth hurried back to her own room and brought forth an armful of her favourites. There was a volume collected from the minor English poets entitled: *Gems of the Hearth and Home.* There was a book called *Self-Control, and How to Practise It.* Stanley's *Darkest Africa* gave a cosmopolitan touch, and a Bible finished the little group.

If Miss Tyson wished to read in her bed in the morning—that was probably her fashion—she would have plenty of suitable books for the purpose.

Mrs. Garth cast a final glance at the room to make sure that all was as it should be, and then went down to her son.

She found him pacing the living room in great agitation; he cast a troubled glance at her, and then fumbled among some scarlet flowers in a tall, yellowish vase, putting them in order. She watched him sadly, and it seemed to Mrs. Garth as if she were looking upon her boy just before he went upon a long journey from which he might never return.

A brisk wind setting up the valley of the Chiluah had turned the night cool, and the great fireplace at the end of the room was filled with burning logs. They made it too warm when one stood near, but they cast a pleasant light over the rest of the room, and, as Edward said, they made the place seem more hospitable. He always connected open fires with comfort, which was a prejudice inherited from the bitter winters of his childhood.

Presently the door opened and a mozo announced Miss Tyson. Garth made a convulsive movement to go, and then recollected himself and asked his mother to meet the girl. She saw that his face was set, and his hands nervous, and her own sorrow gave place for an instant to pity for him and the same dull anger at the girl.

She found Margaret Tyson in the hall in the act of taking off her linen duster. She could not see the girl distinctly at first; she rather saw her own false picture of Margaret, so she went forward with her hand extended and with the crisp rustling of her bespangled dress comforting her ears.

"This is Miss Tyson, I believe?"

She had read that, and the formality of it stayed with her; then the other turned quickly, and Mrs. Garth glimpsed a flashing smile, and very large, very dark eyes. Mrs. Garth felt that small, cold sense of pain which comes to most plain women and to all mothers of men when they see a very lovely young girl. Then the slender, gloved hand was in hers, and she was listening rather to the musical voice than to the words themselves.

The first thing she noted clearly was the simplicity of Margaret Tyson's clothes. But of course those were her travelling clothes, and one cannot be judged by what she wears on the sooty cross-continent trains. Next she noted that she was not being examined in the cool, critical fashion for which she had prepared herself. The girl took everything for granted, apparently. Or was that her art? They went back into the living room, while Margaret was taking off her gloves.

Mrs. Garth dreaded seeing her son standing with his feet spread apart and his arms dangling awkwardly at his sides awaiting Margaret; she was infinitely relieved when she found Edward in the act of pushing up a big chair nearer the fire. He was quite natural and at ease as he greeted Miss Tyson.

They settled down, Margaret sat facing towards the fire, in the centre, with Garth on her right and Mrs. Garth to her left, and as the firelight played over the face of the girl Mrs. Garth's heart sank. It seemed as if a river of feminine might was sweeping down around her son; he could never struggle against it; he could never look beneath that face. She, Mrs. Garth, would have to do his looking for him.

"I've just come from Hal," the girl was saying. "He's very thin—looks rather ill, too."

There was some degree of reproach in her voice.

"Yes," nodded Garth. "He insists on taking the hardest manual labour he can find at the dam. But don't you think it's rather fine for him to adopt that attitude?"

"I suppose you know why he's doing it?"

"Perhaps I do, in part."

"I can tell you."

She turned directly upon Garth, and the elder woman caught her breath. In her day women never stared boldly on men. They observed the trousered sex with side glances, mostly. But Margaret Tyson rested her elbow on the arm of the chair and dropped her chin upon the back of her knuckles and looked at Edward with a steady smile.

Mrs. Garth blinked. She felt as Hannibal might have felt had he watched the artillery tactics of Napoleon at Austerlitz. These revolutionary tactics took her breath.

"I'll tell you why," ran on the charming voice. "It's because Hal is carried away with admiration of you, Mr. Garth. He's actually happy to share your work—even if he is doing no more than swinging a pick or lifting sacks of cement."

It warmed Mrs. Garth's heart to hear that. This was the right spirit to have towards her son; if young Tyson was capable of this, his sister might not be so bad after all.

But: "I'm afraid I shall have a hard time making him go back home with me," said Margaret. "I wonder if he thinks he can make an engineer out of himself by manual labour. Well, I suppose it's more devotion to you than to the work."

There was a certain lightness combined with

perfect poise that shook all of Mrs. Garth's conceptions of what women should be. Everything seemed to run easily off the back of this girl. She was quite unaffected by awe when she talked to Edward Garth, builder of the Chiluah Dam.

These thoughts swallowed the attention of Mrs. Garth for a time until her son rose and went towards the phonograph.

In the interval of silence Mrs. Garth watched the girl's eyes covertly as they moved about the room, and she could see those glances literally pick up object after object and drop them again. It was nothing which the elder woman would have noted ordinarily, but tonight she was super acute, and she read Margaret's mind. Accordingly, she shrank, and then hardened herself and tensed her nerves and her mind.

"What'll you have?" Garth was asking.

"Anything you're fond of," she replied carelessly.

There was that in her tone which suggested that she would probably disapprove of his choice, it seemed to Mrs. Garth.

"Well, most of this stuff is classical."

"Yes?"

There was just the faintest raising of her eyebrows when she said this, and Mrs. Garth flushed.

"Do you care for other things?" asked Garth.

"Oh, yes. I think some ragtime is bully."

"D'you like 'Lucia'?"

"Lucia?" And Mrs. Garth noted with a pang the different pronunciation. "Rather. A little sicky-sweet, though, isn't it?"

"That record cost seven dollars and a half," stated Mrs. Garth coldly.

"Really?" And she turned a dim smile on her hostess.

"Here's a lot of Caruso," boomed Garth.

"Take him all through, he's the most expensive of the lot," pursued Mrs. Garth, intent on being pleasant to the limit of her faculties. Otherwise, Edward would be cross with her. "Queer how much money there is in singing, ain't it?"

"Very. I think the violin goes better on the phonograph than vocal music. Any instrumental records?"

That took Mrs. Garth's breath.

"According to the price list," she announced, "they ain't near as fine!"

"Try anything you wish," urged Margaret, turning. "Select it yourself."

But Garth was discouraged. He came back and took opportunity to cast a thunderous frown towards his mother; she wondered why.

"It's rather late for music, anyway," he said, uneasily, "and we'll have plenty of time to play that stuff later on. Besides, you must be very tired from your trip."

Miss Tyson agreed that she was, and presently she said good night to Edward and went upstairs with Mrs. Garth. She seemed to like the room very much, and Mrs. Garth warmed sufficiently to call her attention to the green-cushioned Morris chair. Miss Tyson's trunk had already been brought up. No, there was nothing she wished.

"If you want to do any readin'," pursued Mrs. Garth, "you may like these books. Travel, poetry, moral writin.' You can take your pick."

Miss Tyson took up one at random: it was the Bible, and it fell from her hand, face down, on the floor, fluttering. Mrs. Garth picked it up with a little exclamation.

"The Book of Job!" she cried. "I suppose that

means awful bad luck—to one of us!"

"Oh, I think not," said Margaret, smiling. "I'm very fond of the Book of Job."

"Are you?" said Mrs. Garth, wondering. "It's very hard on Job, though, ain't it?"

"Yes. I always wonder when I finish it, whether the devil won, or God? What do you think, Mrs. Garth?"

The latter stood agape; and then closed her lips severely.

"I never saw two ways to it," she observed. "Good night, Miss Tyson. If you want anything, please let me know."

And then she fled.

She found Edward walking swiftly up and down the living room, his head bowed; his hands clenched behind him.

"Well," said Mrs. Garth dryly. "D'you like Miss Tyson as well as ever?"

He didn't seem to hear her for a moment, and then he turned and cast out his hands in a gesture of impatience.

"Is it a question of whether or not we like her? Mother, dear, I wonder what she thinks of us?"

"Personally," said his mother stiffly, "I could get along without knowing."

But Garth had resumed his brooding and pacing. For the first time in his life he was walking a path on which she could not join him. She looked at the sway of his broad shoulders, and wondered how there could be any human problem sufficient to stand in his path; and then she looked at the chair where Margaret Tyson had sat. Suddenly Garth stopped and faced her again.

"What's wrong with all this?" he asked, with a broad gesture.

EXPERIENCE THE ADVENTURE AND THE DRAMA OF THE OLD WEST WITH THE GREATEST WESTERNS ON THE MARKET TODAY...FROM LEISURE BOOKS

As a home subscriber to the Leisure Western Book Club, you'll enjoy the most exciting new voices of the Old West, plus classic works by the masters in new paperback editions. Every month Leisure Books brings you the best in Western fiction, from Spur-Award-winning, quality authors. Upcoming book club releases include new-to-paperback novels by such great writers as:

Max Brand   Robert J. Conley   Gary McCarthy   Judy Alter
Frank Roderus   Douglas Savage   G. Clifton Wisler
David Robbins   Douglas Hirt

as well as long out-of-print classics by legendary authors like:

Will Henry   T. V. Olsen   Gordon D. Shirreffs

Each Leisure Western breathes life into the cowboys, the gunfighters, the homesteaders, the mountain men and the Indians who fought to survive in the vast frontier. Discover for yourself the excitement, the power and the beauty that have been enthralling readers each and every month.

SAVE BETWEEN $3.00 AND $6.00 EACH TIME YOU BUY!

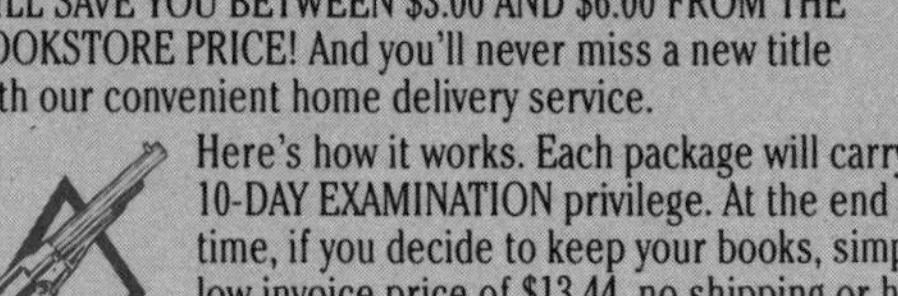

Each month, the Leisure Western Book Club brings you four terrific titles from Leisure Books, America's leading publisher of Western fiction. EACH PACKAGE WILL SAVE YOU BETWEEN $3.00 AND $6.00 FROM THE BOOKSTORE PRICE! And you'll never miss a new title with our convenient home delivery service.

Here's how it works. Each package will carry a FREE 10-DAY EXAMINATION privilege. At the end of that time, if you decide to keep your books, simply pay the low invoice price of $13.44, no shipping or handling charges added. HOME DELIVERY IS ALWAYS FREE. With this price it's like getting one book free every month.

AND YOUR FIRST FOUR-BOOK SHIPMENT IS TOTALLY FREE! IT'S A BARGAIN YOU CAN'T BEAT!

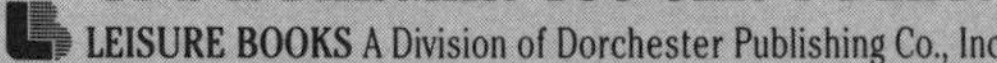

LEISURE BOOKS A Division of Dorchester Publishing Co., Inc.

"Wrong with what?"

"Wrong with the room—wrong with ourselves. Everything was all right until she came; and now everything's impossible! What is it?"

She could have told him, but her greatest wisdom lay in her careful selection of silences.

Twenty-Six
Grapefruit and Other Things

She wore something white, she looked as cool as a flower, and as fragile of colour; she had greeted him pleasantly but without enthusiasm; he had failed to seat her at the table.

These things and a jumble of others filled the mind of Garth as they sat at breakfast. Also, he felt the quiet eye of his mother upon him. He knew that she did not like Margaret Tyson. He knew that she would be trebly pleased if anything should come between the girl and himself.

In the meantime he went ahead, eating absent-mindedly and thinking and trying to plan. In the midst of this, the cool eye of Margaret flickered across him and brought him up standing, so to speak. There had been aversion, contempt, disgust, in that glance. He could not tell what. Perhaps none of the three, but certainly an element of coldness.

Then he discovered that he was squeezing the last of the juice out of his grapefruit into his spoon—and she was hardly started on her own fruit. Heaven alone could tell him how he had progressed so rapidly. He must have been eating like a mucker shovelling coal; and that would explain the quiet content in the eye of his mother also.

"Can you tell me about the hotels in La Blanca?" the girl was saying.

"Certainly," nodded Mrs. Garth.

"Hotels?" echoed Garth heavily. "What do you want to know about hotels?"

"I have to make a choice among them, you know," smiled Margaret Tyson.

His heart fell a vast distance, and his throat became dry.

"Why, you're going to stay here, aren't you, Miss Tyson?"

She seemed mildly, rather coolly surprised. Yet had it not been understood the evening before that she would stay with them while she was in La Blanca?

"You're very kind," smiled Margaret Tyson. "I really can't do that."

"Why not?"

At his blunt question he caught just a flicker of her lashes against her cheek. He had cornered her, he felt, rather brutally, but quite effectually. Then his mother went swiftly and quietly to her assistance.

"Of course you know that you're welcome here, Miss Tyson," she said. "But I understand, well enough, that you'd feel freer in a hotel. And there's a perfectly good hotel in town."

Garth could have browbeaten her like a man for that speech. He cast a sharp, ominous glance at her and then looked back at Margaret Tyson. She was nodding and smiling in relief at Mrs. Garth. Confound these women and their subtleties!

"Hotel?" he growled. "Not fit for a dog. Couldn't think of letting you go there. Not at all. Why, there's only one, and that's full of the greasers. Terrible place, Miss Tyson."

There was rather worry than hesitation in her eyes. Mrs. Garth came to her rescue again.

"Why, what do you mean by saying that, Edward? You know perfectly well that they don't allow the peons in the hotel. Only the upper class Mexican gentlemen are permitted to register!"

"Mexican gentlemen?" snapped Garth. "There isn't such an animal; only difference is in their clothes."

"I'm sure I could stand them for the few days I'm here," said the girl. There was a finality about that speech which stopped Garth's retort. Only a dull rage against the world possessed him.

"You'll take me down there after breakfast?" she was inquiring of him.

"If you want to go," he answered. "Of course."

Then he wanted to curse himself. If she had to leave, why couldn't he be graceful about it? He was showing his hand disgracefully, he felt. And he saw that a thousand impalpable barriers were still between them. He wanted to lean across the table and smash those barriers with a single gesture, and take her hand. Why not? Why not out with it, and tell her that he loved her at once? He glowered down at his cereal bowl, and then stabbed the spoon into it. Everything in the world was wrongly arranged.

He had brought her these thousands of miles across the continent, and here he had lost her in an instant. His own mother was sufficiently to blame for that; he could feel her exultation as she sat with her downward eyes upon the table.

And Margaret? He felt always the cool survey of her eyes, her aloofness. The same sense of shame flooded up hotly in him, which he had felt when Tyson himself refused to dine at Garth's house. Pride! That was the secret of it all. The accursed pride of the Tysons!

Then it happened with the suddenness of thunder out of a blue sky. Rapid feet leaped up the steps to the front door, a hand beat heavily and rapidly, there were loud, excited voices in the hall. And now a white-faced man raced into the dining room. He was one of the foremen.

"Mr. Garth," he cried, oblivious of all the others. "Gas, gas in No. 4 tunnel! Five men were caught, and——"

He gasped and stopped for lack of breath. He had run a long distance.

Garth had risen, and the sudden straightening of his legs sent his chair reeling backward and crashing to the floor.

"Hell!" he said fiercely. "Why wasn't I called on the phone?"

"Phone?" The eyes of the other wandered helplessly. "I didn't think——"

"Five men in the tunnel?" the words came snapping out.

"No, we got out four, and then the gas drove us back. The other poor devil may be dead now——"

"José!" thundered Garth.

Margaret Tyson and Mrs. Garth had risen, staring, white-faced, at each other. Death had stepped into the room. And now, with a single gesture, Garth had whipped off his coat and stood rolling up his sleeves. He was like one prepared to wrestle for his life. All the self-consciousness which had entangled him as he sat at the table was now gone. He was free, clear-eyed, firm-voiced. And Margaret Tyson, wondering, watched him. She caught her first glimpse of the man her brother had prepared her to see.

"José!" roared Garth again.

A Mexican mozo flashed into the doorway.

"The car. Get it out! Be damned fast about it! Bring it to the front."

No confusion of thought. His mind worked clearly and easily. He was meeting the danger. He strode for the door, and Margaret hurried after him, following an impulse.

"Miss Tyson!" cut in the sharp voice of Mrs. Garth. "There ain't anything you can do. Let the men folks handle it."

But Garth, at the door, whirled on his heel and swept her from head to heel with a glance such as had never passed over her in her life before. It probed her, measured her, summed her up in one flash of insight.

"D'you know anything about asphyxiation?" he snapped.

"Yes," she answered quietly. And she felt her heart rise.

"Then you come with me. I may need you."

He added: "There's the car now."

"Just one moment," she said, "and I'll get my hat upstairs."

He threw the door open.

"You come as you are. Quick!"

Even then he was in the car before her, springing in with one leap from the curb, and before she had well settled herself in the seat, and closed the door after her, he had sent the car lurching down the street.

The foreman, yelling for them to wait, raced after, but the car gathered speed like a running horse, and whipped away out of reach of his voice.

It was a big machine, low hung, with a long, grey hood stretching out in front, and it nosed with uncanny speed down the streets of La Blanca.

It turned corners here and there, but went around the last corner on two wheels.

She cast a sharp glance at Garth at that. She had ridden with speed maniacs before, and she knew the type of man who drives hard to frighten a woman; but Garth leaned his broad shoulders forward, and his big hands had the wheel in a death grip.

He was not driving for any motive of pleasure. He was driving with an intent eye fixed before him, and a wrinkle of painful anticipation carved on his forehead.

They whizzed past a cart, and the driver yelled with terror as the fenders flicked under the noses of his pulled-up horses. They skidded past a turn and whirled into the open roadway leading from La Blanca to the dam. And she sighed with relief as the car stretched out on the open road.

But there was no relief in Garth's actions. He did not lean back against the cushions and smile across to her for an appreciation of his fine driving through the traffic. He bent even lower over the wheel, and now the motor hummed up through a swift crescendo as the car stretched out towards the looming mass of the dam.

Twenty-Seven
Concerning Hotels

The wind cut across her face, now, and left her almost breathless. She had never before ridden at such a rate, for the car bowled along, lurching past the uneven places in the road. At every rise it seemed to lift into the air, and landed with a thud farther on, wrenching the heavy body and straining the springs.

Yet she felt, with sudden surprise, that she had no fear. The man knew his car and he knew his road, and he was driving not to break a record or to get a thrill, but to beat death in that gas-filled tunnel up the Chiluah. She felt that he probably was quite unaware of the rate at which they were travelling. His thoughts were already up there at the tunnel gauging the chances of life for that unfortunate—perhaps one of those greasers of whom he had spoken so contemptuously the moment before.

Now they heeled up the slope and swerved down past the rim of the dam, and across the valley.

Where the first cliffs jutted up she saw a dark cavern, perfectly round, and before this there was a crowd of several hundreds already gathered.

The scream of the horn cleared Garth's path, and he brought the car to a grinding stop with foot and emergency brakes at the very edge of the tunnel.

On the ground, hatless, his hair blown up stiffly by the wind, his big arms bare to the elbows, he faced the crowd.

"Is he out yet?" he called.

The only white man in sight stepped up to him.

"No chance, Mr. Garth," he said. "The tunnel is full of gas."

"I know that. Don't tell me what I know already. I asked you if the man was out of that tunnel yet?"

"This is the point," answered the other, flushing, and he produced a blueprint. "The tunnel runs——"

"Damn your plans! I know the tunnel by heart if it's been run as I ordered. Why haven't you got him out?"

"Three times we tried——" began the other, white about the lips with anger.

"Who tried?"

"My men."

"These?" A wide gesture embraced the peons, who stood agape. "Why in hell didn't you go in yourself?"

"I?" stammered the other. "Go into that hell for the sake of a——"

"Bah!" growled Garth. "A life is a life."

And with the word still on his lips he had turned and plunged into the night of the cavern. The foreman stepped back, growling. He looked towards

Margaret with a shamefaced smile, prepared to explain, but she looked through and through him, and to the peons beyond.

"Are you going to let him go in alone?" she cried.

There was a stir among the peons, and then a rumble of voices and a shaking of heads. She stamped in her anger. She would have gone herself, but in case of accident, what could she have done with the vast bulk of Garth? Already his footsteps had echoed away to silence in the tunnel.

Then a voice came from the crowd; her brother stood beside her.

"He's in there," was all she could say.

"Who?" asked Hal, with his usual self-control.

"Garth! Garth, of course!"

"But what's up?"

"Gas. Someone's caught in there, and these—men—won't go in to help him!"

"By the Lord!" cried Tyson, and started forward.

In a sudden impulse of fear she caught at his elbow.

"No, let's wait a few minutes, and see. There's nothing you could do alone if he's overcome with the gas. You couldn't drag out Garth."

Tyson drew out his watch.

"We'll give him ten minutes," he said quietly, "and then we'll go in after him. Here come some white men."

He put back the watch. "So Garth went in after some peon? He's about nine-tenths man, eh?"

"He's all man!" she said eagerly.

"Vulgar sort," nodded Tyson, "but at a time like this he's the kind that's needed. You stayed with them last night?"

"Yes. Is the time up, Hal?"

"Not for five minutes. Don't lose your head, Margaret. By the way, going to the hotel, today?"

"No," she answered. "They've asked me to stay on with them—and I intend to."

"Really?" He looked at her in astonishment, and then chuckled.

"Well, it'll be an amusing experience—living with the Garths. Well, it'll do you good, Margaret. Ordinarily, one doesn't get to know such people."

She looked at him, half angry, half surprised. His viewpoint had been her viewpoint of an hour before. But now she had forgotten it. She had seen Garth in action, and the picture blotted out everything else.

Tyson looked at his watch again, and then called to a few of the white men who had just come up. They consulted briefly, and half a dozen volunteers signified their willingness to go in when the ten minutes should have elapsed.

But before that time came, there was a stir in the tunnel, and then the sound of footsteps. With a rush, white men and peons poured into the cavern; there was a shout; they came out again bearing a limp body in their arms, followed by Garth.

His face was lined and white; he looked like one who has laboured without sleep for a great length of time, and his eyes stared idly about him.

Yet he shook off the arms of those who would have supported him.

"Look to that poor devil," he said. "Found him lying on his face. Air's fresher close to the ground, of course, and he may be alive still. Nasty stuff, that gas."

That was all. His own lungs must have been full of the keen poison, but he had not a word for that. He stood by, watching the men work under the direction of Margaret, working the arms and legs of the stricken peon to clear his lungs of the poison and bring in the fresh air.

And eventually one eye flickered open, and then another. His brother peons, who had not lifted a hand to save him, now shouted with rejoicing. He was lifted to a sitting posture, and grinned vacuously around upon the group.

Then a hand touched the shoulder of Margaret. It was Garth.

"Better get out of this now," he said calmly. "The fellow will have his senses back in a moment, and he'll begin to thank you. Their gratitude sticks like a leech. A man can't get away from it. I know!"

She followed him, mute, back to the automobile. And as they started off, she caught the quizzical eye of Hal Tyson, following them. Let Hal feel what he might, she thought, she had found a man, and she was going to know him better before she was done.

There was very little talk as they jogged back. He was driving with ludicrous caution, now, giving every bump a wide leeway, and only breathing a little deeply to clear the last vestige of the gas from his lungs. But not a word about what he had done.

The thought came to her that his past must have been filled with a thousand things like this; and he had accepted them as a part of his work.

When at last he began to speak, it was of the things they passed; and then, when they caught a vista of the desert over La Blanca, it was of the work on the canals. She heard and she wondered. She had read of simplicity such as this, but she had never seen it.

When they came back to the house Mrs. Garth met them at the door with a single, anxious glance at her son to make out that all was well with him;

Margaret started up towards her room.

"Wait a minute," called Garth after her, "we haven't finished breakfast."

She paused, and stared at him.

"And," he continued, "I've had enough exercise to give me an appetite."

She followed him back to the dining room, and there he sat down, still with his sleeves rolled up, his hair blown stiffly awry, coatless, his elbows resting on the edge of the table, and his cuffs flopping unkemptly about them; yet he was perfectly unconscious; perfectly at ease.

She felt, oddly, that the chains had been struck away, and now the lion was free once more. Put him in clothes of formal perfection, and he would be tongue-tied and miserable again. And she was glad with all her heart that she was sitting opposite a host who looked like a hired hand on a farm—and a rough farm at that! He was looking frankly across at her.

"Coming back to that hotel proposition," he began, a little uneasily.

"If you'll allow me to change my mind," said Margaret Tyson, "I'd like very much to stay on here with you—if it won't put too much extra care on the shoulders of your mother."

"If it does," cried Garth, exultant, "I'll give her a hand myself."

Twenty-Eight
The Padre Intervenes

Tyson had not fasted long enough to devitalise his body; his time of storm had been rather like the drying-out process which fits the athlete for the struggle. In twenty-four hours he was a new man; in forty-eight he could lift the world.

A great joyousness possessed him, a friendliness all-embracing. But though he smiled on the Mexicans they regarded him warily, for they still feared him not a little.

They were used to scorn and contempt from the white men of the Southwest. They were used to treatment such as befits a subject race of inferior mentality. To Tyson, their skins alone were brown; and they responded as children respond to the unexpected kindness of the stranger, at first with dark suspicion and aloofness, and then a sudden and whole-hearted surrender.

If he had been a politician campaigning for their

votes, he could not have taken half so true a course to win them. Already the rumour spread. He was indeed a gringo, but he was a gringo with a difference.

So the whistle sounded the end of this day, and Tyson swung lightly down the slope towards La Blanca. None of the Mexicans offered to accompany him. They would have been glad to do so, but he never thought of inviting them, and without such an invitation they could not go with a gringo. In truth, there was a little atmosphere surrounding Tyson which served to keep them at a proper distance.

He was humming to himself when he entered the town by his accustomed route, and still humming when, by the square, he was stopped by a hail from the side. He found himself looking down into the pale, ugly face of the little padre.

The padre was smiling as he looked at Henry Tyson, a faint smile, as though the joyousness of golden youth struck a dim reflection in his quiet heart. Somehow, that expression exaggerated the sense of suffering which the man bore about him. And the single deep wrinkle which cleft his forehead gave a touch of the wistful to his glance as it rested upon Tyson.

"This is a pleasure, señor," said the padre, in his formal, careful English, with its delightful taint of the foreign accent, "which I have been promising myself since we first met. I hoped I should see you again, señor, that we might come to know one another better."

Tyson was shaking the cold, small, clawlike hand.

"That's good of you," he nodded. "Won't you come up to my room for a talk?"

"I must go back to the mission," sighed the padre. "I am expected there. Will you walk with me? A part of the way?"

"I'm hungry as a wolf, padre," said Tyson, "but I'm glad to go. Eating can wait."

The padre looked up to him, and then shook his head. It had been long since food meant as much to him as it did to Tyson.

He sighed as the youth turned again, and went up the street at his side.

As they walked along, the peons in passing raised their sombreros to the padre, and bowed their heads; but always, just before they passed, their eyes flashed up and their teeth glinted over a smile as they hailed El Oro. Truly, his doings in the cement house had passed the rounds, and the tale of his gambling against Señor Kennedy rounded out the story.

The padre took heed of these greetings in silence for a time. He talked of the people they met, and he spoke of the buildings; he told little anecdotes of the families in the town. He reverted, now and again, with a touch of awe, to the labours of the great engineer who had built all these things in the desert.

But at last he said: "You know my people, Señor Tyson!"

"The Mexicans?" answered Tyson, surprised. "A fine, simple-minded lot. Yes, I like them very much."

"Truly?" echoed the padre. "Well, my friend, a little kindliness goes a long way with them."

He considered his own thought for a time, nodding his head, and casting little side glances at Tyson. Very plainly he could not quite make out the young American, though he was concentrating, for some reason, upon the problem.

So they began to cut up the valley of the Chiluah, the padre lengthening his stride until it extended even Tyson's to keep pace with him.

Watching the swishing robe and the steady, plodding gait of his companion, and the bended, thoughtful head, Tyson began to feel oddly as though he were walking back not only through distance of space, but through distance of time into the days when the mission of San Vicente was first established in the valley of the Chiluah.

The padre told him little stories of those early days, and as they went along he talked enough for Tyson to patch together a more or less broken history of the mission and its work.

They had been hard days for the fathers.

In the first place, the men who established San Vicente had not been taken from old Mexico itself. They were men brought directly from Spain, and therefore they had been ignorant of the ways of the Indians and all methods of approaching them. Which was worse than putting a pedestrian for the first time on the back of a wild mustang and expecting the unfortunate to stick there.

For the flock in the Chiluah were not the peaceable natives who had made the Californian mission rich, for instance. The Indians of the Chiluah were the fiercest warriors on the continent, the savage Comanches, wild as the horses they rode, with tempers as restless as their knives. Yet the patient Franciscans had kept true to their task, and gained slowly in power.

Warriors who came home crippled from distant raids were nursed back to health, and these formed the nucleus of the converts. The neighbouring Apaches looked upon the mission of San Vicente as a shelter and stronghold for their natural enemies, and twice the mission had been stormed and its gardens watered with blood by the onslaught of these cunning savages.

Until one Brother Manuel, "a gentle and pious man," so the quaint old story ran, "took thought with himself and gained from his superior the permission and gathered men, both Spaniards and converts and others, for his crusade; and he went on a far journey, and he struck the Apaches both with sword and fire and humbled them; and he brought back captives in chains and won them to Christ, and they laboured much in the gardens of the mission."

Thereafter, the fame of San Vicente went abroad among the Comanches, and San Vicente became, in a way, their national mission. However, the good brothers were always much troubled, because they could never be sure that their converts were praying to the gentle San Vicente in his true character, or to another San Vicente of their own making—a god of war!

And the stalwart El Toro might well have been one of those grim Comanches of the early days, tireless on the warpath, immune from fatigue, alert as the arrow that quivers on the bowstring. No wonder that Henry Tyson felt as if every step he made carried him deeper into the heart of the old days, when the first mystery was not yet torn from the New World, and God seemed, somehow, closer to the earth and the eyes of men.

The valley narrowed swiftly, they climbed up a brief rise, and in the centre of the hollow which lay before him stood the Mission of San Vicente. Of the lordly rectangle which had once comprised the group of buildings with the garden in the centre, three sides were broken quite away. Only one face remained, the church and the cloisters.

As for the rest, it was mostly a shapeless ruin, with here and there a section of 'dobe wall standing sharply up; but the church and the cloisters seemed at first glance, at least, fairly well preserved. If age and ill-care had dimmed the purity of the walls, yet beside the tawny waters of the Chiluah the mission was clean and white, and the belltower curved proudly into the blue of the sky.

These details Tyson was able to observe, for the padre at the crest of the hill paused a single instant, tightened his belt, and then went down the slight descent towards the mission at a somewhat gentler pace.

As they drew nearer Tyson saw more and more clearly that the first impression of solidity was an effect of distance only, for at close hand there were visible a hundred symptoms of decay. A deep veranda skirted the front of the cloister, and the pillars which supported the roof had mouldered at the edges and were fast passing from square to bluntly hexagonal; and the long roof sagged miserably in the centre, and in the thick walls he perceived more than one fissure, caused by earthquakes, no doubt; one in particular which ran a jagged course on the oblique across the whole face of the wall.

It made Tyson think of the one-horse shay; it might drop into dust at some sudden shock.

Now he stood in the veranda itself. It was paved with great flagstones, and these were worn deeply towards the centre by the shuffling of whole centuries of sandalled and of moccasined feet.

The padre paused before the open door, and then pointed an arm into the dusky interior. Tyson entered, and slowly removed his hat. For a dim atmosphere of sanctity, or that of age which is the nearest approach to sanctity, met him at the door.

He saw some chairs of antique make, painted a dull green, and there were pictures on the wall of Brothers of the Order of St. Francis, and he breathed the air of cleanness and coolness as if the place had just been freshly washed out.

On a wall hung a picture of one of the old brothers seated at a table with a book between his hands—and there stood the very table, and on it was the very book. Tyson turned to the padre.

He was quite old, perhaps, but there was about him that mysterious connotation of youth which clings to so many of the monastic orders—that suggestion of men who have not lived past the first enthusiasm of youth. There was not a line on his face except that deep, perpendicular wrinkle in the centre of his forehead which gave to his entire expression a touch of wistfulness.

"You were good to come," said the padre. "Are you tired?"

"You stole the distance away with your talk," smiled Tyson.

"Ah," he nodded. "The time was when I could have walked with you, but time has put heavy boots upon me. Well——"

His brown hand waved slowly, a gesture of profound resignation.

"You must come out to the garden with me," he said, "and we will sit in the cool while you recover your breath. This way, if you please."

And he led Tyson through a massive arch on the farther side of the room, down a brief passage, and into the open.

"At least, this was once the burial ground, and

some little care of the graves is all my strength permits; so here is all my garden. Do you mind so gloomy a place to sit?"

He spoke slowly, in careful English, but the soft Spanish ran, somehow, behind his English words. A throng of old tombstones filled the space, which was bounded on the three other sides by sagging heaps of ruins, and close to the wall of the cloister were two stone chairs; they had stood there mouldering for centuries, perhaps; six inches of the stout legs were sunk into the ground. Here they sat down.

"Is there only you to take care of all this?" asked Tyson.

"I am the last," nodded Padre Miguel. "Our flock is wasted away; there is little to do except with hoe and spade and rake. And even for that I am a little old."

And he smiled deprecatingly on Tyson. The latter removed his hat, for they sat in the steep shadow of the wall, and in so doing he felt the eyes of the padre shift quickly up to his golden hair and rest there. Not long or boldly; it was only a lingering glance of curiosity.

"And yet," argued Tyson, "are not those new graves—there—and there—and there?"

"Oh, yes. They are the bodies of men who died at the dam. Many of them come here; the Mexican loves the old, you know. It is a long walk, but some of them come here for confession when they are deeply troubled. And when these poor fellows died their last request was that they be buried here in the shadow of dear San Vicente. I was sorry, but their last prayers must be heeded."

"Sorry?" queried Tyson.

"For all these stones and all these graves will be

lost soon enough, señor. When the dam is finished and the waters rise—that will be soon now—all the mission will be quickly covered. And that will be the last of San Vicente."

His quiet eyes grew misty; he sighed.

"It is not a brave place, señor; but even a prisoner will come to love his chains. One of your own poets has said it. Well, there will be many a sad heart among those workers at the dam when the waters rise over the belltower. I could wish that just that could be spared."

"It is sure to be covered?" asked Tyson, and he peered at the old padre.

"You are excited, my son," replied the other, smiling. "But yes, San Vicente has softened many a heart. He has worked great works here within these walls of mud. But there is a period that all things reach, and every sentence has its end. And so—His will be done."

The head of the padre bowed, and Tyson knew that he prayed silently.

"There will be excitement at the dam when the mission is covered with the water," he mused.

"For you see," explained the padre, "they look on it, in a way, as a sacrilege, and it is all that I can do to keep them to their work, a great many of them. They are like children, you see, and the whisper goes to and fro among them, and they shake their heads and say that no good thing will come from drowning San Vicente."

"It would not take much to rouse them to action, I suppose," brooded Henry Tyson.

"Only a leader. But I have brought you here for a purpose, señor, and you will weary when an old man talks so much to so little purpose."

"Padre," answered Tyson, with strange feeling,

"I would have walked thrice as far to learn what you have told me." He looked on down the valley, and frowned at the blunt, looming top of the dam. "Aye, ten times as far." Then, settling back and lighting a cigarette: "But let me hear why you have brought me, if you wish."

"She spoke the truth," nodded the padre, gravely. "You are not like others. I am the more troubled because that is true. Do you guess why I have brought you here?"

"There is only one possible reason. It is the girl. It is Rona Carnahan? She is almost the only person who knows both you and me."

"I am troubled because of her," said the padre, and his clear eyes dwelt steadily on Tyson. "And you have troubled me, señor."

"I shall wager any agreeable sum," smiled Tyson, "that I have troubled you less than she has troubled me."

"I know, I know!" said the padre rather hastily. "But let us be quiet and think before we speak. I do not wish to rush into words and offend you, señor."

And they sat in the silence. It was like the body of music to which the gentle voice of the padre had been the prelude. The shadows slid steadily, quietly across the ground. The moss of the stones breathed its damp, cool atmosphere around the mind of Tyson; he could have believed that by closing his eyes he would awaken in the seventeenth century.

He rallied himself with an effort.

Twenty-Nine
Concerning Truth

"Shall I speak what I imagine?" he said at last. "You fear that I have seen too much of the girl."

"Well?" queried the old man. It was like the clash of a metallic will against Tyson's mind, that short, sharp word.

"My dear padre," chuckled Tyson, "she is a child."

"You will not be angry. I fear this talk, but since I saw that my people love you, I know that you are right at heart. Rona is not a child. She is old enough to ride a horse, run like a man, sing like a bird—and love like a woman."

A little flush sprang up in Tyson's cheek. He had not thought of the girl seriously, but the good padre, unknowingly, was bringing new ideas and riveting them home in the mind of Tyson. He felt now a sense of guilt which had not been with him the moment before.

"I am frank, you see," he said. "I understand you. But Rona will be married within a few days."

"It is an empty promise which is making her marry, señor."

"Padre Miguel," said Tyson sharply, "do you approve of this fellow Kennedy? Have you given him your support with that unsophisticated girl?"

"He is not a very good man," admitted the padre, "but neither is he very bad. He is a simple man, señor, and the simple heart may always be saved."

"Padre," smiled Tyson, "you place a great trust in him."

The priest changed colour a little, but he answered with dignity. "You are not simple, señor. You are youth, and youth is terrible and cruel. You are never still; your blood is fire. And Rona is tinder which a long summer has fired for flame."

"Do you know," murmured Tyson, "that the last time I was with that girl only the ringing of your bell up here saved me from her knife?"

"I know everything which has passed between you," answered the old man, "and it was not until she told me that she had drawn the knife that I began to worry about Rona."

"I'm afraid you have studied more books than women, padre. Is it not so?"

Padre Miguel Vega laid his brown hand on the arm of Tyson.

"I am very serious, señor."

Tyson could not reply. He felt guilty, of what he knew not.

"Tell me shortly: what is the girl to you?"

Tyson looked inward. "I do not know."

"The fiend," said the padre, "works in the dark."

"Come, come! The girl is to be married. Do you think that I have the power to forbid the banns?"

"Would it cost you much," pursued Padre Miguel earnestly, "to give me your word to see Rona no more?"

"My word," said Tyson, "is something which I can neither give easily nor easily retract."

There was a silence between them, and the steep shadow lengthened from the mouldering wall.

"I am going to tell you a story," said Padre Miguel. "It is because she is strange that you hunt her out. She is not beautiful—very. And what could she be in your life? Only an—experience."

Tyson caught the sound of gritted teeth.

"You are not of her order, señor. What you are I cannot tell. You bear the marks of a labouring man, but your eye is not the eye of one who labours. I had a wolfhound once which was fleeter and fiercer, I think, than any living thing."

Here he turned and looked full into the eyes of Tyson. He continued after that enigmatic glance: "But it must be because she is strange to you that you follow her. I will make you know her as I know her. I am sure that is best.

"It was many years ago. El Toro himself was only a boy at the mission then—and a troublesome boy, I warrant you. It was the spring of the year, and in the spring the Chiluah is a pleasant place, silent and green. Travellers have come up the valley at that season, following the river road, and in this spring of which I tell you the father and the mother of Rona came up the river road. They camped among the trees—just over that hill, señor.

"It was plain that they would soon have a child. Indeed, it was for the sake of the child that they came here. For the wife was not well, and her doctor had sent her away from the city to find quiet. About her you must understand, señor, that Mr.

Carnahan was a violinist famous in three countries, and that while he was touring through Italy he met this girl, and they were married.

"And it seemed to me that she was like her husband's violin. In tune, she was most pleasant, but out of tune she was very different. And you know, señor, that it needs but little to make a violin out of tune. It was the same with the young wife. The promise of the child upset her terribly; she could not live in the city; so before the birth the doctor sent her out to find the peace of the desert.

"They were strangely close to one another, this man and his wife. I would visit them in their cabin and watch them with my heart in my throat. For hours, señor, he played his violin, and her eyes dwelt on his face and drank the music, until sometimes it seemed to me that the music was the food on which the young life within her lived.

"So the wife grew stronger and gayer, and the rose came under the olive of her skin, and there was a light in her eyes—a wonderful thing to see."

The padre paused and smiled out to the growing blueness of the hills with the black shadow of the dam between them.

He said again: "To me, señor, it often seems that the Virgin is incarnate in every wife before her motherhood; the Holy Spirit broods within them.

"There was one shadow in the cabin of the Carnahans. He drank much, as some artists will. The burden of his wife's health and the happiness of both lay on his shoulders and bowed him with the weight, and he looked to drink for help. Señor, I have seen him playing to his wife with the red madness in his eyes, and in hers the still, white light. Is it any wonder that my heart would come beating in my throat. The Annunciation, with the voice of Satan speaking; the fiend struggling towards a divine work.

"But one day he had no more to drink. He came to us for help. Alas! we had nothing to give him. He came again a day later and prayed by my side, kneeling near me, for strength. But strength was denied him. Still another day, and he was gone. The violin was silent in the cabin, and the young wife was waiting with blank eyes. I myself went to her and looked into her soul."

The padre broke off with a faint moan; and his calloused fingers were interlaced.

"She knew as I knew why he had gone. But that did not make the waiting less terrible for her. He had gone to the nearest town, and that was a sad journey. Seven days, and now he was overdue. And on the eighth night a great storm broke. Never have I seen such wind and rain. A wall of water eight feet high came down the Chiluah like thunder, and the hills groaned on either side.

"In the middle of the storm I thought of her and rose and went to her in the night."

He paused, and there drove home in the silence a picture of the young padre bowing against the storm, and the wind wrenching at his robe, and the rain crashing about him.

"I came near the cabin, and a bough was torn from a tree above me and flung on my head."

Automatically he raised his hand. There was a jagged white scar that ran from his temple into his thick black hair.

"After a time I roused out of my miserable trance. There was a sad voice blowing down the valley, a wail that went through me. It seemed to come from the cabin, and I thought of the devil that had lived in Carnahan's eyes, and I was afraid and turned and ran down the valley."

The brown hand of the padre rose and pressed against the scar, and all his face wrinkled with pain as though he felt again the torment of that distant moment, and he shivered as if the rain were beating on his sodden body once again.

"I was afraid, señor. And it was long before I had the strength to turn again and go back through the storm. Before I reached the cabin the wails had ceased. I opened the door!"

He could not speak for a moment, but his lips moved rapidly, and pain closed up his eyes.

"It was the voice of the woman's pain—think—which had gone out to me through the storm and turned me back. It was her own voice which had slain her. For if I had come straight on at first—no matter. When I came at last, it was too late. The child was born two months before its time, and the mother was dying—terribly.

"And in that horror, señor, will you believe that I thought still and always of the Holy Mother and the Child and the winter night in Bethlehem? Blasphemy?

"She knew that she was dying, but she did not cling to me and beg for her life. She did not speak a word, but her look went ever from the child to my face, and to and fro and back again. And the child looked at us both with its red, wrinkled, ancient eyes.

"Well, it would have been strange if the mother had lived; it was a miracle that the child did not die. We took it to the mission and cared for it, and the next day Carnahan came back.

"It was then that I was punished with a mortal sin. Consider, *amigo mio,* that I had sometimes looked on the young wife and had remembered that San Vicente must take all the place of woman in my life. And this led me to my mortal sin, for when Carnahan came back I told him all that he had done, and it took his reason from him. To this day his wits live in his violin alone. And that, señor, is my penance, for every day I go to hear him play and to remember the mother of Rona Carnahan. It is true!

"We buried her here—that is her grave. And whenever the moon is full Carnahan comes and plays all night at the grave the same songs he used to play to his wife when she lived.

"Now, friend, I am come to the girl. At her birth she had lost both father and mother, and she got two foster parents—a padre for one, and for the other, the Indian, El Toro. How he came to her is another story.

"But you will see that God and the devil both had parts in her birth, and she has lived her life under El Toro on the one part, and under the padre on the other. So I say to you, señor, that there is a day and a night to her nature—a smile and a blasphemy on her lips—a rose and a dagger in her hand.

"Señor Tyson, she is so simple that she hates the dam and all things connected with it because she knows that the water it backs up will cover the grave of her mother. All her life she has come every day to this grave—you see it there? And she has sat singing. And in her childhood she used to talk to her dead mother.

"Now, the coming of the water is more terrible to her than a second death. Yes, she would give her body and soul to the man who could stop the building of that dam. You see what a child she is? And to you, señor, what could she ever be more than a toy?"

Tyson rose in anger, but the padre rose also and dropped his hands on the shoulders of the young man.

"Think, my son," he urged gently.

"I shall give you my word," said Tyson, flushing, "that before this moment I never thought seriously of the girl. And now——"

"Ah—now?"

"It is a crime that so rare and genuine a nature should go to Kennedy—one of the canaille!"

"And you, señor, what would you do with her?"

"You speak, sir"—this with rising irritation—"as if that wild woman were in the hollow of my hand."

"No. I only fear. I appeal to your honour."

"Honour," said Tyson coldly, "cannot go in leading strings."

"Ah, my son," murmured the padre sadly. "You are filled with double purposes, and I only follow the shadow of your mind. Beware! Beware of pride! Today I feel you are clean of body and mind. But tomorrow you may be viler than the leper. God Himself could hardly cleanse you. Pride, my son, it is a canker that eats the heart of a man. Today you feel yourself a proven man. Tomorrow your pride may be hurt, and when it is touched you may become a wolf, tearing all things around you."

Tyson frowned impatiently, and the padre lifted his hand for silence. A light, sweet whistling, like that of a strong songster flying up the wind, came to them over the wall of the cemetery.

"It is she!" muttered Tyson.

"And your face lights with danger," said the padre gloomily. "Alas! my son, I fear there were no evil thoughts in your mind before I put them there today. Our Father forgive me if it is true. And so you will give me no promises?"

"Padre Miguel," said Tyson, his voice hard, "you are not young."

"It is true," said the padre, and smiled calmly into the angry face of the youth.

"I am going to meet her," said Tyson.

"Ah?" said the padre.

"And I shall try to act always as a man of honour should act. Does that please you, sir?"

The padre made a singular gesture of resignation.

"The wind pleases me and the calm also," he said softly; "the drought and the rain as well. The will of our Father is all."

Tyson whirled on his heel and stalked away, but the Padre Miguel followed the retreating form with the same undecipherable smile.

Afterwards he resumed his place in the stone chair and remained for a long time gazing down the valley, where the blues of the evening climbed the sides of Cabeza and Blanca, though rosy light still rested on their heads.

"It is true," said the padre, and he spoke softly in the solitude. "I am no longer young."

A faint echo nodded gently back to him from the ancient wall.

Thirty
Pride Washes Clean

As for Tyson, he swung down the valley at a rapid pace. Expectancy put a spring in his step, expectancy of what he could not know.

The good father had worked quite the opposite of what he hoped. For the life of Tyson had been singularly clean, strangely free of the usual faults of men of his own leisure class; the companionship of Margaret had been an antidote for the atmosphere of sin in which so much of his life had been spent.

Rona had been to him only a diversion, an oddity, with just a touch of novelty and beauty besides. But he would probably have seen her a thousand times in full innocence.

The pride of caste held him in bands of iron. All the world he admitted to his acquaintance. The brown, simple Mexicans, rough-handed Garth, they were all free to occupy his ear and receive his thoughts. But into his intimate personal life only the elect could enter. Yet now the padre had planted a new thought, and such thoughts grow quickly.

For the poor padre had suggested that he, Tyson, had an influence over the girl, that she was interested, intensely; and Tyson felt suddenly the thrill of possession. Not that his thoughts went far. Of marriage he would as soon have thought as of leprosy; not even the thought of any affair with the girl was firmly implanted in his mind.

All Tyson knew, as he swung down the valley, was that an adventure lay before him, and he was prepared to taste the full zest of it—and retain his honour. A gentleman's honour; who has ever stopped to consider what its whitest portions are, and where pride begins and honour leaves off?

He was bearing straight for the sound of the whistling. Apparently it lay directly ahead of him down the river path, but now the sound came to a sharp period. In a moment he passed the point where she should have been, according to the loudness of the whistling an instant before. But the path was empty both ways, and the hush of the evening lay heavily around him. There was not a trace of Rona Carnahan.

"The devil fly away with her," said Tyson angrily, and he turned his back, somewhat sullenly, upon all thought of the girl.

Yet he had hardly made a pace when a voice behind him said: "Señor Tyson, if I were a man, I should horsewhip you for that!"

He turned with an exclamation and found her leaning against a tree, the tree which had concealed her. Her senses must have been of hair-trigger sensitiveness to have warned her of his coming in time for her to hide. She was dressed like an Indian, in a garb of freedom, more masculine than feminine, in a sleeveless buckskin jacket, wide sombrero, and short skirt. Her hair hung in two long braids, one over each shoulder, with the light twisting along them like the path of a torch down a river at night.

"You passed so close," she said, "that I could have stolen your hat."

"Why did you hide?"

"I knew you were looking for me, Señor Tyson."

He frowned at this complacency.

"You knew?"

"I saw the necktie, señor. I knew then that you had come to boast."

He removed his hat and rubbed his forehead, for he was heated by the walk.

"I have busy days ahead of me, Rona," he said, "and only a short stay on the Chiluah, I fear. I have come to say good-bye."

"The Chiluah will miss you," answered the girl, and covered a luxurious yawn.

"Here's a fallen tree for a seat," she went on. "Sit down and say good-bye. It is easier than standing." She followed her own advice and sat down on the trunk. "Besides," she continued, "I want to hear about the fight."

"What fight?" queried Tyson, and feeling ill at ease standing there before her, he took a place at her side.

"Where did you shoot him? And will he recover?" asked the girl.

"What are you talking about?"

"Kennedy, of course."

"Fight?"

"Will he grow well again?"

"I see now. You think I fought him for the necktie?"

She started.

"Did you steal it?"

"I won it from him, gambling."

Her teeth shone.

"He did not fight a stroke for it?"

"Not yet."

She brooded.

"He looks like a man," she said, and then: "You should not have won it from me!"

He caught himself leaning close to her, and recovered with a start. What he thought of then was the pale, pure face of Margaret; and then he felt this new sense of guilt. He held out his hand. "It may be long before I see you again. Good-bye, Rona."

If the padre could have seen that, how his heart would have leaped, surely. The renunciation!

But she paid no attention. "You have just left the padre?"

"Yes."

"I told you he would send you away. Did he frighten you?"

"Frighten me?"

She smiled. "The big man will deny that *you* frightened *him*."

"You've a poisonous tongue," he answered angrily. Then he mastered his irritation and extended his hand again.

"I'm in a hurry," he said. "It's late, Rona, and I have a long distance to walk."

She took his hand and retained it in a steady clasp.

"I don't want you to go," she asserted. "I will tell

Padre Miguel that, and perhaps he will let you stay."

"He has nothing at all to do with my going," said Tyson in a louder voice.

"Yet you are going, señor."

"Why should I stay?"

"Because you like me."

"You will marry Kennedy and be happy ever after; so busy plaguing him that you'll forget me, eh?"

"I shall not marry him," she said earnestly, "if that is sending you away."

He turned to face her squarely, and he searched her as a strong light plumbs the darkness, but he could not read a thing within her.

"You have promised him," he said.

"A promise is a word, and a word is a breath." She inhaled slowly. "So, I take back the promise with the breath. Is it not true?"

"Padre Miguel will have another opinion," smiled Tyson, "and so will poor Kennedy."

"However," she insisted, "I will not let either of them hurt you."

"Dear God!" burst out the man. "Do you dream that I'm running away because I fear an old priest and a bull-throated gambler?"

"Of course," answered Rona Carnahan, "they cannot hear you now. I am glad of that."

It needs a rare man to bear the imputation of cowardice from the lips of any woman; and Tyson was worried. For the first time he regarded Rona seriously, because for the first time she had seriously disturbed him. She had passed into sudden change as the moon dips behind a cloud and leaves the skies dark with midnight. She sat with an elbow on her knee, and her chin resting on a clenched fist, and her eyes probing a gloomy distance—like a feminine "Thinker."

"What shall I do," asked Tyson, "to prove that I'm not afraid of them?"

She did not answer.

"Yet I haven't time to waste on the padre and the gambler," he concluded, rising, "so it's good-bye, Rona."

She paid no heed to his extended arm, and Tyson frowned.

"Good-bye," he repeated. "I'm sorry to leave you in anger, Rona."

"You will come back," she said, and was silent again.

He stared after her, but found an expression which he could not decipher. Perhaps there is nothing that makes a man so uncomfortable as silence in a woman; for her natural weapons are grace of body and music of voice and the charm of small, speaking ways; but when she is silent the deadly weapon of thought takes the place of all these.

It is puzzling, as a boxer is puzzling who keeps his right hand extended instead of his left. It is difficult to explain the peculiar and insinuating power of silence; perhaps it is that we endow the silent one with strength from our own imaginings.

At any rate, it became extremely difficult for Tyson to meet the solemn eyes of Rona. It was as if the girl were judging him, and reading his values with a pitiless accuracy. It was not long—that pause—but while it lasted Tyson forgot the lessening light, and the swift trees, and the blue hills on either side, and he saw only the large, dark, thoughtful eyes of the girl. There was no place for words. What meaning could words have to her?

He turned on his heel and strode down the valley. The atmosphere of thoughtfulness which she had established stayed with him. He was picturing her in a thousand attitudes, critically, and remembering that in none of them had she been beautiful.

Yet the impression she gave was that of beauty; he tasted the thought of it, and being a connoisseur, he knew; it was like seeing the sun through a smoked glass—it did not look like the sun, but he knew that the brilliance was there.

There were other puzzling things about her. Not the least of these was that at this moment he did not feel as if he had left her forever; there was none of that definite sense of oblivion which a final parting brings.

It shot home to him that that might have been what the girl was thinking when she sat there with her chin on her fist, studying him. Was it calm confidence that he would return? The idea brought him to a sharp stop, and, throwing back his head, he laughed shortly.

So doing, his eyes fell upon the heights of La Cabeza, and there he saw, indistinctly, lost in shadows, a mighty face.

He closed his eyes, he rubbed them, and stared again; the face was gone. For a moment he felt a vast relief; the thing must have been a mirage. He studied the top of the mountain. The last light of the day played dimly across the crags, burying one prominence in darkness and lifting out another, as a worker with charcoal uses the broad, soft end of his stick and changes his composition with strong, slow strokes.

Yet a moment of thought brought back the disturbance. In spite of the fact that he could not find it again, the features of the face remained clean-cut in his mind; or, rather, the featurelessness of the face. It had been like one of those antique sphinxes of Egypt, with nose and eyes and lips and chin obliterated by time; yet the impression of the face is only the sharper for the ruin.

A smiling face—a mocking smile. With an uneasy spirit Tyson circled the hei[illegible]e dam, and swung down towards La [illegible]perstitions do not rest easily on th[illegible] century mind, and it was little wonde[illegible]yson walked with his eyes upon the ground.

Thirty-One
The Shadow of Thought

In the mind of Garth's mother thoughts moved as slowly as the tortoise creeps, but they plodded on with equal sureness of gaining their end. Into the train of her thinking burst an interruption that shattered the quiet of the room. It was Margaret Tyson, who whirled in through the door carrying the sunshine with her.

"Edward is upstairs changing," she announced. "We're going motoring around the dam. Won't you come with us?"

Mrs. Garth adjusted her glasses so that she could look up more easily. It always made her wince to hear the girl call her son Edward; and she had not been with them for ten days! She gathered her sewing more closely in her lap, for when Margaret ran in, in this manner, it affected Mrs. Garth like a disturbing wind.

"I think not," she answered slowly. "No, I guess I won't go."

Margaret dropped to the footstool before her, clasping her lithe hands about her knees.

"Why not?" she asked. "Do you *have* to do that sewing?"

Mrs. Garth blinked, for in the new position a shaft of sunlight set the girl's hair afire. Mrs. Garth often winced like this when Margaret came close, as she would have winced if a chain of great diamonds had been flashed in her eyes.

"I guess I won't go," she announced in the same mild voice.

"Why not?" repeated Margaret Tyson. She laid an impulsive hand on the knee of the elder woman. "You sit here so much, so many hours every day, that sometimes I feel as if you must be unhappy."

Mrs. Garth dropped her eyes and could not answer for a moment. When she sat by that window in the old days, she had been waiting for the coming of her boy with the night; she had been waiting for him—the goal of every day. But now when he came home there was someone else to welcome him and receive his smile.

She found a swelling coming in her throat at the thought. This day, this Sunday, for instance, she and Eddie would have sat about, talking a little, until the evening came, and then they would have gone for a short stroll down the street in the cool. But now? Surely it was not good for him to go gadding on his one day of rest.

"I'm just restin'," answered Mrs. Garth in her thin, quiet voice.

Margaret Tyson slipped to a position behind the other's chair and leaned her elbows on its back. Her hands were folded just beside Mrs. Garth's face, and the latter watched, from the corner of her eyes, the gleam of them in the sun. Just a ray which played about them. And when Margaret spoke, the rich, full tremor of her voice, tense with good spirits that overflowed, sent an uneasy quiver through Garth's mother. She was like a shadow, she felt bitterly, compared with this brightness of youth. No wonder Eddie was dazzled.

"Look out there through the window!" urged Margaret gently. "Look at the sunshine! Don't you want to get out and fairly bathe in it? Aren't you hungry for it? Come with us and get the wind in your face, Mrs. Garth. I love the wind. Don't you?"

"It's always blowin' things," answered Mrs. Garth. "And bright sunlight ain't any too good for the eyes, Miss Tyson."

She could not see how Margaret stepped back and looked down, puzzled, at Garth's mother. But Mrs. Garth felt the greater distance, and breathed more easily. Sometimes, when the girl was so close, she felt as if she were fighting away an intoxication. It was like a spiritual danger leaning over her. Besides, really good girls, homemakers, were never so gay and confident as this Margaret Tyson. The latter made one more attempt, after starting to turn away.

"It makes me really unhappy," she said earnestly, "to see you here all day—and most of the night—with that dark shawl around your shoulders, like a sign of mourning."

Mrs. Garth lifted her glance at that, and the mistiness cleared from her eyes a little.

"When you get to my age," she said, "you'll have things to sorrow over."

"Not if I live to be a thousand. Sorrow is a habit. If you would come out——"

"Oh, Margaret!" called the deep voice of Garth.

"I'm in here!" she answered. Then the door opened.

"We're losing the prime of the morning. Let's start before the crispness is out of the air."

"I'm trying to get your mother to come."

"Oh, mother?" Mrs. Garth tensed herself. "Don't worry about her. You can't pry her out of that chair. Come on, Margaret. Good-bye, mother."

The door closed on them as Margaret went out, and the current of Mrs. Garth's thoughts started again at the point where they had been broken off. Her son should not marry Margaret Tyson. That was the beginning and end of her ponderings, the period to each idea. Margaret Tyson should not marry Eddie.

It was not that she really disliked the girl, but there was a mortal strangeness about Margaret which was worse than dislike. She felt that if Eddie married her, his mother would for ever after be an outsider in his home. Even now the girl was carrying him away into new fields.

She did not actually think that Margaret loved Garth. That was impossible. She had seen those keen, short side-glances now and again. Sometimes they rested on the furniture and sometimes they rested on the face of Edward—at such moments, for instance, as when he talked of pictures, or music.

Other times, when he spoke of his work, his plans, his future, the girl was an intent, fascinated listener; but every now and then that keen, cold, penetrating glance darted out and transfixed something to the heart. Obviously, she could not love Edward. But sometimes, in this twentieth century, women did not marry for love. It was not like the old days. Margaret might be ambitious.

Yet it puzzled Mrs. Garth more and more as the days went on, seeing the growing intimacy between the two. Margaret was above her son's class, and no good came from mixing classes. Edward himself often said that. He talked of it in Henry Tyson—the difference between that fellow's pride and the pride of ordinary men.

But of course he was blind to the pride of Margaret simply because that pride was covered with feminine softness. And she, for her part, was not blind to the faults of Edward—witness those keen glances many a time. But something seemed to charm the girl.

For one thing, she was continually reverting to what "Hal" said of Garth. In the eyes of her brother, it appeared that Garth was a great builder, an important man. Indeed, it seemed that the whole basis of Margaret's regard for her son was based on what Henry Tyson had told her. On that she built. To that she constantly reverted, and would not let the other jarring notes call her away from the main trend and tenor of the big man's mind. He was a creator. And she talked of him as another girl might have talked of a poet.

All this was strange to Mrs. Garth, but she felt vaguely that Henry Tyson was at the base of the trouble. He was the leverage through which Garth had been raised to such a height in the eyes of Margaret.

They must not marry!

She had tried various ways of opening the eyes of Margaret. Whenever possible she talked of the old, poor days. That grated on the girl, she saw. But always Margaret shrugged the unpleasant tales of poverty away, and brought Edward back to thoughts of his great work—the reclaiming of the desert.

They must not marry!

She fastened the idea more securely with every stitch of her needle. She felt a certain confidence in her ability to handle her son. Indeed, she had directed the course of his life in far more ways than he himself was aware.

Her power was the power of the water dropping upon the stone. In the first place it was her gentle, steady, relentless insistence which had forced her boy to go through school. She had starved to provide the funds many times, but she had never let him know that she suffered. In times when he was tempted to give up the long preparation, she had been there to lay a hand on his shoulder.

She kept her faith in God; and in Edward's future. She had a vague feeling that she had gone into partnership with the Father, and that between them they had turned out this masterpiece.

And now, to have that masterpiece taken from her by this girl—no, that could not be. She stitched the certainty more firmly home. They must not marry!

The morning wore on.

What would be Edward's life with Margaret? Already he was changing. It began with the dissatisfaction with the furnishings for which he had paid so much. Then there had been consultations between him and Margaret, and then a rearranging of the rooms. The very room she sat in was now so strange to her that she hardly recognised it. There were not half so many things in it. Also, the girl had strange ideas about harmonising colours, and Edward had listened as if to a dictator.

He sat like a pupil at the knee of a teacher, and

Margaret grew interested in the teaching. Also, there were the evenings when he played the phonograph, and she talked to him about the music. And there were other evenings when she sat at the piano and played for him, and stopped now and then and talked again, and then played once more.

The education of Edward was beginning over again, and along lines to which Mrs. Garth was a stranger. They must not marry!

What would it be like if Edward were to have to meet the friends of Margaret, friends who must be like that terrible, proud brother of hers, of whom Edward talked so much, with something approaching dread? They must not marry!

A door opened and slammed, so that she started. Then steps; then voices, one deep, and one light and musical, playing over the other like sunshine over water.

They had returned!

Thirty-Two
The Alliance

They did not come directly to her, but she heard them first about the house, the heavy footfall of Garth sounding here and there, and his booming voice, and then the laughter of Margaret.

She hearkened to that laughter as a bird past its singing days might listen to the whistling of a young songster which makes music for its mate in spring. Eventually they came in to her, Margaret first, and Garth, with a roll of paper under his arm, stood back nearer to the door as if he grudged his mother even this moment of delay. With the precision of sadness she noted it all.

"Back so soon?" she asked quietly.

"You *must* come with us now," burst out Margaret. "We've found the most wonderful place for a house."

Not a muscle stirred in the face of Mrs. Garth. Indeed, she had been schooled in pain; but in her heart there were ashes and dust.

"A house?" she echoed carefully. "Ain't this a good enough house?"

"It's well enough while the dam is building," broke in Garth, irritated, "but of course it won't do afterwards. This isn't a permanent home. Will you come along with us, mother?"

No life in his invitation. He hurt her more than the girl had done, yet she very naturally laid all her sorrow to the credit of Margaret.

"It's up on La Cabeza," ran on Margaret happily. "You know where the side to the east slopes out into a shoulder?"

"Yes."

"That's the place for the house Edward is going to build. We came back for paper, and now he's going to go up there and sketch the outlines for the plan. Perfectly wonderful site. You see, when the dam is finished, and the water backed up the valley, it will be a regular lake. That will be the back view. There's to be a patio, with the house surrounding it in two wings, a sort of hexagon."

She began to draw the idea in with her hands, fixing the plan in the air so that she kept one eye upon it and one eye upon Mrs. Garth. "Imagine the outlook from the centre of the patio! One way we'll look down on the desert——"

"It won't be a desert then," put in Garth.

"Of course not. All green, and every inch of it due to your work. That will be in front, looking away down through the front wings of the house. Think of that when the blue comes in the evening and draws across the green things. And then towards the back we'll look down on the lake—miles and miles of water going up the Chiluah. Those sloping hills will make wonderful beaches, Edward."

"I hadn't thought of that. Coming, mother?"

"I guess I'll stay here." She saw his relief, shook her head at Margaret, and a moment later the pair were gone again. It seemed to her as if their voices grew more joyous as soon as they were away from her.

A house! There could be only one meaning in that. She knew that when a girl begins to plan a home with a man she generally, consciously or unconsciously figures herself in it. So far Margaret was probably going ahead innocently enough. Edward had not asked the important question, that was plain. But while they conned over those plans, while they sat together imagining the furniture, anything might happen. Mrs. Garth sat bolt upright in her chair, staring, as if a ghost faced her.

Of course it was the impulse of the moment which was sweeping the girl away. She was several thousand miles away from her own home and people. She lost her perspective and judged Edward as he wished to be judged—in his own setting, where he was a king among men. Afterwards, in the time of awakening, she would begin to make comparisons, and then life would be hell for them both. If only some of Margaret Tyson's own New York friends were there to keep her in touch with facts—at this point Mrs. Garth actually cried out, a low, hoarse note of exultation. Then she rang the bell beside the chair.

To the mozo who opened the door in answer, she said: "Have you heard of a certain Mr. Henry Tyson here in La Blanca?"

The mozo frowned to collect his thoughts, and then shook his head. Mrs. Garth drew in her breath impatiently. It was stupid that she did not know the man's address, though his sister lived in her house.

"Miss Tyson's brother," she explained eagerly. "A young man with yellow hair like that of Miss Tyson. Ain't you heard of him? Yellow hair, and——"

"El Oro!" cried the mozo, and his eyes and teeth flashed at once. "*Sí, sí, señora!* El Oro! I know him well. I know Rodriguez, and Rodriguez is his friend."

"Go bring him here. Go tell him that I wish to see him at once—please!"

The mozo stared an instant, for he was unused to such precise commands from the little old lady; then he nodded and disappeared. And Mrs. Garth picked up her sewing and the broken trend of her thoughts. They must not marry!

It was not more than a half hour before the mozo appeared again, breathless, and his eyes shining. He had seen and talked to El Oro, and he had many things to tell his fellows about the strange man.

"El—Señor Tyson is here," he announced. Then he burst out: "Señor El Oro himself, señora!"

"Bring him here to me!" commanded Mrs. Garth, and she centred her attention on her stitches. She was perfectly cool and collected now, just as she had always been perfectly cool and collected on those other times when Edward had been ready to throw up the burden in his early days—those years of starvation before he got his first really big commission.

Then she heard the door open, and a light footfall tapped on the floor. She felt the new presence rather than heard his coming.

"This is Mrs. Garth?" queried a pleasant voice.

When she looked up, she started, the resemblance to Margaret was so great, but her second glance showed her differences.

For instance, his chin ended in an abrupt square instead of the rounded finish, and his cheekbones were more pronounced, the forehead higher, the cheeks thinner. Moreover, from the eyes of this man, as from Margaret's, there came a fire, but it was a gentle flame in the girl, and in the man it was a consuming thing.

He was such a person as Mrs. Garth could never imagine unpoised, uncontrolled, unsure of himself. He looked straight into her eyes, smiling.

"How are you," she said, and took his hand. He kept her from getting up, and slipped at once into a chair. She saw that his pale hands were reddened on the inside, a sure proof that he had been doing common labour, and his clothes were ingrained with the dust of cement, and shining from ineffectual brushing. Nevertheless, he gave a singular impression of cleanliness.

"We been wishing you'd come to see us," she began, a little uneasily, "but Eddie says that you won't come to visit; not while you're workin' on the dam."

"I couldn't play the rôle of your son's friend and a common labourer," he answered. "Of course you see that. And I really shouldn't stay here long now. It won't do for the men to think that I have a stand-in with the big boss."

She looked at him narrowly, but there was no double meaning on his face.

"I won't keep you long," she said. "I got a little thing to speak to you about."

"Don't let me hurry you," he answered. She saw his glance wander about the room, first carelessly, then with sudden interest. "By jove," he said suddenly, "this is very pleasant."

"The arranging of the room is your sister's work," she answered pointedly.

"Oh?" he queried politely.

"She and Eddie," nodded Mrs. Garth, and watched him shrewdly. But it was plain that the coupling of the two names meant nothing to him.

It was hard for her to break in upon the main thread of her talk, for there was something airy and easy about this fellow which embarrassed her.

"It's about your sister and Eddie that I want to talk to you," she said.

And she folded her hands over the sewing and looked him in the eye. He had started to nod casually, but now he sat up a little straighter and stared.

"Yes?" he said, rather breathlessly.

"I'd like to know if your sister has been talkin' to you any about my son?"

"About Garth?" He kept his intense eyes upon her. "I've seen very little of Margaret since she came, and when we talked—yes, she has often spoken of him. Quite enthusiastically. Why do you ask?"

"Because Eddie has been talkin' a lot about her."

There was no doubt of her meaning by this time. She saw a sharp flush dye the cheek of Tyson, and his jaw set.

"Mr. Tyson," she said, throwing diplomacy to the winds, "I ain't in favour of it. Are you?"

He could not speak.

"They ain't the same kind of folks," she went on, scoring her points rapidly, "and they'd regret it later on."

She saw his throat muscles bulge, and then he

controlled himself with an effort that left his hands clenched and his face colourless.

"They're not the same——" he echoed, and then, half under his breath: "Good God, Mrs. Garth, what do you mean?"

"Just what I'm saying. Seeing a lot of each other is pretty dangerous for young folks, and Eddie and your sister have been seeing a pile of each other lately. I been watching."

"Do you mean to say that your son—Garth—is dreaming of——"

It angered her to see his incredulous unbelief, his scorn.

"But don't worry," he muttered, settling back in his chair. "I'm sorry that he's drawn false impressions. Margaret is always a little too friendly, and people are apt to put wrong constructions upon it. I'll speak to her. Very sorry this has happened."

"They been planning a house," she said noncommittally, and she could have laughed in spite of her pain to see him writhe.

"A house?" he said heavily. "Margaret has been planning a house with your son?"

He rose from his chair—jumped up almost—and began walking back and forth with a quick, light step. She could see that he was enraged; she saw more than that; that he was containing his wrath by a great effort.

"How long has this been going on, Mrs. Garth?"

He turned as he spoke, and the words went snapping at her.

She took up her sewing again and began to work, and every stitch was riveting her original idea: they should not marry! She had won the great first step; Tyson would help her.

"It's been goin' on ever since Eddie saw Margaret."

"Ever since——" He sat down suddenly, staring. "You mean," he added, lowering his voice to a murmur that went thrilling through her, "you mean that it began when he first visited us in New York?"

"It begun when he saw her," said the remorseless old woman. "He made up his mind that she was to be his wife. And what he wants he most generally gets."

"His wife; Margaret his wife," repeated Tyson. "God!"

The idea crushed him first, and then maddened him.

"The only reason he brought you out West——" she began.

"He didn't *bring* me," cut in Tyson coldly. "I came of my own accord."

"The only reason he brought you out here," she insisted, "was because he knew that he wouldn't have no chance with Margaret if he stayed with her in New York. He knew that he had to get her out in his own country—where manners and things like that don't count so much. So he brung you because he knew that she'd come trailin' after."

And she heard him breathing quick and hard.

"A double purpose?" said Tyson.

There was a long pause. She became afraid to look into his face, yet there were few things which Mrs. Garth feared.

"All that talk about hardening me up, giving me a taste of the real iron of life——" He stopped. "I thank you for letting me know this, Mrs. Garth."

"And now what are you going to do?"

He stood with the knuckles of both hands grinding into his forehead. When he looked at Mrs.

Garth again, his eyes were blank, like the eyes of a child which cannot understand some difficult explanation. "Garth brought me here—me—because he wanted to——" Tyson broke off with a strong shudder.

"It is—wrong!" he said, with white lips. And it was as if he had named a leprous thing. "And shall be—prevented."

Mrs. Garth looked narrowly at him. She remembered the massive shoulders of her son, and she remembered what Garth had also told her of their boxing. There were unknown reservoirs of strength in this fellow. What she perceived of him was a very dim hint of the mind within, and yet there was just a touch of fear, even in her cool mind; and there was deep rage also, for she felt the clashing of classes in this conflict between Tyson and her son.

Even in the silence she felt that the crisis was there. The battle was commenced. She saw Tyson staring blankly into vacancy, his face white; and she knew that he was inwardly writhing with pain, shame, hate.

Thirty-Three
Pride Lifts its Head

When, later in the afternoon, she heard the sound of the closing front door, and then the voices, she smiled grimly to herself. They came expecting to find a lamb, and instead they would walk in on a tiger. And she looked up at Tyson with something akin to affection. He would fight her battle.

Garth was calling as he came: "Mother! Oh, mother!"

The door flew open, and he stood with a lighted face, the gleam was in his eyes, the smile of triumph on his lips.

"Mother," he said again, "I've——"

And then he saw Tyson, and his voice stopped.

"Well," he said, his colour rising, "this is a surprise. How are you?"

He began to approach, but the voice of Tyson in his greeting checked the big man at a distance like a stretched out, invisible hand.

"I've come to see Margaret," he said quietly. "Do you know if she's in?"

The embarrassment of Garth was increasing, and the heart of his mother went cold. She knew that the battle had indeed commenced, and the first part had gone against her. As plainly as if he had spoken it in words, she knew that her son had come to tell her that he had asked Margaret Tyson to marry him, and had been accepted.

"Yes, she's in her room, I believe. By the way"—he checked himself again—"I'll show you up, if you wish."

"No," said Mrs. Garth, rising, "I'll take him up."

"Then I'll be waiting for you down here, mother. See you later, Tyson."

And Mrs. Garth led her champion out of the room. Once the door closed behind them, shutting out Garth, she reached for the younger man with a fumbling hand, found his arm, and clung to it. Her dizziness lasted only a moment.

"It's happened," she said. "I seen it in Eddie's face. Mr. Tyson, what're we going to do?"

"I think I shall find something," he said.

They started up the stairway, and even in her agony of pain and suspense she noted the graceful ease with which he helped her, his hand under her elbow. And she felt the steely, flexible strength of his arm, and when he spoke there was a quiet ring to his voice.

She compared him with her boy as one compares a rapier of tempered, priceless steel with a battle-axe of ponderous metal with a chopping edge. A different sort of force, but one fully as deadly, she felt.

If she had warned this man in time—but it was useless to talk of "ifs." She clasped his hand in both of hers when they stood just outside Margaret's door.

"God teach you what to say and do," she prayed in a fervent whisper.

And he answered in an ordinary speaking voice: "Thank you very much."

She watched with hungry, yearning eyes as he rapped at the door and then disappeared within the room.

He found Margaret in the very act of throwing off her linen duster, and she turned to him with flushed cheeks.

"Hal!" she cried. "Hal, dear, you couldn't have come at a better time."

He stood by the door, making no move to greet her.

"I don't believe that I could," he said.

They studied each other, she with the smile dying on her face, and he with a smile growing, an unpleasant smile to see. Then he went and sat easily on the foot of the bed, very close to her, and swinging one foot. He might have come to gossip about the weather, to watch him.

"Now what's all this nonsense about?" he said directly.

She stopped with one glove worked half off her hand, and the colour of her cheeks became a flare of fire.

"Edward told me he wouldn't tell you till I had had a chance—Hal, you don't mean you disapprove?"

It was as if she had struck him across the face with a whip. He became a sickly sight.

"It's true then, Margaret? You've promised to marry that——" He stopped.

"Don't look at me as if I were a leper," she answered hotly. Then, bewildered: "In Heaven's name, what's wrong with you? Isn't Edward the man you praised as if he were a sort of demigod, a new Titian, a builder, an empire maker? I forget all the wild terms you used!"

"One praises a strong horse for much the same reasons."

"So that's it! Because his fingernails aren't manicured? Because he can't take a quip, or make one? Because he has no parlour tricks?"

He stood up straight, and caught both her hands firmly at the wrists.

"Pull yourself together," he said, and though his voice was low it had that quality of metal in it which Mrs. Garth had noted. He changed it subtly to a note of appeal and horror: "For God's sake, Margaret, remember what you are, and what he is!"

She was fully as straight as Tyson, and her glance clashed on his without flinching.

"And what am I? Part of the flotsam of the world; part of the worthless driftwood. And he——"

"Is a superior bricklayer; a very competent ditch-digger."

It was odd to see how nearly alike they became in their anger. His nostrils quivered, and her jaw set in a line almost as stern as that of her brother.

"Hal, I warn you not to talk like this. It's both foolish and useless."

"I had rather be foolish than shamed."

"Ashamed of Edward Garth? Ten days ago your voice shook with pride when you merely mentioned what he was and what he had done. I tell you, I've never had the echo of what you said out of my ears."

"I did. God knows I was a fool; but it's not too

late to undo the foolishness."

She started to speak, but he rushed on in the emphatic whisper of the desperate: "Think, think, think! Margaret; he's all big hands and burly arms and scientific mind."

"With the soul of a poet!"

Tyson released her, and groaned.

"He—poet; dear God, this is my own work coming back on me like a boomerang. That heavy-footed dullard the soul of a poet? Margaret, I'll tell you what he has done—this honourable man, who——"

"You don't need to tell me why he brought you out here. He told me about that."

"And you approve of it?"

She flushed, but her anger kept her keyed.

"It was a trick at your expense, but—he loved me, and that would justify a great deal. Oh, Hal, he was desperate; he told me everything today."

He was shaking with passion, but he began to smile.

"Very well," he said. "If that's your viewpoint, the only way to make you see the truth is to remove the thing that lies in the way."

He started back towards the door, but she intercepted him.

"What do you mean?" she panted. "Hal, remember yourself. You look like a demon. I know what's in your mind."

"Please take your hand away. I'm going to smash him, my dear, as any man would smash an unclean creeping thing that crawled into the heart of his family. I don't know how I'm going to do it, but I'm going to destroy this hulk, this double-dealing, crooked, brazen-faced cur."

She stood away from him at that, saying coldly:

"You've spoken quite enough."

"Not yet," he went on in the same deadly manner. "I came out here and learned to look up to this fellow as the soul of honour—a diamond in the rough. I've gone through hell trying to conform to his standards and learn his ways of living. And now I find that I've been using a thieving trickster as my model. I don't know yet what leverage I'll find, but I'm going to ruin this strong man, this giant."

She tore open the door.

"Then go down and tell him that to his face!"

He bowed to her formally.

"I hope you will always retain the instincts of a lady, Margaret."

And he disappeared into the hall.

Thirty-Four
Spoils of Victory

At the entrance to the living room he stood quietly, and found Mrs. Garth sitting sewing, while Garth, with a downward head, paced up and down the room anxiously. At the sight of the newcomer, he wheeled towards the door and started forward.

"My mother has been telling me of an unfortunate conversation she's had with you, Tyson, and I want——" The pale face before him, and the ironical smile, stopped him. "What's the matter?" He began walking forward again. "Listen to me, Tyson——"

"Stay where you are," warned Tyson. "I find it difficult already to breathe this air. It seems to be tainted, Mr. Garth."

A sharp fear turned the big man grey.

"You've seen Margaret, and she has changed her mind?"

"You need have no fear about her just yet," answered the other. "She's still worshipping an idol I helped set up for her. Before long she'll see the clay knees and scrape off the rest of the gilt."

"You can't anger me, Tyson. I know that I have done you a rather shabby turn in bringing you out here with a double purpose. But I've confessed everything to Margaret, and she's absolved me. Don't you see, Tyson, that in my peculiar position I had to resort to unusual means?"

Mrs. Garth made no further pretence of sewing. Her eyes flicked from face to face; hope and despair.

"I think," said Tyson evenly, "that I understand you perfectly."

"Don't talk like that, man! Forget broken bones. I'll spend my life trying to make it up to you, if that's any good. Good God, Tyson, every man in the world has metal in him that will tarnish—and may be burnished again."

"Except gold," answered the other.

"Tyson, don't tempt me too far!"

"Tempt *you?* You cur!"

"You've said something that requires retraction."

"To a man of honour retractions cannot remove stains."

"Tyson, I'm in my own house."

Mrs. Garth was pale as a lichen, but she did not flinch. She raised her head like an ancient warhorse who hears the trumpet.

And her giant son went on, grinding his teeth to keep himself in hand: "Call up an old saying, Tyson: all's fair in love. I had to do what I did. And I'll prove that I'm right by making Margaret happy the rest of her life."

"I suppose you're right," said Tyson calmly. "All's fair in love—and in war. I came out here and kept my head in the clouds for a while, but now I'll get it back to the earth with a vengeance. Garth, you used me as a leverage to pry your way into my sister's heart. Now, by fair means or by foul, I'm going to smash you—smash you!"

"You have a free hand," said Garth. He balanced himself with his feet spread far apart. "Smash me?" He laughed harshly. "Tyson, unless you're a fool, you'll see what I am out here, and see yourself in comparison. Look there! Can you undo that?"

And he pointed through the window at the looming dam.

"Who knows?" murmured Tyson. "Who knows, Garth? I've seen stranger things done. I suppose I look like a pygmy, Garth, in your eyes, but give me a few days to try myself out."

"As much as you want," sneered Garth. "Tyson, before you go too far, I offer you my hand. I'll forget the things you've said. And I'll spend my life trying to make Margaret happy, and be a member of your family you'll be proud of. Tyson, I swear it on my honour."

"Your honour?"

"Damn you!" I tell you frankly, Tyson, I've never liked you very well. There's always been a distance between us."

"Thank God for that!"

"There's always been this devil in you that shows now. And now I say: no matter how I've won Margaret, I'm going to keep her. If I've used a trick, I'll cover that trick with honest gold. Anyway, she's mine. I've fought for her, heart and soul, and to the victor belong the spoils."

It was a moment before Tyson could answer. He was shuddering like a branch in a windstorm, and his face was terrible.

"A very good maxim, Garth. To the victor belong the spoils, and the battle is not over."

He raised a forefinger and pointed his words: "Mark me, now. The contract between us is broken. From now on I'm existing simply to smash you, Garth. Watch yourself! Once a crook always a crook. And I intend to show Margaret an intimate view of your heart."

He turned on his heel and strode from the house. The Mexican mozo in the outer hall saw him pass, and at the sight of his face the little servant shrank away and crossed himself.

"The devil is loosed!" he muttered in Spanish, and started as the door clicked softly shut behind the departing figure.

The stronger the purpose which guides a man the greater is the strength he feels within him, and as Tyson went down the street he looked towards the towering mass of the dam. The street he walked had been paved for the workers upon that dam. The houses he passed were occupied by the builders. Yet in spite of the myriads who had laboured on it, the dam seemed too vast a work for human hands. Nevertheless, the task before him was the ruin of the man whose brain had conceived the labour, and whose will had executed it.

A thought that would have bowed the heads of most men, but Tyson walked with an upright, springy tread. For one thing, all methods were open to him, good and evil, and when a man admits any possible means of attaining a given end, his resources are infinitely increased.

Full of these thoughts, he saw little about him until he turned aside and leaped up the steps in front of Mrs. Casey's boardinghouse. At the head he checked himself with an exclamation, for he had almost collided with a brilliant figure in blues and reds—Rona Carnahan. She, too, started back, but at once she controlled herself.

"Rona!" he exclaimed. "By the Lord, I've been eager to see you. Stand over here. Let me look at you!"

"Why," she said suddenly, the topic uppermost in her mind coming out, childlike, "why do people smile when they look at me—white people, I mean?"

"*I* never smile."

"You did at first."

"Then I was a fool, and the others who smile now are blockheads. I'll crack their sconces for 'em if I ever see 'em doing it, I promise you that. Rona, give me your hand again. I haven't realised how I've missed you."

And he spoke the truth.

"Then why have you stayed away?"

He thought of his last talk to her and his farewell; and he thought of the good old padre; but last of all the words of Garth rang through his mind: "All's fair in love—to the victor belong the spoils." And was he not committed to any course, good or evil?

"I said good-bye, but I've changed my mind about that." He brushed the past away with a wide gesture, and then smiled on her. "I'd like to begin again if I may. Did you really come all the way down here to see me?"

There had been just the glint of a coming smile in her eyes, but she threw a curtain over them now.

"No."

"No? Then why? Ah, it was Kennedy!"

"Bah!"

She tossed the thought of Kennedy away with both hands.

"Then why are you here?"

"To find out if you were sick—you've been away so long."

"You knew all the time that I would come back?"

"Of course."

He chuckled, watching her with new eyes of observancy.

"You seem thinner, Rona. Have you been ill?"

"No, I have been sad."

Every man has a taint of the cad at heart—unless he is a saint.

"Sad?" queried Tyson eagerly.

"Because the dam is nearly finished."

She turned and shook her fist at the corner of it which was visible around the edge of the house.

"When it is finished the water will rise in the valley. And San Vicente will be drowned. Poor San Vicente! Tell me, señor, is it not a crime against the dear saint to cover his house with water? How can men do such a work?"

When the ground is ploughed, any seed will grow in it. Tyson caught a deep breath.

"How can men work at it?" he echoed thoughtfully. "The Mexicans—I wonder!" He continued solemnly: "For my part, I shall never raise my hand again to help at the work. *I* repeat."

"It is well, señor," said the girl sadly. "But that will not save the grave of my mother. It will be covered with water. I shall never be able to talk to her again!"

"Rona, you would be glad if the dam were stopped—if the water never rose? If all that work went for nothing?"

"If a man could stop that," she cried eagerly, "I'd

fall on my knees. I would worship him, I——" She made a little sign of despair. "But it is as easy to move La Blanca as to destroy the dam. Only an angel could do it. Ah, Señor Tyson, why does not the good San Vicente rise against it?" She sighed. "It is late. I must go back."

"Come along then. I'll walk with you."

She started to smile, and then shook her head.

"No," she said, "the padre does not wish me to walk with you in the valley."

"But you are here?"

Her eyes flashed.

"He did not speak of the city."

"Will you come again, Rona?" The devil which dwelt in the new mind of Tyson made his heart leap and then set a thought in his mind. "Listen. Tomorrow I am going to move to another place. I have been living in this hovel as a jest—a novelty, you understand? Tomorrow I am going to get new rooms. Will you come to see me there, Rona?"

"How should I find you?"

"I shall leave directions at this place. You can inquire. Or I shall come and take you."

"No, no. The padre——"

"Hang the padre! Rona, will you come?"

She looked at him with her head canted to one side, wistfully.

"Will your new house be very beautiful? Flowers in jars, and silken curtains, señor?"

"That and more."

She shook her head with sudden decision.

"No, señor."

"Why not?"

"I cannot tell, except that I shall not be there."

"Listen to me——"

But she brushed past him and raced down the

steps. He felt that it was useless to follow, and turned with a muffled oath back towards the door. For that reason he did not see that she paused, not far away down the street, and looked back.

Thirty-Five
The Third Chime

As for Tyson, he went slowly up the stairs inside towards his room. He went slowly, and for every step he had a thought. It had all happened very strangely and swiftly. That morning he had wakened perfectly happy and contented. He had stepped down into the world of labour, and at last he had won a place for himself in that world. He had accepted a new model of manhood, with a youth's passion for a hero, and Garth filled the pattern of that new model.

Now, in the evening, not a vestige of his old ideas remained. Garth, the idol, lay shattered and broken—to him, and his purpose in life was to crush the big man—break him to helplessness. One great lesson, indeed, he had caught; might is right, and to the victor belong the spoils.

He embraced the idea with a savage joy. To stop the rise of water in the dam meant the smashing of Garth, the opening of Margaret's eyes, the winning of the wild, lovely girl, Rona.

The door of his room stood ajar, though he generally closed it. He paused there and called: "Well?"

In reply, there was a slight click, and he saw the tall form of Kennedy standing under the light with his arm still raised above his head. Tyson closed the door behind him. Then Kennedy spoke, briefly, like a man who has come on a business errand.

"Have you a gun?"

"No."

"Then I've two," said Kennedy, "and you can take your pick." He produced them with a quick gesture, and laid them on the table—ponderous forty-fives of amazing length.

"So you've come to shoot me up, Kennedy?"

"I've come to shoot you down," said the big gambler calmly, "as I would any other thief and rustler."

His eyes fastened at the throat of Tyson, where lay the yellow-and-black necktie. Tyson understood, for he drew it forth, full length, and smiled.

"Ah," he said, "you've seen Rona, and she's given you a bit of her tongue. When I saw her last she was a bit surprised that you hadn't fought for the sake of the necktie. But it's too late now, Kennedy. She's made up her mind about you."

"You're a bold man, partner," said the Westerner, and he caressed the gun nearest to him. "And you've played a strong game. You've done well with your hand, but now it's called. That's all."

He chuckled deep in his throat, and his eyes probed the body of Tyson as though picking the places where his bullets should strike.

"You're a good man, Tyson, but at this game I think I'm a bit better."

"It's very clear," Tyson nodded. "You apparently think that the only passport you need back to her favour is the necktie?"

"You got the Bible beat for thinking," agreed Kennedy.

But Tyson was fallen into a muse. There are times when discretion is the better part of valour, and he thought now of the uncanny ease with which Kennedy had produced the two big guns. The man was an expert in their use, he knew, while for his part he had never fired twenty shots with firearms of any description.

Moreover, there were reasons why it would be most inconvenient to be put even temporarily out of commission; for now was the time to raise a tide to sweep up against Garth; his voice was needed to give it direction. It was a hard thing to do—harder than almost anything he had done in his life.

"It's a strange thing," he said, "if we should fall out about a piece of coloured silk. I've had my fun out of it, Kennedy, and now you might as well have yours."

He raised his hand to undo the tie, while Kennedy stood frowning in astonishment, with a palpable sneer lifting the corners of his mouth. Yet the slender fingers of Tyson never tugged loose the knot of the tie; they stopped as they touched it, for he saw, again, the picture of the face, dim as the obliterated features of a sphinx, that had appeared at the crest of La Cabeza.

The old legend said: love within a year after that vision, or death. And here was death looking at him out of the keen eyes of Kennedy. To struggle now was like gambling against fate, and Tyson loved above all else the gambling chance. His hands fell from his throat, and he smiled upon Kennedy.

"I had forgotten," he said, "that there's another score between us that makes it impossible for me to give you the tie. I'm sorry for it. It's a little thing, but I can still feel the tingle where your fingers struck my face the other day. For that reason, Kennedy, I'll have to accept your offer of a gun."

He rose, and as he did so, by chance, a bell from the church in the town began to toll, slowly, with whole seconds between the beats.

"A knell for you, Kennedy," smiled Tyson. He continued: "Unfortunately, I don't know a thing about guns. So when we fight we'll have to leave the result to chance. Let me have the guns—so! Now stand back a pace from the table, as I do. Good! You see, Kennedy, there lies a gun with the muzzle towards you. There lies a gun at my end of the table with the muzzle towards me. The thing we each must do is to reach our gun at a signal, get it by the trigger end, and then blaze away. That makes our chances equal."

Kennedy forced a laugh.

"It's a good joke," he said. "The next time I have a drink I'll laugh over it."

"I'm as serious as a minister."

"Fire across this table?" cried Kennedy.

"Not so loud," warned Tyson. "Why not across the table?"

"Murder, plain murder!"

"But we've equal chances."

"A man couldn't fail to hit at a single yard."

"Exactly. It all depends, you see, not on marksmanship, but on ability to get to the gun first. It makes up, you understand, for my poor marksmanship, and we start even."

Kennedy changed colour.

"But here?" he queried. "In this house?"

"To the dead man," said Tyson calmly, "it will make no difference what happens after the shots are fired. And for my part, I'm willing to take a chance on what will follow."

Kennedy stared.

"If you begin to feel shaky about it," suggested Tyson.

But the other broke in hotly: "Make it any way you will. I'm not the kind that bluffs out. You can tie our left hands together, if you want, and be damned to you!"

"Of course," nodded Tyson, "that would be surer still; but I want to give you some chance. Listen to the bell of the church. We'll count by that. The next stroke is our first count, and at the third stroke we go for the guns. Hear!"

The clapper of the bell sent out the next dull, wavering vibration. They faced each other; the eyes of Tyson were glued to the face of his opponent; the eyes of Kennedy were lowered to his gun. And so the seconds passed, till the second stroke of the bell.

At the sound Kennedy started, body and eye, lurching for his gun. But he recovered himself in time, and stepped back in place. The move, however, had betrayed his hair-trigger nervousness, and like a gambler who has betrayed his hand to a foe, Kennedy flashed up a sullenly defiant glance at Tyson.

With his gaze once fastened on the smaller man, he could not again change its direction, for Tyson held him, as it were, with the superior strength of self-confidence. He had not started at that second stroke of the bell. Hand and foot and eye had remained true to him, and the admission of weakness showed in a sudden pallor that swept over the taut features of Kennedy.

In contrast his eyes grew large and very dark, and his forehead gleamed with perspiration. More than all, there was a visible quivering of his arms—the gun would wabble crazily in that hand even when he had seized the butt.

They waited for the third stroke of the bell, while the humming of the last fell and died slowly away to a sound thinner than the strain of a muted violin. But the third stroke never came. Tyson raised a forefinger.

"Luck is with you, Kennedy," he said, and smiled.

The blood rushed back into the face of the gambler. He leaned over and scooped up his weapons.

"Another time!" he muttered, and strode from the room.

From the hall Tyson caught the sounds of muffled, rapidly lessening curses, and then as he sank into his chair, and a not unpleasant sense of weakness slipped through his limbs, he knew perfectly that Kennedy would never have the courage to face him again.

A new sound roused him from his thoughts. It was a faint tapping, and the sound seemed to come from above him. It stopped, then it began again in a sudden, rattling volley. Rain!

He ran like a panic-stricken fugitive at the cry of fire, and looked out of the window. That was the meaning of the sudden darkness in the early evening. He had been too wrapped up in his thoughts to look, but now he saw that the sky was sheeted in dull grey, here a furling reef, and there solid sheets. Rain!

And the waters would soon be rising behind the dam. There was no time to be wasted.

Thirty-Six
A Word in Time

Outside, he found that everyone was pouring out into the streets to watch for the starting of the downpour. For when the rain commenced in the valley of the Chiluah it was no light thing. The skies emptied themselves in a gush. So far there were nothing but minute guns which announced the approach of the storm, and far-off thunder growled in the hills. La Cabeza had put on a sullen hood of vapour.

Little water had fallen, but enough to spot the streets and send up a sharp alkali scent. It was almost as if the dead earth were crying aloud for drink! But Tyson noted these details with an anxious eye, and then pushed straight for the quarter of the town where Rodriguez lived. When he reached the street he commenced walking with downward head, as one who broods over a great sorrow.

As he had expected, Rodriguez sat in his doorway with his guitar across his knees. He rose with a gay shout at the sight of Tyson.

"Señor El Oro!" he called, and then, after he had shaken hands: "What is wrong? Where is your sunshine gone? Why are you so changed, señor?"

"I——" began Tyson; then hastily: "I must not speak!"

"So?" and the heavy eyebrows of Rodriguez lifted.

"But I must be on," murmured Tyson, and turned away.

"Señor!" cried Rodriguez. "Señor El Oro! What is your sorrow?"

Tyson turned slowly back.

"I grieve," he said sadly, "that so many men should be damned for a sin of which they do not know."

Rodriguez caught his breath.

"What men—damned?"

"You—I—all of us who work here!"

The Mexican crossed himself; his eyes were starting from his head. "Señor!" he gasped.

"*Adios,* Rodriguez."

"But the sin? What sin, señor?"

"If I should speak it might cause great trouble. I cannot speak."

"The sin, the sin! Ah, Señor El Oro, open my eyes to my wrong, and I shall go to the good father——"

"Rodriguez," answered Tyson sternly, as one who sees a divine thing tampered with, "can you undo with prayer daily a sin which you daily work at with your hands?"

"Merciful Virgin!" breathed the big man, and drew a noisy breath through his expanded nostrils.

"But I have talked too much," muttered Tyson. "Once more, *adios,* señor!"

But Rodriguez was before him, blocking the way.

"You are my friend, señor," he pleaded. "I have seen it many times in your eyes that you are the friend of poor Rodriguez! Tell me all!"

"I tell you," cried Tyson impatiently, "if I should say what I know it might work a great harm. Yet," he mused, "you are a good man, Rodriguez. I am sorry for you."

"I have five children. What would come of them?"

"I truly grieve for you, poor Rodriguez!"

"In pity, señor!"

Tyson bowed his head in a long silence in which he seemed to be struggling with himself.

"Then to you, only, Rodriguez, for it tears my heart to think of your damnation. It is the thought of your five children that moves me, my friend."

"The saints will save thee," said the Mexican, in a voice that trembled with solemn emotion. "Speak, and I shall not breathe a word of it to a man, a woman, or a child."

"Saving your own?"

"My own. Yes, yes; saving my own, señor."

Tyson drew close. There was a strong scent of strange liquors and of onions on the breath of Rodriguez, but Tyson controlled his shudder and approached his lips to the very ear of the big foreman.

"Up the valley of the Chiluah," he whispered, "there is a holy place."

"San Vicente!" muttered Rodriguez hoarsely.

"And the dam," continued Tyson hurriedly, "will back the waters high up the valley—will cover San

Vicente to the bell-tower. The work of God will be destroyed by the work of man—and on the soul of every worker on the dam there will rest a weight heavier than lead, dragging his eternal spirit down—down—to the fires of hell—to burn for ever!"

Rodriguez reeled back and caught at the lintel of his door for support.

"God be with us!" he stammered.

Tyson bowed his head. "We are lost," he said heavily.

"But the father—Padre Miguel—why has he not warned us?"

"The padre is an old man."

"True, true!"

"And old men think little."

"Señor El Oro, that is also true. My old grandfather—but we—what shall we do?"

"What can we do?"

The Mexican groaned. "Ave Maria——"

"What will prayers signify in the ear of the Lord," warned Tyson solemnly, "when the sight of the dam is ever in His eyes? Do you think that He will forget the sin of the least of us who have worked upon it?"

"My wife—my children——"

"Ah, Rodriguez, my heart is heavier for you than for myself."

"I shall not lift another sack of cement!"

"It is well, Rodriguez. It may save you still. Repentance is great in the books of Heaven! Neither shall I labour."

"But my friends—my so many friends—shall I leave them to blunder blindly to hell?"

"Remember, poor Rodriguez, that you have promised. Yet I shall release you so far as this:

Those who are dear to you you may warn. All others——"

"The saints have sent you to warn us. I knew—did not I tell Bianca—that you were no common man. The hand of the Lord has put a sign upon your head. Ah, señor, upon my deathbed, I shall remember."

"And what work you have done upon the dam, pray that it may be forgiven you, Rodriguez."

"This night——"

"It is well. *Adios* again, Rodriguez. I feel that there is still hope for us if we can but change our ways."

But Rodriguez gathered him in a mighty embrace against a sweaty bosom, and then rushed into his house, and the sound of his loud voice rattling forth the terrible tidings to his wife followed Tyson down the street.

When he had gone a little distance he turned at a plaza and looked back upon the town. The shadow of the great dam rose over it, and Tyson began to laugh, softly, to himself. He was hailed in the midst of his laughter and saw before him the little Mexican for whom he had gambled at Kennedy's place.

"You are gay, Señor El Oro?" asked the other, and he grinned in sympathy. "Yes, it is good to watch the rain!"

"Gay?" frowned Tyson. "I was laughing, my poor friend, to think what fools we have been. Look back at the dam! It casts a shadow over us; it blots out half of Heaven, and in the end it shall blot out our hopes of eternal happiness."

"Ha?"

"I shall tell you," said Tyson. "Walk on with me."

And as they went down the street he began to

talk rapidly. Before his tale was five minutes old, the little man was quaking; at the end of six, he was a pale-faced, nervous wreck.

"San Vicente reward you for warning me," he stammered. "Señor El Oro, twice you have saved me. You shower your favours like the water from the sky. Only one thing I beg. Let me speak with my poor friend, Pedro Juachez. Let me give him the word."

"To him only, then. *Adios,* señor."

The other waved a hasty hand and fled at the full speed of his withered legs. And Tyson grinned after him. The devil was up. In two hours, he knew, every peon in La Blanca would have the tale in his ears, magnified a thousandfold by repetition. Let Garth save himself if he could. He would need all his power now.

In the meantime he would live no longer like a pig in the squalid sty of Mrs. Irene Casey. Before the stores of the town closed, Tyson visited two shops. One was a Mexican renting office; the other was a furniture shop which, from the need of providing both well-to-do whites and the Mexicans, contained a really wide variety of stuffs. In this place, Tyson spent most of the evening.

And he took occasion to put certain secrets in the ears of the proprietors.

Thirty-Seven
The Crisis

Murmers of the gathering storm passed through the heavens that night, and murmurs of another nature passed among the peons of La Blanca. Overhead the thunder rolled and chattered, and now and again long lightnings leaped across the sky, splitting it like an axe into two jagged sections. In the Mexican quarter of La Blanca, underneath, human voices continued until dawn.

Here and there groups gathered on doorsteps. Now and again there was some house bursting with illumination where hidden hoards of tequila had been brought to the light, and pulque, mysteriously produced from nowhere in particular, washed down the more fiery liquor as chasers.

And always the talk went fast and quickly about the board. The name of El Oro was often on the tongue; and likewise they named Garth, the big boss. For him, they made their teeth glint like suddenly bared knives. So the morning came.

At dawn the sky was thick and heavy, and occasional gusts of rain had drenched the houses and sprinkled the dusty streets of La Blanca; yet it was not to the sky above them that the inhabitants turned their eyes.

They stared to the north, for the tops of the mountains were obscured by a mist, low-hanging, streaked with deepest black, that moved continually nearer. And all men knew that the rain was descending in sudden torrents through the upper valley of the Chiluah.

Be it understood that rain fell seldom even in the mountains, but when it did come there it rushed down like a cloudburst; and the older inhabitants gathered here and there to tell of storms of the past, and how they had seen walls of water plunging down a valley—a sheer rise of three to eight feet sweeping along with a sound like thunder and gutting away the banks on either side.

In a raincoat Margaret Tyson hurried through the first scattering drops of the downpour. She was going to the office of Garth, from which she could watch when the first strong torrent of water struck the dam and backed up. However, the rain did not follow her all the way to the office; it turned into a thin mist whose falling was barely perceptible; but far up the valley the clouds gathered more and more thickly and the long lightnings lunged close to the horizon, flickerings of light.

When she reached the little office building Garth was not there. His secretary brought her in and seated her; Garth had gone to the dam, said the secretary, and might be back at once—urgent business had kept him from filling his engagement to meet her at his office at this hour. And having said this, the secretary fairly turned his back upon her and stood at the window.

"Look!" said Margaret suddenly to him. "There's some trouble out there!"

The entire vicinity of the dam was black with men, but along the surface of the works there was not a crane in motion, and hardly a column of smoke arose from the donkey engines. Those men, who were darkening all the slope, stood idle, or mixing blindly, one group with another. Not a hand was lifted in useful work.

"Perhaps they're waiting, like us, for the coming of the water," suggested Margaret.

The secretary cried out beneath his breath, stood for another instant transfixed at the window, and then rushed to the door. As he threw it open they heard the deep voice of Garth saying: "Stand off! I'm not a dead man yet, as they'll learn before I'm done with 'em."

And Garth himself stood at the door. Blood streaked one side of his face, which was set and grim. He strode across the room without taking the slightest heed of anyone and seated himself at his desk. A cloud of other men appeared at the door.

"Delaney!" bellowed Garth, and an old Irishman stepped in. His eyes were fixed upon Garth as upon a miracle. "Do you know the man who fired that shot?"

"Ay, sir. Rodriguez."

"The foreman in the cement house? I thought I recognised his black face."

"Here's the marshal, sir," broke in Delaney. "Shall I have him swear in a posse?"

"To fight that army of fools? No!"

The marshal broke through the group at the door as Garth spoke. He was one of those low, broadly built men who seem designed for battle—like bulldogs.

"Got your message, Garth," he said as he entered, "and came right up. Give me the straight of it and I'll have these greasers in order in jig-time." Here he caught sight of the bloody face of Garth, who kept his handkerchief pressed against the wound. "By God, they nicked you!"

"It's nothing," answered Garth. "The point is——"

"Wait one moment," said Margaret quietly. "I can take care of it." And she stood beside him. The marshal jerked off his hat and stared stupidly; it was no place for a woman. But Garth flushed almost as deeply as the blood upon his face.

"You!" he said huskily. "I forgot——"

But Margaret had already turned away and was taking a small first-aid cabinet from the hands of the secretary, who was palsied with excitement. She opened it, and set to work quickly, washing the shallow scalp wound and dressing it in haste and with precision; but even while she worked the marshal was asking questions.

"Open up," he said. "The quicker the better, because I'll need to swear in a posse. Just what happened?"

"The water from the mountains is due on the rush," said Garth. "An hour—two hours—three hours—I don't know how long. It all depends on how hard and how steadily it rains in the upper valley."

"That's plain."

"I've got to catch that water, Marshal Vance! When it comes it will come like an ocean tide, and every cubic yard of water that gets through the gates means golden dollars lost. You understand?"

"Sure. Close the gates, man. The gates are built in, aren't they?"

"They are. And the dam is high enough to hold the first week's run of water. I sent out orders to close the gates this morning as soon as the rains started. The man I sent brought back word that the dam was covered by greasers who refused to work and who wouldn't allow anyone to approach the dam."

"A strike?"

"Call it that. I went myself to close the gates——" He paused a moment and flashed a glance up to Margaret as she finished her swift bandage. Not a word of gratitude—only the silent look. "When I reached the dam," he went on, "I was stopped by the mob. They grew bolder. I tried to force my way through. Someone of the greasers drew a knife. I knocked him down. Then a gun was fired and the bullet glanced across my head, stunning me. As I dropped some of the boys who were with me—Delaney and the rest—dragged me back. The Mexicans didn't follow. They were satisfied with keeping me from the dam."

"Are they striking for higher pay?"

"They're striking to keep the dam from being finished. They're gathered to keep the gates from being closed."

"Easy," nodded Marshal Vance. "I'll swear in twenty boys I know, and we'll make short work of that gang. Say the word, and swear to the necessity, Garth, and I'll have those gates closed in twenty minutes."

"With an armed force?"

"Only way to handle the greasers. I know 'em!"

"I know them also," said Garth, "and there's one subject that they value more than their lives."

"Eh? Their religion?"

"Right! I've heard chatterings of it since last night. Some devil has spread the word among the Mexicans that if they let the dam be completed the rising of the waters will cover San Vicente up the valley, and the soul of every man who has worked on the dam will be lost. They're frightened out of their wits, and they'll fight as men fight to save their souls."

"Then," barked the marshal, "there's only one thing to do. Call in the State militia."

"The moment you show armed force, Vance," said Garth, "those fellows will use dynamite, and blow the dam from its foundations."

"God!" breathed the marshal. "Then what's the hope?"

"One small hope. I've sent an automobile up the valley to bring Padre Miguel from San Vicente. The priest from the mission itself will surely be able to convince them."

"Will he try?"

"I think he will. The men I sent will tell him exactly how the case stands. I know Padre Miguel. He has the courage of a crusader. They'll be back in a moment, and we'll see from the windows what he can do with them. I want him to make a talk to the crowd, and I think he will."

Margaret's heart went out to the pale, drawn face of Garth, and yet it beat with pride in the strength of Henry Tyson. With his single hands he had set a force in operation which in a night could check all the powers of Garth.

Garth would win, in the end. She even yearned for a man's form so that she could fight at his side, but she was glad from the bottom of her soul that the victory must have its price.

For Garth had told her, briefly, what passed between him and Tyson the day before, and at the end Garth had smiled.

Thirty-Eight

La Paloma

There was no flinching in Garth in the crisis. He talked quietly with the marshal, taking up one plan after another, like a purchaser examining samples, and laying them down again, unsatisfied, but with the determination to go on until he had what he wanted. Now and again, when a fresh roar of shouts rose from the hordes of peons who covered the dam, he raised his head a little, and a cold gleam came in his eyes.

Yet, on the whole, he was cool as a general who directs a victorious army under fire. She was seeing what men can be, and she rose to the occasion, for there was in her the blood of the fighter.

"Now," said Garth, raising his great bulk from the chair, "here comes the padre—and the crisis for the dam."

"And for Edward Garth," murmured Margaret to herself.

The clouds over La Blanca had broken up under a stiff breeze, and now a shaft of the morning sun struck in behind Margaret and made her bright hair like a halo around her face; and she sat with her head far back and her eyes and her smile for Garth alone, though every other glance went out of the windows towards the dam.

An automobile had swung up the slope from the valley and from it dismounted three men who walked still higher up the slope behind the Padre Miguel. His head was bare and the morning light gleamed on his bald head, and the rising wind twisted at his rusty robe.

Straight towards the thickest of the crowd of Mexicans he walked. They gave back before him, opening a broad pathway. The word seemed to pass with the speed of rumour through the idle host; from the outskirts they packed in increasing numbers towards the left flank of the dam, and when at length the padre stood on a rising bulwark of concrete there stretched on all sides of him a black mass of humanity with bronzed faces upturned, and the light of the morning sun struck aslant across that bronze ocean.

The wide murmur of the multitude swept up from the dam and reached the office of Garth and the silent group within it. A silence followed over the entire scene; the padre had lifted his arm.

They could follow him from period to period by the slow gestures of his arms. They knew, from the office of Garth, that when he swept his arm up the valley he was speaking of the mission of San Vicente. And there was a sad solemnity about the thought of the old priest, talking there before the throng, and pleading for the destruction of his own church. They could tell the power of his words. For most of the crowd nearby followed the gestures of the padre with ripplings here and there. At length he stretched out both his arms and raised his face. Of one accord the whole mass fell upon their knees.

"He wins!" cried Garth, in an indescribable voice. "They are praying. And at his feet!"

The secretary beside him called suddenly: "The water! It comes! The gates, Mr. Garth!"

And far up the valley they saw, clearly, with the morning sunlight upon its face, a downward rushing wall of water, dark brown, carrying great trees in its forefront as easily as sticks and straw. Two yards high, it swept on with an increasing murmur.

"Now!" pleaded the secretary. "May I give the order? May I send out the men to the gates?"

"Let this rush of water go," answered Garth, straining his eyes towards the priest. "It's hard, but what does an hour's flow of water amount to? It's the padre! Can he hold them in spite of the flood?"

For now the wall of water, striking the broader cañon just before the dam, spread with innumerable foamy rushings, and the sound of its voice went in a deep roar up to the office.

"Can he hold them?" repeated Garth. "Can the padre keep them to their prayer? If he does, we have won! Listen!"

There was a wavering and a lifting of bent heads in the crowd as the sound of the water poured up to them, but the padre stepped forward on his broad bulwark. They saw his arms stiffen. His head went farther back. They knew he was raising his voice and making it battle with the rushings of the water.

And he conquered! For one by one, and by degrees, men who had risen to their knees to watch, dropped back to their attitudes of devotion. They saw the movings of brown hands making the sign of the cross; peering more closely they could even make out lips that moved in the prayer. It held for a long moment, and then another sound rose.

It began, thin and weird and sad with infinite distance, infinite yearning. At first it was something to be guessed, rather than known, like the voices and the choruses of the winter wind, but at length it grew, it gathered volume, the watchers and the listeners around the big form of Garth heard now the unmistakable strains of "La Paloma!"

For another moment the strain gathered volume slowly, and the padre was seen to be exerting every effort to keep his flock from listening—to hold them to their devotions.

It was in vain. In a wave, every throat in the crowd suddenly burst into song. Every devotee sprang to his feet. A swell of mightily chorused singing swept up the valley side and burst about the walls of the office building.

Patriotism had been cunningly blended with superstitious fear by him who started that singing, and the combination of the two elements was too much for the host of peons. Still the poor padre strove against the music, but all backs were turned to him.

The song rose higher still, shrill with an ecstasy of triumph. The Mexicans danced on the top of the broad dam. Their wide sombreros flared to and fro. They shrieked and called to the brown rush of precious water below; they struck each other over the shoulders in a nameless delight. San Vicente was saved, and a thorn was placed in the crown of the "gringo"!

But Padre Miguel? He turned slowly away, at length, and made his way as slowly up the slope towards the little office building, followed by the three others as a sort of rearguard.

Garth began to laugh, a thin sound like the laughter of an hysterical girl, and terrible coming from his great throat. He turned upon the group.

"My friends," he said, "I have lost. San Vicente is stronger than I!"

And he dropped heavily into his chair behind the desk and sat with his great head supported in both hands. Not a sound, then, from all the room; and the jubilant yelling from the dam surrounded them, with a keen note of barbarian triumph which roused Garth from his stupor of the moment. No blank stare in his eyes; but there rose in them a sharpening gleam of the battling instinct. The door opened; Padre Miguel entered the room.

His eyes encountered those of Garth, and his head failed.

"Señor," he said, "I have been too weak."

Big Garth rose and moved with that ease which told of strength more than the budging of great weights. He took the padre by the arm and seated him in a chair beside the desk.

"The devil," he said, "is a fairly strong foe—even for you, good Padre Miguel!"

And this man was not a gentleman? With all her heart, Margaret wished that Hal could have heard.

"But tell us what caused you to fail, padre. Was it the sound of the rushing of the water?"

"It was not that, señor. When I spoke before those many men there came a strength in me, señor, that made my voice loud, so that those who heard me kneeled, and even over the noise of the flood I still made them hear me. I had a thought while I stood there that the noise of the water was the voice of the fiend; and I struggled against it."

He smiled deprecatingly around the room, and his mild eyes flitted from face to face. "It was a sinful and proud thought, and I was punished for it. But think, ah, think, señor! In another moment I should have had them all as gentle as sheep to do as I bade them! The water came. I raised my head and spoke more loudly. Still they heard. They were chained. They bowed their heads and prayed. It is good for the soul of man when he turns his eyes on the dust and sends his thoughts up to God. So!

"And as I spoke I fixed my eyes on the edges of the crowd. For there were some who could not hear me. I tried, and though some of these kneeled even as the closer ones, a few remained standing. More and more dropped to the ground, and a sense of power came in me.

"Then I saw, far off on the edge of the crowd, the face of a man whom I could not touch. He had a pale face, not like the brown ones around him. And I thought that I could catch the glitter of his eyes even at the distance. The morning sun, see you, was upon him.

"Towards him I directed my eyes and my voice, and my thoughts. But I could feel that he was smiling.

"Presently he turned to those near him and spoke, with many gestures. And after a moment, they began that song—'La Paloma!' "

Garth closed his large hand.

"Padre," he said softly, "good padre, can you name that man?"

"I can, señor, and the Lord have mercy upon his sinful heart. It is Señor Henry Tyson."

Thirty-Nine
A Gentleman's Agreement

"Tyson!"

Garth turned in his chair until his eyes met those of Margaret—and then he smiled frankly at her.

"Gentlemen," he said, "I shall ask you to leave me alone with Marshal Vance. McIntosh, will you take Miss Tyson back to the car? I'm coming on myself later on."

The crowd moved away, and Garth went with Margaret to the door.

"Are you afraid?" he asked rather grimly.

"You're going to win," she answered with confidence. "I'm certain of it."

His hand closed over hers; then she was gone.

When Garth and Marshal Vance were alone in the room they looked at each other intently, silently, and when they spoke they went to the point with a rather brutal curtness, which is sometimes the way with men of action. They knew and respected each other, and accordingly they wasted no time; the cards of each were laid, face up, on the table, so to speak.

"Sheep follow goats, and Mexicans follow leaders," said Garth tersely. "Who's leading that crew of brown fools, Vance?"

"I heard the talk around town. It's a young white renegade—Tyson."

"No one but a renegade—a no-good hound—would herd with the greasers."

"I had that idea—I imagined Tyson was behind it. What hold has he on them, the greasers?"

"I can't quite fathom it. I worked a brace of stool-pigeons through the greasers, and it seems they call him the El Oro."

"I knew that."

"He's done a couple of things that caught their eye. Among other things, he beat Kennedy out of a large bunch of coin."

"The gambler, eh?"

The marshal grinned. "Gambler? Of course there's no gambling in La Blanca."

Garth set his jaw as he snapped out: "We've got to get this Tyson out of the way. Vance, can you do it for me? Trump up a charge against him?"

"We haven't even a shadow of a crime to lay against him."

"Damn legality. I want his hands tied. Is he the one who started this chatter about saving San Vicente's Mission?"

"Right."

"He's got to be handled."

"The law can't touch him, Garth."

"Then—simply close your eyes to reports if you hear that Tyson has disappeared."

The marshal grew even more sober.

"How far would you go?" he asked.

"Vance, I give you my word that I'll do him no bodily harm, but he's got to be shunted out of the way. This Kennedy—what do you know about his relations with Tyson?—Enemies?"

"Haven't heard much about them."

"Kennedy himself. What is he?"

"A cool-headed gamester. Fighter. He has a past, but I haven't worked it up yet. Listen!"

A fresh wave of water came thundering down the Chiluah with a sound like a heavy wagon rumbling over cobblestones. Garth watched it foam and roar through the open sluice gates; and on its heels the rain began to rattle like machine guns.

"This is hard on you, Garth—that water getting away. Maybe the spring rains will be long this year; maybe there'll be enough to fill the dam after this first rush."

"Maybe," said Garth bitterly. "Vance, take me back to La Blanca in your car, will you?"

Which indirectly explains why Kennedy, not many hours later, stood before Garth in the latter's home. The gambler had answered the call hurriedly, anxiously, for he knew that his place, as well as every other den of the same nature, existed only by the sufferance of the Big Boss.

They were tolerated, not because Garth approved of gambling, but because he knew that Mexicans must have their games, and he kept an eagle eye upon them; half a dozen different houses had been closed for crooked work. Kennedy compressed his lips with anxiety as he faced the big man.

"You're Kennedy?"

"Yes, Mr. Garth."

"You run that house a block south of the plaza?"

Kennedy felt his doom was upon him, but he knew that it was useless and worse than useless to attempt to deceive Garth. He nodded.

"What do you know of a man named Tyson?"

Kennedy drew a great breath of relief.

"El Oro?" he repeated. "I know him. Want him, Mr. Garth?"

There was a rather sinister eagerness about the fellow which made the rest of his way easier for Garth, yet he stammered a little as he continued: "Kennedy, the law is a useful thing now and then."

"Yes, sir," said Kennedy cautiously.

"But there are things which the law cannot do, because now and then perfectly justifiable acts lie outside of the law."

"There ain't any doubt of it!" nodded Kennedy heartily.

"For instance, sometimes men get in the way of each other."

"Ah?"

"And sometimes one man may block a big work. You can imagine that?"

Kennedy was silent, but his eyes shone.

"And when the law cannot remove the obstacle, then it may be necessary to use means which are not legal. You follow me?"

"Sort of."

Garth drew a short, deep breath of impatience; he measured Kennedy's very soul.

"Kennedy, Tyson is in my way."

His voice was very low, and after he had spoken the two eyed each other solemnly. Kennedy slipped closer and dropped a hand on Garth's shoulder. With that last speech he seemed to have shed his awe like an inconvenient cloak.

"Dead dogs don't bark," he whispered.

Garth struck away the gambler's hand with an oath. In an instant of revulsion he seemed about to strike the other with his fist, and Kennedy stood bewildered.

"Not that, you fool!" growled Garth. "Not a hair of his head injured. But—I want him out of the way."

"Ah," murmured Kennedy, who had found himself and his man he thought. He drew out a cigarette case and extracted his smoke. "Have one?" he queried. "Smoke, Garth?"

The lips of Garth twitched as he noted the omission of the usual "mister." He shook his head, but Kennedy eyed him coolly while he lighted his cigarette and puffed a cloud towards the ceiling. He flicked the match so that it described an arc outlined by a film of smoke and then tapped on the floor, at Garth's feet.

"When?" he said.

"Now; as soon as possible."

"Not before night."

"Very well. Your terms, Kennedy?"

The latter smiled—on one side of his face only—and closed one eye slowly.

"Between you and me, Garth, there ain't any terms. 'S that all?"

"One more thing. You're sure he won't be injured?"

"Not more'n necessary."

"Take enough men so that it won't be necessary, I tell you. And don't underrate him. You'll find him just so much wildcat if he has a chance to fight."

"There's ways of persuadin' him," grinned Kennedy.

"Keep him safe—two days—three days. I don't

know how long. Maybe in twelve hours you can turn him loose again, but I have to keep him away from the Mexicans."

"Partner," drawled Kennedy, "not even daylight will see him in the place I'm going to put him. Anything more?"

"Nothing."

"So long, then. Glad I met you, Garth."

He paused at the door to wink back once more, significantly, and then slowly disappeared without. Once he was gone, Garth threw open the window and stood in front of it drawing deep breaths. He felt as if his hands had been dabbling in a murder.

Forty
Suspense

It had been the hope of Garth that the terrific downpour might drive the Mexicans from the dam and to cover, giving him an opportunity to rush the dam and close and lock the sluice gates, but though the majority of the peons did take shelter from the storm, an amply sufficient number stayed on guard, and they were heard actually singing as they stood in the rain; a religious devotion seemed to sustain them, and the brain of a white man seemed to direct them. Garth could guess whose that brain was.

Meantime, from his house, he received telephoned reports every few minutes, and transmitted the important messages to Margaret. Millions of gallons of priceless water were rushing away through the gates, and only if the spring were extraordinarily wet would they be replaced. Millions of dollars were thrown away by that delay.

And now the news had travelled apparently all over the country. Wires began to arrive from his Eastern backers, anxious wires urging him to do something, and he felt that he was tottering in his position. After all, his whole reputation was staked on bringing the dam into effectual operation this year; another delay would make him anathema with his investors.

So he ground his teeth, and thought of Tyson. Who could have dreamed that the fellow might have this power of destruction? It seemed to Garth as if his own big muscles had been chained in an invisible leash. He was helpless—until Tyson was removed. And he yearned with all his heart for the coming of night and the message from Kennedy.

Margaret also waited for the dark. All day she sat at the window watching the thick, parallel lines of rain, which blotted out the closest hills and obscured even the houses across the street. She knew that this rain was the fortune of Garth, and that the fortune was slipping through his fingers; she wanted to be with him and help—but very wisely she controlled the impulse and stayed away.

And so night came, with a gradual dimming of the mist of rain outside the windows. Something was to be done that night about the dam. This much she knew, and no more. It was then, just before the grey outside the windows turned into pitchy black, that one of the mozos brought up word that Padre Miguel Vega waited below to see her, and Margaret was glad of his coming, glad of anything which might break the suspense of waiting.

She found the good padre in the big empty living room. No one had thought to light the fire of logs at the end of the apartment and there was only one floor lamp to illumine the place. It was as if the house of Edward Garth were preparing for his ruin. The padre rose from the chair, where he sat with his hat resting on his knees, and the raincloak turned back from his shoulders. He came a few steps to meet her, his earnest eyes on her face.

"I am Miguel Vega," he said simply, "and you are the Señorita Tyson."

"You know me?"

"By your brother, señorita."

"Sit down, father. I'll have the fire going in a moment."

"Not for me. I have come only for a few moments in a matter which needs speed. Señorita, it is a hard thing I have come to say. But an old man may speak frankly to—a lady."

He made a pleasant little pause of emphasis before the word, and Margaret flushed with pleasure. In La Blanca she had almost forgotten that men could be courtly.

"Whatever it is," she assured him, "I hope you will speak openly."

"I must, and hastily. It is a matter of your brother's name and honour, and the soul of one who is dear to me. In the valley—yonder—there is a simple, childlike girl living with a half-demented father. Her name is Rona Carnahan."

"And Hal——" began Margaret, changing colour.

The padre raised his hand.

"Permit me to tell you more, señorita. If the story is half told, you will not understand."

And he sketched in briefly the history of Rona and her father. He told swiftly of how Tyson had met the girl, and of how he, the padre, who was more than half father to Rona, had vainly striven to prevent further meetings.

"And this evening," he went on, "in a lull in the storm, I went to see if the floods had disturbed the Carnahans, and on the way I met Rona hurrying down the valley. I stopped her and asked her where she was going, and she answered with pride, señorita, that she was going to meet your brother."

"You stopped her," breathed Margaret. "Thank Heaven, you met her!"

The old man smiled sadly.

"I tried to stop her," he said, "but it was like trying to stop the rain and the thunder. I tried to speak to her of sin, but to her your brother is a saint, one of the elect, because he has kept the water of the flood from covering the mission."

"I see it!" cried Margaret, striking her hands together. "He keeps the water from the grave of her mother, and she is grateful."

"More. She is beside herself, and she has gone to him."

"Why did you not command her back? Father, you are law to her!"

"Until today. But I could not stop the dam; and your brother has done the great thing. Therefore she turns from me to him. When you see her you will understand."

"I shall go at once," muttered Margaret. "But it can't be that Hal—Father Miguel, his life is clean. I know it!"

"It is ever hard to find the sin in those we love," said the padre sadly.

"Let us hurry!" she cried. "You will show me the way? You will go with me?"

"To the door, but not within. No man, not even one of a holy order, can interfere with another in such a matter as this. But you, señorita, are a lady."

He followed her to the hall, where she whipped a raincoat about her shoulders.

"Will it be too late?" she pleaded.

"Our Father alone knows," said the padre simply. "I have been praying for both their souls!"

And they went out into the whipping storm.

Forty-One

Revelation

From Mrs. Irene Casey, Rona learned the direction to Tyson's new lodgings, information which the good lady imparted with sufficient tartness, and she hurried on towards the place. There was less rain, now, but the wind blew a hurricane. Once, as she twisted around a corner, the gale caught at her like a hand, and jerked her back against the wall; but she went on with her head lowered. She was all compact with strength; besides there was enough sunshine and excitement in her heart to flood the world with brightness and warmth.

So she came, in due time, to what seemed to her an imposing building; certainly it was one of the superior buildings in the Mexican quarter. It was erected on the pattern so familiar in Mexico City—a two-story structure with the first floor devoted to the porter's lodge, and space for storage, kitchen, chickens, horses, cattle. The upper floor was reserved for the living rooms. At the gate she met a little old woman swathed in shawls and cursing the storm softly under her breath. She looked like the caricature of a round ball with a face set upon it. Yet the ancient creature opened the gate with surprising swiftness even before Rona had time to knock.

"You are expected, señorita," she said, and Rona knew by her voice that the hag was grinning. "Up these stairs, and open the first door."

And as Rona passed, a skinny hand hovered in front of her, palm up; but Rona brushed by.

"Scum!" she heard muttered in Mexican behind her.

She turned on the stairway.

"Scum yourself!" she cried shrilly. "You call me names!"

The other rolled herself from side to side, apparently to get her wrath and her vocabulary ready for launching, but before her words began to spout, the door at the head of the stairs opened, and in a square of light Rona saw Tyson. He was so transfigured that she hardly knew him, for he was dressed in white, and the light from the room behind him set his hair shining like golden wire.

"Come up, Rona. Don't mind the old lady."

The latter scurried out of sight, and Rona resumed her journey.

"I would have wrung her skinny neck," she informed Tyson, "but I thought I might make you angry. What have you done to yourself, señor?"

And she stepped away as far as the narrow landing would permit.

"My clothes?" he chuckled. "I've called in a wizard named money, and had him working for me."

Working overtime, in fact. An exchange of wires

to New York had brought Tyson a handsome sum of money, and with it he had done a great many things in the past twenty-four hours. The living rooms were a sufficient proof.

He showed Rona first into the little reception hall, and while he closed the door she stood gaping. It was indeed a surprising place, considering the rather dingy mud exterior of the building, for on each side of the door stood a potted palm with the branches joining overhead, so that she stepped, literally, into an atmosphere of green coolness.

On the dull-green tiles stood at one side a high-backed hall seat, and opposite the palms there was a pair of tall, rectangular mirrors, so cunningly arranged that they repeated the images, and Rona found herself looking down a long vista of palms. She turned a look of wide-eyed wonder upon her host.

"Señor Tyson—magic," was all she could say.

He laughed while he stripped off her wet cloak, and then blinked. For she was wearing a broad, red hat, flashing with gold and silver lace, and some matador had bequeathed his jacket to her, and, apparently she had added embellishments of her own design. All her gala splendour, however, was confined to the upper part of her costume. Otherwise she wore a short khaki skirt and low-cut, heavy shoes. Tyson drew a breath and contained his smile.

"This way," he directed, and led her into the living room.

She followed him silently, stepping as though there were thin ice underfoot. At the entrance he heard a sharp exclamation, and when he turned he saw her throw out her arms and then catch them back to her breast; her eyes were afire with joy. She made him think of a child at the border of fairyland.

He himself was satisfied with the room. Here the dull-green tiles, as everywhere in the house, were repeated, the large stones being fitted with true Mexican cunning, so that one seemed to be walking on a single solid slab of stone, unbroken by any crevice. The world has no finer natural stonemasons than the Mexicans. The prevailing note of the place was Japanese, however, with which the jade green of the floor harmonised perfectly.

There was a blue and buff Japanese rug; at the windows print curtains displayed the wavering figures of gaunt cranes; cream-coloured wicker chairs were comfortably cushioned with chintz, and to the side was a lovely table of Japanese lacquer, gold and black. It caught the eye first, and the eye was content to rest upon it.

Above all, on such a night as this, was the great fireplace, which filled half of one of the end walls, for the room was a long rectangle, and the yellow and crimson flames from the logs made colour notes repeated all around the walls by jars of brilliant flowers—unfragant, tropical blossoms.

Rona advanced by slow degrees to the centre of the apartment, and her glance went methodically from place to place; she seemed like one who drank. There was the same starved expression, and it went oddly to the heart of Tyson.

"This way now," he said gently at last.

"More?" she whispered, incredulous.

But in the bedroom her strength failed her. She sank back into a chair and gaped almost stupidly.

Rest is the most necessary requirement for life in the hot Chiluah, and this room was almost as large as the last one. That gave an opportunity for plenty of air circulation. Everything was the purest white . . . curtains, walls, and ceilings, bed and wicker chairs. The very cushions of the chairs and the chaise longue were white. And on the jade floor lay a goat-skin rug, with long silken white hair.

However, there was one variance, at least. For here stood a jar of flowers on a stone bench, and the yellow blossoms branched up against the wall; and by the bed, on a small table, stood a bed lamp with a broad shade as green as the floor. These were the two spots of colour, and they lived. The rest was lost in that exquisite white.

He turned, naturally, towards the girl, but she could not speak. So he unveiled the crowning wonder. He opened the door of a deep, broad closet, turned on the light within—and behold the place was filled with a riot of colour, springing out of the darkness, silken sheen, mists of tulle, glimmer of brocade, richness of velvet—the closet was crammed with lovely gowns.

"Yours, my dear," said Tyson. "If you want to change, I'll wait for you in the living room."

He left her, mute as a statue, and closed the door softly behind him. Before the fire he selected his cigarette automatically and smoked slowly, smiling in meditation through the blue drift of the smoke.

It was very pleasant. It was indeed like opening the gates of fairyland to a child's heart. There was both sadness and happiness in Tyson. When he looked around him, the room was changed by her coming. The silence was peopled for him.

He closed his eyes and remembered how she had thrown out her arms when she saw the place; and then he sighed: something of the tender reverence was coming up in his mind. He had to frown and shake himself to banish the new emotion.

To the victor belong the spoils!

"Honest" Ed Garth had said that. And after all, it was truth. For instance, consider Rona Carnahan. In due time, her father and the padre were sure to die, and then she would be left unguarded in the world. That would mean only one end of her. Or—suppose he, Tyson, had not come into her life. It would have meant her marriage with the gambler, Kennedy, and certainly this life with him was better, cleaner, almost, than marriage with that fellow. Besides—to the victor belong the spoils!

Good! He would grapple that idea to his heart. Garth had built his life along those lines. Why not Tyson? As for the other side of the matter, to be sure, he had kept himself indifferent and clean all his life. But what of that? There was his sister. She was among women what the diamond is among gems, and yet she was willing to throw herself away on the heavy-handed vulgarian, Garth!

After all, such silent arguments as Tyson now turned over in his mind always end in one way. "Purity," he decided, "is merely a matter of habit, an affair of the mind, a way of thinking."

A door opened, not with a sound, but he could feel something look in on him; when he turned, it was Rona. At least, his senses told him it was she, but not his eyes. For the wild girl of the reds and blues, the khaki skirts, and the heavy shoes had disappeared, and in her place was a figure clouded in white, with the lines of her grace just hinted at, and all the mystery of feminine loveliness about her.

He could not see details at first. She came on his sight like music on the ear, a burst of beauty that set his nerves tingling, a wave that drowned his senses.

After that, he could see more clearly. All in white, her olive skin might have semed too dark, and the instinct of the artist which lives to an extent in every young girl, made her recognise it; so in her hair there was one of those yellow blossoms, and at her breast there was another spray of them. She was perfect, from the heavy coil of the black hair, low on her forehead, to the slender, white, slippered feet.

How had she known how to dress like that?

Forty-Two
Danger

"Look!" she was saying. "Can you believe it? Is this I?"

"I don't know. I doubt it."

"See what you've done?"

She whirled around, her arms outstretched. A dancer would have envied her that motion. And now she faced him, flushed.

"I've done this? Only a blind agency, Rona. Sit down here. Let me look at you."

She came and slipped into a chair opposite him, so poised that she seemed almost on the verge of springing up again.

"Look and look and look!" she cried, and the yellow of the fire was doing strange things with the cloudy white of her dress, and setting a leaping flame in her eyes. "I could hardly leave that mirror in there. Who am I? What is my name? Oh, Señor Tyson, what has happened to me?"

It made his heart beat so fast that a chill touched him. She was quiveringly eager, alert as a bird on a branch; light enough for the wind to sway.

"Talk to me," she said, "or something will break in me. Talk to me!"

And she added: "And don't tell me when I must go. Just for a minute, I'm going to dream that it's all really mine, like a dream that isn't a dream!"

"I tell you, Rona, it's daylight reality. Go? You'll never go! And everything you see is yours."

"Señor!"

"Everything!"

Her lips parted at that, and then, with a stroke, all the mystery and all the aloofness were gone from her, and he could look into her and through her as deeply as the sunlight may strike through the window into a dark room. He felt as if someone had poured his hands full of jewels.

She was speaking again, and what a voice. It was low, and there was no tremor in it, but it pierced him like an edged sound: "Is it true? Señor Tyson, if you give me all this, how much you care for me! I shall tell you. I have hoped that you might, but then there were times when I thought that you laughed at me, and I almost hated you for it. But now I see that all the time you were not laughing more deeply than your lips. But tell me—did you guess when I went in my rags that I could be—like this?"

"Not all like this. But I knew you were lovely, Rona."

"Lovely?" She drew in her breath, and leaned back in the chair with eyes half closed, faintly smiling at him.

"Tell me again!"

"Beautiful, Rona."

"Once I found in a book words like these you are saying." She sighed happily. "It is true! You care much for me. Tell me: More than the padre cares for San Vicente?"

"A thousand times more."

"Ah? More than my father loves his violin?"

"Far more."

She looked slowly away from him towards the fire, still with that faint smile, and now she raised her hands slowly and pressed them over her heart.

"And you?" he asked.

"I? How could I help? The clothes have changed me outside; but do you see I am changed within? When I looked in the mirror, I could not speak, and then I wanted to weep, and then I wanted to laugh; and last of all I remembered that you had done all this, and something inside me grew big—big——" She made a vague gesture. "It was sad, like being far away from home. It was beautiful, like La Cabeza at sunset. It was . . ."

She broke off suddenly. "How many times I have made you angry! But you will teach me to be otherwise. You see, there are times when I am unhappy if I cannot make everyone angry. There is so much sin in me, that sometimes when I make the dear padre frown and my father swear, I could sing for happiness. The little, small devil takes me by the hand. But you—*amigo mio*—who are strong enough to tear down the dam, are strong enough to change me."

He was thinking with furious speed. Garth would be done for now in a day or so, if the dam were kept with the gates open. Then a little while longer, to make sure that the big man was smashed, and he would be gone. What could he do with the girl then? If he took her away with him, there would be what sort of a life for her in New York—and for him? It would be different in Europe, of course.

And then the girl. She might change in time, begin to regret as she learned more. And what did she know now? And what was her knowledge of the world? He leaned back in his chair and began to question her, half tantalisingly.

"All this is yours, Rona. And very soon I shall leave you here with it alone."

"Alone?" She canted her head and considered the idea seriously. "No, I shall not like it if you are away."

"But I am going on a very long journey."

"I have always wanted to travel. Perhaps as far as Mexico?"

"Much farther! This journey may have no end!"

She clapped her hands.

"Good! Only a fool could wish to live in one place for ever."

Plainly there was no shaking her on this point. It was like threatening a bird with a fall through the air. Perhaps, however, there was a touch of the mercenary about her. She had often talked of money.

"But it will be hard for me to make money for us both to live on."

"Money? Why, you are rich!"

"All I have is here, Rona."

She made a little moue of aversion.

"And I don't like to work, my dear."

"Well, I knew that when I first met you. It is true and right. A man is not a squaw. He should not work."

"But who *would* work for the money?"

"I."

"For both of us?"

"Of course. Señor Kennedy would often tell me that after we were married I would never have to lift my hand. All things would be done for me. When I clapped my hand servants would come running. The big man also would come when I wished, and not otherwise. Bah! As he talked I despised him. He was like a squaw. I wanted to beat him with a stick."

"What work could you do?"

"Once as I walked in La Blanca I sang, and after a moment people came to doors and windows and threw money at me. But why should I care for money, then? I walked on and let the money lie, but for you, I would pick up every cent."

"Well," murmured Tyson, "I love leisure. It would be an easy life. But there are other things. If we travel unmarried——"

"Shall we not be married?"

He started a little, and stared at her until she saw his astonishment. When she understood her colour did not change a shade.

"Well, marriage is nothing. I have seen one. The padre talks while a man and a woman stand together. Then there is a ring given. Bah! It is nothing but words."

"But consider, Rona. When a man and a woman are not married, few people come to see them. They stay by themselves. They have no friends of their own class."

She answered instantly: "If they are true friends, they will not care what words have been spoken over us. If they are not true, what do we want with them? Besides, there are only two real friends—a horse and a gun!"

She might be ignorant of the world, but she had

a certain cool wisdom that hit at the heart of things.

"Rona," he said solemnly, "if you mean this, then I'll make a compact with you, to be kept until——"

Someone knocked at the door, and he started and turned guiltily. Again the knock. He rose, angered, and started to answer the call. He had told his porter to allow no second person up the stairs. So, in his temper, he jerked the door open roughly and found himself staring into the face of Margaret.

Forty-Three
The Lady

His first impulse was, childishly, to close the door in her face, in his panic. His second was anger. In some way she had learned, and now there would be a scene. So he stepped back and waved her in. She had no eye for the place. She merely took the cloak away from her shoulders. The streams of rain pattered on the tiling.

"Hal," she said in a whisper, "tell me it isn't true!"

"That what isn't true?" he fenced, but his colour changed.

She drew her hand back from his arm as though he were a leprous thing, and her face turned sick with disgust.

"I wouldn't believe it!" she said, through white, numb lips. "I can't believe it now! Hal, for God's sake, come away! Come away with me now."

She tried to draw him through the door, but he shook her roughly.

"Lower your voice," he warned, and then gestured towards the next room. Then: "Don't lecture me, Margaret. It's useless. I'll tell you this: my life may sicken you, but the thought of you and Garth is the same to me."

"Henry!"

"I tell you it is."

"But that poor child—that half-wild creature——"

"Come with me and meet her. Child? Come with me, Margaret."

She hesitated an instant, and then went impulsively after him. Rona sat with her arms crossed behind her head, and she turned and smiled up at them, calmly, unembarrassed.

"Rona," he said, "this is my sister, Margaret. She has heard of you, and is anxious to know you."

That brought her to her feet.

"Your sister?" she came swiftly to Margaret, her hand stretched out. "I am *so* happy, señorita!"

No girl of perfect training could have done it better. And Tyson smiled openly at Margaret's astonishment. She had taken Rona's hand without a word; then she slipped down into a chair as soon as her fingers were free.

"Oh!" murmured Rona, concerned. "You are tired. The wind is like a wild bull tonight. Come closer by the fire."

Automatically Margaret obeyed.

"So!" She had caught up a cushion and arranged it behind her visitor's head. "You are more comfortable?"

Margaret turned her eyes in dumb wonder towards her brother, and then her glance came back, fascinated, to the girl. As for Rona, she stood back a little to look at the picture.

"Now I can see," she nodded. "Of course you are his sister."

She drew up a chair close to Margaret and sat far forward in it, resting her chin on the palm of one hand, and down from her wrist fell the cloudy shower of her sleeve and left her arm bare to the rounded elbow.

"I have a thousand things to ask you, señorita. They are chiefly of him."

"I'll answer whatever I can," said Margaret slowly, "but I am afraid there's a good deal I don't know."

"Of course. Who could know everything about him? First——"

The door to the bedroom shook slightly, as though the wind had struck it.

"What is that?" asked Rona, starting up, alert in an instant.

"The wind," said Tyson.

"No. Something——"

The door swung wide, and in it stood a masked man with a glint of blue at his side—a long, heavy Colt forty-five.

"Tyson," he said, in a rather muffled voice, "come with me; you're wanted."

The three were on their feet at the apparition, Margaret with a faint scream.

"Take it easy, lady," said the masked man. "There ain't any harm comin' to him if he don't make a fight."

"Look here," said Tyson quietly. "If you've come for money, you'll get it. Over there——"

He made a step, and the gun flickered up from the side of the visitor and covered him.

"Stand fast! No funny work, my fine bird, or I'll

drill you clean. Stick up them mitts while you're about it!"

"Don't be alarmed," said Tyson calmly to his sister. He raised his hands as required. "There's no danger."

"There you are, Bud," said he of the gun. "Go through him, will you?"

He stepped forward into the room, and showed two more masked figures behind him. They both entered, and one of them went to Tyson and ran his hands swiftly over the pockets and belt of the latter.

"Nothin' on him," he announced.

"Now, Bud," said the first speaker to Tyson, "are you goin' to come quiet, or do you need a rope on your hands? Better tie him, I figure. All right, pal!"

Rona Carnahan, white about the lips, but her eyes as steady as steel, had slipped back to a corner where a small writing desk stood. Now her hand moved out behind her and the fingers gripped a heavy inkstand.

In the meantime, one of the other two had put away his revolver and now produced a small coil of twine.

"Turn around, cull," ordered number one, "and cross your mitts behind you. Make him——"

The arm of Rona jerked convulsively over her shoulder, and the inkstand flashed across the room. Fair and true it sped to its mark, and a fractured skull would have been the doom of the first gunman if some premonition had not made him jerk back his head and glance around. As it was, the heavy glass, with the stream of ink still falling through the air along its course, glanced with a sharp thud from his forehead and he dropped like a poleaxed steer in his tracks.

The suddenness of it saved Tyson. He had seen the flash of the coming inkstand, and now he put his weight behind a smashing blow that clipped him of the rope squarely on the point of the chin.

The fellow went down with a curse that was bitten in two in the centre, and while the third gunman reached for his weapon, Tyson had whipped up the gun of number one and covered his quarry. A fraction of a second covered the entire action; now he was master.

He took command without even raising his voice, though it rang like bell metal, softly.

"Rona, take a look at this fellow you floored. I think you've broken his head. Get those hands up, you fool!" (This to number three.) "You on the floor, stand up and get over there beside your friend, and keep your hands over your head, or I'll finish you!"

The orders were obeyed in heavy silence. Rona spoke, on her knees beside the unconscious man.

"Heart beating; breathing. He'll come back to life."

"Take off his mask."

It was done, and a blockish, deeply jowled face appeared, with the mouth sagging open horribly. A thin trickle of blood ran down from the cut temple. Presently he groaned, and sat up.

"Sit quiet, my friend," said Tyson, moving back a little so as to keep all three within easy range of his gun. "Now, Rona, get the guns from that pair."

She obeyed him swiftly and stood with the heavy weapons in her hands, flushed and alert. It was a great game to her.

"You, over there; lower your left hands—mind, you, only the lefts—and pull off your masks. I'm going to get under this little affair."

Number two obeyed with a snarl and flicked his mask on the floor. A chunky fellow, he appeared now, with a rosy, stupid face, but number three, after pulling his hand down a few inches, kept it stationary.

"Off with that mask!" ordered Tyson, raising his voice a little. "I won't warn you a third time, my fine fellow."

"Then be damned to you!" growled the man, and tore away his mask. A pale, scowling face looked out at them.

"Kennedy!" cried Tyson softly. "I knew there was something to be learned."

"You!" burst out Rona Carnahan. "You!"

Kennedy stood motionless, speechless with rage and shame.

"Now," said Tyson, "you two over there can clear out."

Amazement widened their eyes, and number one removed the handkerchief which he had kept pressed to his bleeding temple, to stare at this incredibly lenient captor. They were as speechless as Kennedy.

"You can clear out," continued Tyson, "because I don't think you'll come back." They made a lurching movement towards the door. "Wait a moment." They paused.

"Take these along with you. You probably know more about them than I do."

He held out their weapons, taking them both from Rona's hand and extending them to the thugs, butt first. They stood well armed, and two to one against him, but they flashed a single glance from one to the other, and were of one mind. The round-faced fellow blurted out: "Sir, it don't take no two looks to see a toff and know 'im. If you was ever to need a handy man, sir, just be thinkin' of——"

"Easy, pal," snarled the other. "Don't be talkin' your life away."

"And please use the front stairs going out," smiled Tyson. "Stand steady, Kennedy!"

The last remark came like the click of a hammer on the cap, as Kennedy strode after his companions. He faced about to Tyson.

"What's up?" he said, half sullen, half suspicious. "Are you framin' something for me?"

The door closed lightly after the two departing guests, and Tyson smiled gently upon his victim.

"I'm framing a question, Kennedy, that's all. What put you up to this? Was it——"

His eyes finished the question by throwing a glance towards Rona.

"Her?" sneered Kennedy. "*I* don't chase after that kind."

He glowered at the girl, and Tyson followed the glance. He expected to find Rona in one of her passions, but he was astonished at what he saw. She was looking steadily at Kennedy—through him, indeed, rather than at him—and a smile of utter indifference touched her lips.

The eye of Tyson ran over to his sister, and he started, for her expression was that of Rona, except that it was tempered with a touch of horror and fear as she gazed at Kennedy.

There was the same fine contempt in both of them, the same aloofness as from a thing infinitely below them. And very swiftly Tyson followed up the comparison.

He saw for the first time a fineness in the wild girl, like the fineness of a blooded horse. He thought of tales he had heard of mustangs which reverted to the original Arab stock of the Spaniards. The girl was suddenly become strange to him, new.

A little shudder ran through him. He felt like one who picks up a stone to throw and sees the glitter of gold in the rock just as it is about to leave his fingers. His attention came coldly back to Kennedy. He must get the dirty work over and quickly.

"Kennedy," he said, "you don't leave me till I have the truth out of you. What sent you here?"

Kennedy maintained his glowering silence. His head bent a little and he stared up at Tyson through his heavy brows. Tyson made a step closer, and his face became a study in cruel resolution.

"Kennedy," he said softly, "I warn you for the last time. Give me the truth or I'll—mark you—so that you'll carry the brand. Out with it!"

The last words cracked out sharply, and Kennedy winced as if he felt the whip.

"If you want the truth, take it," he snarled. "Go ask Garth."

A heavy silence dropped on the room.

"Garth!" repeated Tyson slowly, stunned.

"It's false!" cried Margaret. "Hal, this fellow can't tell the truth!"

"Can't I?" sneered Kennedy. "Go ask him. Go ask Garth. Him and me, we fixed it up."

"For money?" said Tyson.

"Nope. It was a gentleman's agreement."

The smile of Tyson went to Margaret, and found her white with disgust.

"And what was the agreement, Kennedy?"

"To put you out of the way."

Tyson started.

"Death?"

"No," said Kennedy. "But to get you safe."

"With guns?"

"That was left up to me. I wasn't going to harm you none."

Tyson thought a moment. "I think that's all. You can go now, Kennedy."

The latter started hastily towards the door, but with his hand on the knob, distance gave him courage.

"You've won two hands, Tyson," he threatened, "but luck will come my way."

"You forget, Kennedy," smiled the other, "that a horse with a poor heart never wins. Good night."

The door slammed after the intruder; his heavy footfall went down the steps, and then Tyson went to Margaret. She had slipped down into a chair and sat with her face buried in her hands. Tyson laid his hand lightly upon her shoulder.

"I'm sorry, Margaret," he said gently. "I'm very sorry."

She lifted a grey face; she seemed to have aged.

"It's the shame, Hal," she said brokenly. "I—I'm sick." She caught her breath. "How could he do it? How *could* he?"

"My dear, we won't talk about it."

A perceptible shiver ran through her.

"And I have to go back and speak to him again. How——"

A light click interrupted her; Rona had withdrawn into the bedroom and left them to talk alone together. Even in her grief Margaret looked her wonder at such perfect tact.

"I leave tomorrow, Hal," she said. "And you?"

He answered quietly: "We've both been pretty near to a messy time. Thank God we've come to our senses."

"You're coming with me?"

He was silent.

"I haven't a word to say," she murmured. "I haven't the right to advise you, after what's happened. But oh, Hal, if you go on, you'll regret it. Hal, she's a lady!"

"I know it," he answered solemnly. "As soon as you leave, I'm going to take her back to her father."

"And tomorrow?"

"I don't think I can leave with you. I've got to see that Garth is finished."

She closed her eyes suddenly, and swayed a little, but she said nothing.

"You still care?" he asked.

She looked at him through a long moment, and there was such anguish in her eyes that he had to bow his head. She rose.

"The poor padre is waiting in the street for me."

"Tell him that he has no cause for worry. You can give him my word, Margaret."

And so they parted, and he watched her down the stairs. When he came back he rapped on the door of the bedroom; it flew open, and the lighted face of Rona was before him.

"Change back to your old clothes," he said. "We're going up the valley, and we're starting now."

Forty-Four
The Battle

Tequila and Mescal had been flowing freely for twenty-four hours in La Blanca, and the devil was loosed in every Mexican peon in the town; accordingly, when morning rose, they gravitated naturally towards the centre of trouble. There was a sufficient detail guarding the dam, for they had not yet worked themselves to the point when dynamite would be used, and they were contented simply watching the water rush away to waste through the open sluice gates.

The others by hundreds moved towards Garth's house. At first it was only a group of two or three who stopped to shake their fists at the worker of evil. They made the nucleus. Others joined them, not knowing why, and then a rumour ran abroad and started the peons from every distant corner of the city.

There was something about to happen at the

house of the big boss, and so they hurried and swept up in waves and droves, choking the street with tossing sombreros and brown faces, and flashing eyes. They had no purpose, beyond mischief in general, and so they waited. Bottles passed freely through the mass, and the noise gathered head.

Through the thick 'dobe walls that noise penetrated in dull, heavy waves of sound, inarticulate as the rushing of the wind, and Garth got up from his chair and raised the shade to look out.

A shrill yell of hate greeted him, so he turned and went quietly back to his chair. Opposite him sat his mother, and in her lap was the inevitable sewing, but today, for the first time in years, the needle was idle.

Something had gone wrong. She had gained one great purpose, and now Margaret was in her room packing her things and waiting for the train. She had won that great point, but in pulling one stone, she had destroyed the equilibrium of the whole building which her life work had erected, and now it was crashing about her ears.

Each fresh yell from the mob was the crumbling of another wall; each shrill, single-voiced burst of Spanish mockery was the toppling of another pillar. If she had not been able to hear it in that uproar she could have read it graven in the face of her son.

He had sat like that in his chair ever since the girl had spoken to him, late the night before. Now and again he rose and walked up and down the room. Then he returned and sat there. It was not despair, to all seeming. It was rather the calculation of one who cannot understand a great calamity without careful thought.

Not once had he reproached her, either in word or look, but he bowed and accepted the burden of her existence, she felt, as a horse bows to the burden of a crushing rider. He accepted her without anger or hate, even though she had worked the ruin. And as that hand of pain closed over her heart she felt like the artist who in a fit of blind sulkiness destroys the inspiration of his canvas and leaves not even a slight sketch of the great idea.

If she could have gone to him and touched him, and consoled him, she would have had at least one outlet to her sorrow; but when she came too close he winced, silently, and it stabbed her with remorse.

She could have prayed from the bottom of her soul for one outburst of hate and rage that would clear his mind of all rancour against her; but now she knew that this thing would go on working in him for ever. He sat thinking, thinking, and he showed no sign of emotion, except that he could never look out upon the looming mass of the dam that blocked the Chiluah.

Telegrams were pouring in, now; he allowed them to lie unopened on the little table beside him. The foreman of the dam, even Marshal Vance, could not reach him. A thousand miles of desert could not more effectually have cut him off from human society than this burden on his brain.

A heavy step came through the room from the end opening on the stairs. It was a mozo carrying two heavy suitcases. Mrs. Garth silently prayed that her boy would not see the fellow, but he lifted his head and looked—there was not a shade of change in his expression.

The mozo looked out through the window, shook his head, and retreated. When he came again, he was carrying the travelling bag, and Margaret Tyson walked before him.

She seemed perfectly poised and calm, but her face had not a vestige of colour, and Mrs. Garth closed her eyes to shut out the sight. She knew it all perfectly now. Pride—the same terrible pride which had roused Tyson to action—was now driving Margaret out of Garth's life, but still she loved him. She was not the kind of woman to give her heart twice, and Mrs. Garth, with her eyes closed, saw the truth more clearly than she had ever done when they were open.

Now the adieu!

It was the quietness of it that froze the heart of the mother. The girl came straight to her and took her hand for an instant, murmuring something about thanks for the care Mrs. Garth had given her. Then she was bowing to Garth.

Would he hear? Would he see? It seemed not, at first. He raised his head and looked blankly, and when he finally rose and bowed it was with a bewildered expression, like one who is stunned.

That was all, and thank God it was over!

Now the girl was at the door which the mozo opened before her, and now she descended the steps. The door was still open while the mozo gathered up the suitcases. He was strangely slow about it, and Mrs. Garth saw the brown wave in the street open, and then close around Margaret. Only the white feather in her hat was visible, bobbing.

A few steps only. Then it paused.

For a fresh clamour had risen from the crowd. Someone shouted a shrill phrase in Spanish, and a gust of harsh laughter went up. The crowd was dense around the girl, and Mrs. Garth saw a big Mexican take off his hat and bow to Margaret. He was standing directly in her path, and Mrs. Garth noted the mockery of his broad grin. The mozo stood undetermined on the porch.

Then it happened with a terrible suddenness; a new roar from the mob, and then, splitting the thick noise, a tingling cry, a woman's cry. It floated back, it rang through the room.

And it had brought Garth to his feet like a sleeper awakened.

One dazed glance he flung about him, his fists already clenched, then he saw. And he charged through the door with a bellow.

"You're unarmed, Eddie!" screamed his mother, starting from her chair, and catching up from the drawer of the table Garth's automatic. As well have tried to tag a storm wind. Garth was down the front steps from the porch; a shout of triumph from the Mexicans greeted him—savage triumph—then the current of the crowd swished around him like the skirts of a woman walking against the wind.

Straight towards the girl he clove his way. She was in no danger apparently, but the touch of some drunken peon had probably terrified her, and there was big Rodriguez still with hat in hand before her. She could neither shrink back nor go forward through the solid mass.

It seemed impossible that any one man could work a way through the mass of humanity, but Garth smashed through them resistlessly. His lunging shoulders bowled them over. Here and there a knife flashed over the heads of the rest, but before they swung down a pile driver fist crashed into their faces, blotting out features with a red smear.

The whole street was tossing like waves in a

chopping cross current. Hands were darting up, and clenched fists, and knives. But in their struggle to get to the point of contact with the enemy, they tangled themselves into an inextricable knot. Twice, in despair, Mrs. Garth raised the automatic to fire, but it wabbled in her withered hands.

And still she saw Garth wade on. Then his heel ground in the face of a fallen man, and as he staggered a knot of Mexicans heaved up from the centre and shelved off with arms and legs writhing in the empty air. Only an instant Garth paused to get his direction.

"Margaret," he shouted.

And a thin, clear voice answered. She was facing towards him, struggling to get back.

He charged again. It was appalling to watch him fight. He struck them as if with a thunderbolt from either hand. Each surge of his shoulders sent the nearest men staggering. Now they commenced to bear away from him, those nearest, for they had learned the meaning of those red, dripping hands. They fought and clawed their way back; they made a clear wake behind him. But those beyond them pressed them still towards the big man.

He swayed back a little, now, and then flung himself forward at the last group which surrounded the girl; and he split them as a snow-plough splits a drift. Instantly she had slipped behind him and sped dodging down the wake he left and back to the house; panting, white, she was beside Mrs. Garth at the open door.

Garth turned on his backward journey, a terrible figure. His coat was literally torn from his back by clawing hands, and the shirt beneath it was in tatters, his hair framed his head wildly, and a streak of crimson flowed down one side of his face. The

Mexicans, wild for revenge, thronged back into his path towards safety. And everywhere, now, there were knives.

He could not have lived a second, had not the press of the crowd chained the hands which carried the flashing, naked steel; and now and then there was a scream where a blade went home in the wrong flesh. Margaret caught Mrs. Garth by the shoulders and shook her fiercely.

"Do something!" she cried. "Call the servants. Get those guns. For God's sake, don't stand there, frozen!"

Then she saw a trembling mozo crouching at a corner of the room, and she groaned in despair. She turned, and saw Garth battering his way forward. A score of hands reached for him, but he was tearing his way through them, and the brutal hands struck down form after form before him, only to find his way clogged with a fresh mass of fighters.

But the fearful exertions were already telling on him. He stood head high above the mass of the peons, and his mouth was open, his lips grinning back from the teeth, as he gasped for his breath. It was a grim face—like a distance runner struggling towards the finish—or one caught in the pangs of death.

Another thing caught her eyes. Off there, down the street, a second figure was working through the crowd, and thrice as fast as Garth. This other did not come by the use of downright brutal force, but he slipped in a snake-like way, literally writhing through the mass.

It was Henry Tyson, and he came with desperate speed, shouting, but his voice was drowned in the clamour. No sound to break through that save the roar from the bull throat of Garth. Would Tyson come in time? No, he was a score of feet away, and the mob grew denser towards Garth. Even if he reached them, could he control that blood-maddened lot?

Still Garth came on. The tugging hands set him reeling now. Again and again clawing groups closed over him, and each time he shook them off with more difficulty. And his blows staggered men now, but rarely dropped them under his struggling feet as heretofore.

And she saw, coming from behind, the big Mexican who had first blocked her way down the street. He was very tall, almost as large as Garth himself, and one hand, held high above his head, was gripping some weapon—a stone, or a fragment of a 'dobe brick.

On he came, swiftly, brushing through the thinning crowd just behind Garth. He was close. He was upon the fighters. And Margaret saw his teeth flash as he straightened his arm and brought it down.

The weapon landed straight upon Garth's head, and he went down limp; a wild yell came from the peons.

No hope for him. Probably a dozen knives were already buried in his body before he struck the ground, but she knew with a terrible certainty that she loved him, and him alone, forever.

The gleam of the automatic which Garth's mother held caught her desperate eye. She seized it, not as a gun, but as a club, and rushed across the porch and down the steps, and then, as her hand closed round the butt of the gun, she felt the trigger—the cartridge exploded, the muzzle of the weapon jerked up, and a thin mist of bluish smoke, like that of a cigarette, went curling upward.

Again, again, again she fired wildly into the air, and the peons scattered as if she had sprayed them with molten lead. They screamed as they ran, for the sound of guns in the Southwest means only one thing to the Mexican. They spread out, fighting to get away, heedless of the fact that a single girl stood armed before them, and out of the press leaped the form of Tyson, and stooped beside Garth.

"Keep them back!" he shouted to Margaret. "Fire in their faces if they come again!"

He was slipping his arms under the shoulders of Garth, and now he raised the inert bulk and staggered towards the open door. But there was no need of another shot from Margaret's gun. The Mexicans had rallied swiftly, indeed, when they saw the limited extent of the danger; but now they were seeing the bare, golden head of Tyson, and a mutter ran through them: "El Oro! El Oro!"

What was he doing, rescuing the servant of the devil, this inspired man?

Up the steps Tyson dragged his burden, and through the door. He laid Garth upon his back and stared stupidly down at the blood-stained face. Then there was a clatter as Margaret tossed the heavy automatic carelessly across the room. She faced her brother.

"Look!" she cried fiercely. "See what you've done! You!"

And then she was on her knees beside Garth, and Garth's mother weeping beside her.

The roar of anger was growing in the street again.

"Thank God!" Margaret cried. "He lives!"

And Tyson went out to face the crowd.

Forty-Five

The Sacrifice

After all, there is nothing men love so much as mystery. The peons knew that Tyson had been the force which first attacked the big boss, and now they saw him talking for the big man. They could not understand, but they were too interested to protest.

For some strange reason El Oro wished them to disperse quietly to their homes. Therefore they would go, and afterwards El Oro could give them a clue to the mystery if he chose. He was not such a man as one could question lightly to his face. When he ceased talking from the veranda before Garth's house they were already in motion down the street—those who had felt the weight of the fists of the big boss limping in the rear; and Tyson went thoughtfully with them.

All that he had done had worked against him, like a preordained doom. He had thrown himself violently into the line of Garth's habit of thought. He had accepted the cruel maxim—to the victor belong the spoils—but first he had let Rona slip from his power; and now Margaret, who was to have been cured of her love for Garth by the crushing of the big boss, had been finally won to him by the very act of his fall.

It staggered Tyson. He tried to put his ideas together, but he was lost. Rona had left him the night before, bewildered and sullen at his sudden change of mind, and now, in the house of Garth, his sister worked to recall the man she loved to health and happiness.

One thing remained of his work of destruction. The dam was still open—the water still coursed to waste down the Chiluah. But of what avail was that to him? He had crushed Garth—even to the dust—but the purpose for which he had crushed him was lost.

But one great picture remained with him, overshadowing all else: the memory of Garth battering and smashing his way through a crowd of peons like a bull through a mob of half-starved yearlings. It made Tyson lift his head and smile. Ashamed of a family alliance with such a man? But whether or not he were ashamed, Margaret had made her choice for life. For her sake he must restore the work of Garth's life.

It was not easy. The force of superstition which he had set in motion against Garth must be met by a pull of superstition in the opposite direction. He must find some way to console them for the drowning of San Vicente's mission. Automatically, as he pondered, Tyson turned up the valley towards the mission.

The sky still thronged with clouds, but the rainfall had abated. Far to the north, indeed, the vapours flung down in black mists about the higher mountains, and vast bodies of water were falling there; that was why the Chiluah grew larger and louder every hour; that was why wall after wall of water lunged down the valley with the roaring of a thousand bulls.

He was knocking, at length, at the central door of the mission, and the padre himself opened to him. When he saw Tyson the face of the old man lighted; he made a quick mute gesture inviting him in, and when Tyson stepped through the door, he saw the reason. For in a chair near the smouldering, irregular fire sat Rona Carnahan.

She rose when she heard the new voice, and Tyson saw her gladness first, and then her conscious restraint. She was waiting for some explanation from him before she would resume the old relations; and he had come to destroy the last remnant of her faith in him! The irony of it made Tyson smile without mirth.

"I know everything," the old padre was saying in a shaken voice. "God was with you, my son! He saved you at the crisis! If you wish to speak to Rona alone, I shall step out and leave you together—freely—freely! I shall trust you now, señor, with an absolute trust!"

He wrung the hand of Tyson while he spoke, and then they both lifted their heads to listen, for the wind brought a rattling burst of rain against the side of the building, and shook the crumbling, 'dobe walls.

"No," said Tyson, "I have not come to see Rona, but you, padre."

"I shall go, then," said the girl, and she flushed,

but whether with anger or disappointment he could not tell.

"No," protested Tyson. "Stay where you are. You'll want to hear what I have to say, I suppose. Padre Miguel, I have come to speak of the mission."

He looked about him. It was a low-ceilinged room. The rafters were bare, and had so rotted and wasted with time that a few of them were cracked across, and all of them bowed and sagged in towards the centre of the plastered ceiling. Along the walls ranged pictures of the padres who had done notable things for San Vicente, grim faces, most of them, half pioneer and half monk; but the paint was corroded and cracked by the dry air of centuries.

"Try this chair," said the padre.

It creaked and groaned under the weight of Tyson, as if it protested against maintaining so much youth and energy. He sat with bent head, considering the puddle which spread from his soaked boots. They were costly affairs of elkskin, soft and pliable, perfectly fitted, and he wore whipcord walking trousers above them.

He felt the eyes of Rona upon him while he drew off his gloves of rough, dark-yellow leather. She was measuring him, gauging a distance, it seemed, which his clothes and her tatters set between them.

"You are wet and cold," murmured the padre. "Rona, my child, you know where the wine is. Bring the Señor Tyson a bottle. It will warm your blood, my son."

"I need no wine," answered Tyson bluntly. "What I have to say will make me warm enough."

He laughed a little uneasily, with his eyes upon Rona.

"Your will is my will," nodded the padre.

"Padre Miguel," said Tyson abruptly, "I have come to bury San Vicente under the water from the dam."

Rona sat with black face, and the padre, after a moment of motionless astonishment, moved his chair so that he could look more fully into the eyes of his guest.

"I am an old man and a plain man," he said, "and my brain cannot follow these jugglings. Do I understand, señor, that you will allow the gates of the dam to be closed and the great work of Señor Garth to go on?"

"No, padre," said the girl, breathless. Her voice rose with an angry ring in it. "No, he does not mean that."

Tyson looked fixedly at her: he could see the flame blow up and ebb away in her eyes, and he had never thought her so beautiful as now, when he was about to give her up. For surely it would mean this.

"I mean it," he said gravely. "The gates of the dam may be closed."

The padre blinked as if at a light.

"My wits buzz," he muttered. "For Rona you kept the gates wide. And now—what do you mean by this?"

"Yes," pleaded the girl. She shed her anger. She was all soft appeal now. "Speak to me, señor! What is it you mean?"

"I have not come to discuss meaning," said Tyson heavily. "Padre, you will do what you can to help me?"

"And make the desert bloom? Yes, yes. With all

my heart. As for the house of San Vicente, it has served its time."

"Listen then. What caused the peons to rise was the whisper that the drowning of the mission was the subtle work of the devil."

"You, señor, should know best about that whisper."

"Perhaps." He shrugged his shoulders. "But what is it they prize? These bare walls?"

"The altar and the cross and the holy places here."

"Then consider this. We make a picture for these childish fellows. We form a long procession, with you to head it. We take up the holy relics and the shining cross and we carry them up from this old mission and form a new church on the hills, high above the reach of the water. We raise a new church to San Vicente."

"With the cross glittering far across the desert? Señor, the blessed saint himself has inspired you!"

"He has chosen a strange vehicle for his inspirations, then," said Tyson, dryly.

"But my mother," whispered the girl. "*Madre-cita mia!* Oh, what of her?"

"Hush, child!" said the padre. "This is a holy work!"

"It is a work of the devil—the devil!" She ran towards Tyson. "You and your lies and your promises!" she cried. "I hate you!"

"Rona," he pleaded. "Let me tell you how——"

But she brushed away his arm and raced away through the door. On the threshold the blast of the wind struck her and staggered her, but the next moment she was out of sight. Tyson, with a muttered oath, sprang after her, but the padre blocked his way.

"Señor," he said, "it is useless—it is dangerous to follow her now. Surely you counted the cost before you did this thing and formed this plan?"

And Tyson bowed his head.

Forty-Six
Going Home

No fortnight had ever worked such changes in the valley of the Chiluah. High on the side of Mount Blanca rose a glittering cross which had once showed from the belltower of the old mission; and around the former house of San Vicente the rising waters backed up from the dam now lapped.

All the lower valley was filled by this time, for there had never been such a spring flood in the history of the Chiluah, and since that day when the procession wound up the side of La Blanca and the new church was consecrated, since that day and the closing of the sluice gates, the water had risen swiftly, inch by inch and foot by foot, up the strong face of the dam.

Several days before almost the entire force was taken from the dam and put to work at the levelling of the ground and the construction of the permanent canals through the desert outside.

Now the system was complete for many a mile, from the big laterals to the little, wandering channels which crossed and recrossed in an infinitely complex tangle, feeding the checks.

It only needed that the sluice gates be opened, and for the first time the sands of the desert would be flooded by the will of man.

To be sure, the water was not so high as it would eventually reach, but there was enough for experimental purposes and the first flooding to settle the sandy channels. Afterwards the gates would remain closed until the waters topped the walls of San Vicente and brimmed the very top of the dam.

It was a great and formal ceremony, that opening of the gates. All other work had ceased. Already the peons thronged the mountainsides and the top of the dam, waiting till the waters should leap out at the signal.

The signal itself was to be a solemn one—the chiming of the bells from the new church of San Vicente on the hill; and the signal for the chiming of the bells would be the rise and fall of Garth's hand. He sat there in his office on the slope, commanding a wide view over the desert, and waited. He was quite pale, now, but the bandage had been taken from his head the day before. Margaret sat beside him.

"They're growing impatient on the dam," she warned Garth. "You'd better wait no longer. Hal may not come."

"Another ten minutes," answered Garth, consulting his watch anxiously. "It's his work in a way, as much as it is mine. Why isn't he here?"

Margaret knew well enough, but she would not answer.

At that very moment Tyson stood with the padre

in sight of the deserted mission. He had come there wholly at the padre's persuasion.

"Shall we go down," the padre was saying, "and take a last look through the walls?"

"You are gay today, father," answered Tyson, and he looked narrowly at the old padre. "If you were another man, Padre Miguel, I should say that you had a double purpose in bringing me up here. However, we shall go down."

But as they went down the slope a sound came up to meet them, thin and sharp, whistling through the trees. Tyson started, and then stopped and faced the padre.

"It is true, señor," he said sadly. "The old man is playing his violin in the burial yard, and she is with him. I had hoped to bring you two together once more."

Tyson asked curiously: "And why that, good padre? Have you not told me yourself that when she even hears my name she frowns?" He sighed. "I fear you have a grudge against me, padre. You would show me to her as the hunter shows the hare to his greyhound."

"No, no, señor," replied the old man, seriously, "it is true that she looks black at your name. She knows that you might have kept the water from the grave of her mother; and for all I can say she will have it that the dam is the work of the evil one. So she has been saying to herself over and over again these days, that she hates you, Señor Tyson. But if she sees you again——"

"What then?"

"Why, señor, when the rain falls the ground will be wet, and when the wind blows the trees must sing whether they will or no."

"This," said Tyson, musing, "sounds more like poetry than reason."

"When I was a young man," said the padre, "we never spoke of women and reason in the same breath. Let her only see you, señor. Her reason may say one thing, but her heart will say another. Will you come on with me?"

But Tyson looked up and back to the glitter of the new cross on La Blanca.

"If she should run on you in a rage," said the padre simply. "I shall stand before you, señor."

Tyson smiled, but he grew serious almost at once.

"Are you so confident?" he asked. "Has she spoken kindly of me—even one syllable since the gates of the dam were closed?"

"Señor," said the padre sadly, "I am not a brave man. I have not had courage to name you. But I know that she loved you once; and you, señor, still care for her."

"I cannot spend my money and have it still in my purse," said Tyson, smiling that same mirthless way.

"Will you let her go in this careless manner?"

"There is nothing in the world," he replied coldly, "that one cannot forget."

The padre considered.

"Then come with me to her," he said. "*Show* her that you have forgotten her."

"But why should I do that?"

"Because it may help her, señor, to forget."

"I will go," said Tyson at last. "But I fear that she will be the lightning and I the rod."

The padre eyed him with wonder.

"If you were to die, señor," he said, "you would still have a jest on your lips. But let us go down.

Hurry. The water already laps about the outer walls!"

It was, and fast rising; for though clear sunshine poured over the lower valley, to the north the vapour of the storm hid away the tops of the mountains, and increasing torrents rushed down the valley and filled it with sound, in pulses, where a wall of the water passed and spread out in a great wave through the artificial lake, and then the intermediate silence.

Already the upper edge of the lake glimmered around the southern walls of the mission, and the 'dobe sagged with the consuming moisture which drew it back to mud. The channel of the river itself ran so brimful that it had washed away the bank on either side. And the narrow, wooden footbridge that crossed it to the mission shook under the feet of Tyson and the padre.

"We have no time to spare," said Tyson, as the meaning of the situation dawned on him. "Another wall of water may take up this bridge and knock it to kindling, and this is the only way to the mission; see there! The water is swinging around there on the northern side."

The padre, grey with concern, answered not a word, but hurried on, almost at a run, and as they went the sound of the violin rose into a singing outburst.

"Listen," panted the father. "This is his way of talking to the dead! No power on earth can convince him that his wife does not hear his music."

They tossed open the door of the building; it seemed as if the air within were already damp and dark with the foreknowledge of the coming destruction, and through the first chamber they ran out into the burial ground. Old Carnahan stood leaning against the wall, his violin in one hand and his bow in the other, and his singular red-stained eyes stared blankly at Rona as she strove frantically to draw him from the place. Already a pool of water was growing in the southern part of the cemetery.

"Thank God!" she sobbed, when she saw them. "Oh, padre, you are barely in time. I thought you would never come!"

"Señor Carnahan!" cried the padre, shaking the musician by the shoulder. "Waken! It is I! It is time to go home!"

The other brushed his forehead with his bow hand. He looked like one newly awaked from sleep.

"Yes," he murmured. "I must go home. I am about to go home. I have only one more question to ask her before——"

He was already putting his instrument under his chin when Tyson slipped a strong arm about him under the shoulders and brought him easily, gently, forward. Rona drew him from the other side, and as they worked together her eyes flashed across and dwelt on his with mute gratitude.

Once in the open the full extent of the danger was clear. The Chiluah already ran bankful, and even the few moments they had been in the mission had raised the lake around its walls; and now, a line of white far up the channel, a new wall of water swept down to raise the flood.

No time to lose; Tyson and Rona shouted to the padre to run on ahead, and they took Carnahan by a shoulder on each side and hurried on.

He went willingly enough, to all appearances, though he murmured to himself words which Tyson could not understand. And so, panting with haste, they reached the bridge.

It staggered under them, but they crossed safely enough and stood on the other side on firm ground, with the roar of the white, onrushing wall shaking the earth.

It was almost at the bridge when Carnahan started and pointed towards the mission. "Do you hear?" he cried. "Padre, do you hear her voice? She is calling me."

And wrenching away the arm which Rona still carelessly held, he leaped away and was instantly upon the bridge. Tyson did not need the scream of Rona to spur him on. He sprang in pursuit with the white froth of the wall of water gleaming only yards from the bridge; his foot was barely on it when the bright mass struck.

It picked up the slender bridge and snapped it in two. One portion it carried tossing on its way. The other fragment it flung back on to the bank, and with that it flung back on to the bank Tyson with stunning force against the slope.

He rose instantly, but it was far too late to aid poor Carnahan. The musician was already splashing his way knee deep to the door of the mission and even while Tyson staggered to his feet a great wave rolled up in the lake and plunged after the fugitive.

He reached the door in time, and the water lunged against it the instant he was through, and then leaped up the wall as if exulting in its strength.

"Get higher up the slope!" urged the padre. "Quickly, what is lost cannot be reclaimed—and there is no danger here. Señor, help Rona."

She went blindly, her head bowed, and they climbed until no possible danger from the floods remained. They stood, now on a lofty shoulder of the hill, and looking far down the valley they saw the solid-sheeted water of the lake, and beyond that the rim of the dam, and still farther across the desert and the intricate tracery of the canals which reached out towards the horizon—a brilliant sky, for it was now sunset time.

All around the mission the waters of the rising lake tossed, now, and while they watched a great section of the wall sagged, swayed, and then belched out with a mighty rushing sound and cast a yellow wave far out on the water. It left three storeys of rooms visible for an instant, and then the returning wave sank hungrily into the aperture.

That sound fell away, and now the thin whistling sound of the violin rose clearly and sweetly from the mission.

"Our Father, forgive me!" groaned the padre. "Now I understand. Indeed, she is calling him home."

Still the singing of the violin rose, small but clear. It was no solemn and tragic strain; it was a sound of rejoicing, dancing like the waves of the lake, and keen as the light of the waters.

A loud and tumultuous crashing shut away the music as the whole southern wall spilled out across the lake, and the besieging water swirled closer.

"Listen!" said the girl suddenly. The horror seemed to have fallen from her like a cloak. Was it the murmur of the padre at his prayers for the dying that she meant. No, for once more the sounds of the violin rose, sharper. The music was winged, and flew to them, and hovered around them; and it was more beautiful than ever, and like all perfect things there was a soul of pain within it.

"He is playing for my mother," whispered Rona.

"And it is love. Ah, he is playing for us as well. Do you hear?"

With a single gesture Tyson caught her close to him.

The music soared to a pitch of triumph, rose to an incredible pitch, and then there was a bellow of falling walls, a splitting and rending; the lake rolled out and then swept back again, and from four sides the wave met in the centre and leaped exultantly towards heaven.

Far away, the bells of the new church of San Vicente began chiming. They looked by instinct towards the shining cross and then beyond the dam, where the water was spreading with incredible swiftness through the laterals.

Now it passed beyond the slant, blue shadow of La Blanca. Now it slid out through a myriad of the smaller canals. The colours of the sunset fell upon that running water. First it was like keen fire, but now it was rich, molten gold that ran tangling through the darkening desert.